The Wincheste

The St Cross Mirror

Larry Jeram-Croft

Cover photograph: The ancient Hospital and Alms House of St Cross, Winchester

Also by Larry Jeram-Croft:

Fiction:

The 'Jon Hunt' series about the modern Royal Navy:

Sea Skimmer
The Caspian Monster
Cocaine
Arapaho
Bog Hammer
Glasnost
Retribution
Formidable
Conspiracy
Swan Song

The 'John Hunt' books about the Royal Navy's Fleet Air Arm in the Second World War:

Better Lucky and Good
and the Pilot can't swim

The Winchester Chronicles:

Book one: The St Cross Mirror

The Caribbean: historical fiction and the 'Jacaranda' Trilogy.

Diamant

Jacaranda

The Guadeloupe Guillotine
Nautilus

Science Fiction:

Siren

Non Fiction:

The Royal Navy Lynx an Operational History
The Royal Navy Wasp an Operational and Retirement History
The Accidental Aviator

Prologue

Sarajevo. Sunday, 28 June 1914, 10:45 am

Gavrilo Princip stood outside Schiller's delicatessen. Princip was a small man seething with anger. His deepest rage was focused, as it had always been, on the Austrian Empire but he had an even more urgent and grating anger with his comrades. Five of them had lined the streets where the Arch Duke was to travel that morning and all they had achieved was to throw one grenade that missed the Duke's car and exploded under the next one. The resulting speed of the convoy as they fled the scene had made it impossible to do anything more. What should he do now? His comrades had all disappeared. If anything were to happen it would be up to him now. The fat Duke had given his speech in the Governor's residence but it was now rumoured that he was going to attend the victims of the morning attack in the local hospital. So here he was on the most logical route that they would take. He glanced anxiously up and down the road. Surprisingly, there was no sign of policemen or for that matter any soldiers. After the alarms of the morning, it was almost laughable that the authorities were not taking any extra precautions. For the thousandth time, he felt in his pocket for the reassurance of the cold metal of his FN 1910 pistol. Each time he did so, his resolve became firmer. He was going to strike a blow for Slavic independence whatever the risks.

Suddenly, his thoughts were interrupted by the sound of motor cars down the boulevard. His senses leapt into overdrive when he was able to see that it was indeed his target. The target and his wife were sat in the open in the third car. Archduke Franz Ferdinand was clearly very brave or a complete idiot. Gavrilo's teeth ground in frustration when he realised that the convoy was once again moving too fast for him to get close. What was he to do? Taking a shot at a moving car with a small pistol was far too unlikely to succeed. Whilst he dithered in indecision something strange happened. The two leading cars suddenly turned left up a side street and after only a hundred yards they stopped. Clearly, there was some sort of altercation taking place between the drivers. The Duke's car had

1

followed them but seeing the problem ahead, the driver had started to reverse. It became immediately clear that he wasn't a very good driver and was having trouble guiding the clumsy vehicle backwards.

It was the chance Gavrilo had been waiting for. As he ran across the road, the Duke's car had stalled. He tugged the pistol free. Within a few seconds, he would have the perfect, close range shot at both his target and his fat ugly wife.

Just as he ran up to the back of the car, its engine roared into life. The driver's foot must have slipped off the clutch because it shot backwards so fast that Gavrilo had no chance at all. Two tons of wood and steel smashed into him knocking him flat. The last thing he saw was one of the large rubber clad wheels milliseconds before it ran directly over his head and the world went black.

Chapter 1

I've always liked the William Walker pub. Set in the corner of a block of ancient buildings it has an air of permanence. I idly wondered just how many people had come inside for a drink over the centuries. Apparently, it was one of the oldest pubs in the county. The décor was dark oak and red plush chairs and seats. However, it wasn't pretentious in any way, not the least because there wasn't a horse brass in sight. It used to be called the Cricketers Arms. However, some clever entrepreneur must have realised that naming it after the famous diver who had spent ten years of his life diving under the foundations of the massive cathedral opposite, with sacks of concrete, to stop it from literally sinking would be good for business. Not that any of the myriad of bars and restaurants in the town were short of business these days. Because of that, I had timed it so that I was early for the lunchtime rush. I was able to take my pint over to my favourite seat and enjoy the view.

Yes, the view, a grand sight in so many ways. Through a curtain of beech trees was the aforementioned ancient pile of Winchester Cathedral. Not the prettiest piece of medieval architecture by far. Indeed, many people called it ugly with its squat, square tower. What it did have was a grand presence, a testament to almost a thousand years of dominating the city it had been built for. However, to me, it also represented all that was good and wonderful about the city it resided in. Or should I say cities? Because that was the other thing about the view from this particular window. From here the sight was really timeless. Vehicles were not allowed down this part of the road outside and there were not even any lamp standards in sight. Just the entrance to the cathedral grounds guarded by a wrought iron gate, the trees and the building itself. It was timeless, literally.

The beer was perfect as usual. Locally brewed, room temperature and with the appearance of old dishwater. My American friends would never understand. After half a pint, my thoughts began to mellow slightly. Coming back to the city after so many years away in London had felt like coming home. In some ways, the intervening years working as a policeman in the Met had simply become part of another person's life. That said, I could

3

hardly take up where I had left off. I had left as a schoolboy and come back a man. The fact that I had come back at all was something of a surprise at the time. My parents had both passed away a few years before and the brief visit to their funerals had been far too emotional for me to reconnect with the city. No, it was the death of my uncle, the one I hardly knew, that had proved the catalyst in more ways than one. He had died a bachelor and I was an only son and also the closest living relative, so to my utter surprise, I had inherited not only his lovely old house but also quite a decent sum of money. Enough money, in fact, to mean I wouldn't have to work for the rest of my life if I didn't want to. At the time I was going through a particularly unpleasant time at work. A new boss had come in and was making everyone's life a misery. It was with the utmost satisfaction when he had hauled me over the coals for the umpteenth time for some imagined misdemeanour, that I had simply told him to fuck off and turned my back on London and policing forever.

This time the city welcomed me back. I even looked up some old school friends and reignited some old friendships. My uncle's house was on the outskirts of the town in a place called St Cross. The area was part of a medieval church and hospital most of which still stood despite Henry the Eighth's depredations and was flanked by the slow moving river Itchen which had carved out a massive area of beautiful water meadows all along the east of the city. It was an area I knew extremely well from my childhood and to be living within its confines had proved delightful. Well, at first, at least.

Of course, nothing ever stays simple. The old house needed some TLC and that kept me occupied for a while as did reacquainting myself with the area and old friends.

Then, one day, I was walking down the old High Street, now a pedestrian area, intending to visit a book shop near the bottom of town when someone called my name. I looked around and at first couldn't see anyone I knew. Then I saw a young woman waving at me. She was remarkably pretty with her dark hair in a ponytail. She was wearing tight jeans and a bright yellow T shirt that showed off a slim but well endowed figure. For the life of me, I couldn't place her face but I was sure I had seen her somewhere before.

'Tony? It is you, isn't it? I heard you had moved back from London.' Then seeing what must have a blank look on my face she

4

laughed. 'You don't remember me, do you? I'm Carrie, you used to go out with Hannah, my older sister when we were all at school.'

The penny dropped but the last time I had seen this girl she must have been no more than fourteen with braces on her teeth and her hair in pig tails. To say she had blossomed was an understatement and what was even more surprising was that she remembered me. Mind you, I did remember her hanging around rather too much when I was courting her sister.

We got to talking and then had a drink. She was amazingly frank, admitting that she had fancied me like mad when I was going out with her sister. From the look in her eye, I felt that some of that infatuation might still be there. She was a teacher now at the Peter Symonds sixth form college. It had been a boy's grammar school in my day when I was there. We talked for ages and found we had a great deal in common, not the least that we were both single. I told her about my inheritance and she seemed very keen to see the house so I invited her back and one thing led to another. She stayed the night and to be frank, has so far stayed for the rest of my life. If it were only that simple because soon after that everything changed.

I sat back in my seat and took another long pull at my beer. What was I to do about Carrie? Both of her.

Chapter 2

I guess I really need to go back to when all this started. It was the day the letter arrived. The one that changed my world forever. I had been working nights for a week on a very boring surveillance job. After yet another eight hours sitting in a van listening to nothing happening at all in our mark's house, I was just about all in. As I pushed the door open to my flat there was the usual scraping of paper behind the door. I almost kicked all the letters aside in order to get to bed but there were so many this time I reached down and retrieved them. As usual, there were the standard offers of credit cards I neither wanted nor needed. There were flyers for double glazing and the local fast food joints. However, amongst all the dross was a large buff envelope and my name and address were written on it by hand, in clear almost copperplate writing.

It was enough to wet my interest so I pulled open the flap as I wandered into my kitchen in search of a coffee and something to eat. I knew I would never get straight to sleep even if I had been having trouble keeping my eyes open in the van. I was now just too wound up. As the kettle started to heat up, I looked at the letter. It was on very smart embossed headed paper and the address was that of a solicitor's firm in Winchester. I immediately recognised them as they had dealt with the probate when my parents had died some years previously.

The contents of the letter were a complete surprise. My first thought was that someone at work had discovered who these solicitors were and it was all a wind up. But that didn't make any sense. But who the hell was this uncle? I had distant memories of my father mentioning that he had a brother but that they didn't talk or meet. Something to do with a family argument many years ago. That must be who this was about. Apparently, he had died and as I was the last living member of the family he had left everything to me. What the letter didn't say was what the estate actually comprised of. I looked at my watch and saw that is was after nine so they should be open. Grabbing the phone, I rang the number on the letter, said who I was and asked to talk to Mister Simpson.

He came on the line very quickly. 'Anthony, you've obviously seen my letter. I'm sorry, I should probably have telephoned you over this matter but I tried your office first and they told me that you were working some major case so I thought a letter might get to you quicker. Was I right?'

I immediately recognised the solicitor's voice. 'Yes Mister Simpson, it was probably the best idea. I'm on night shifts at the moment and hardly get a chance to be near a phone in daylight. Now come on, what's this all about? I vaguely recall my father mentioning he had a brother but that's about as much as I know. Who was he and is this bequest important?'

'Goodness yes. Your uncle Peter lived in Winchester as you may know and I understand that he never spoke to your father, although I don't know the reason for that. There are a great number of papers at the property. I'm sure you will find out all about it when you read them.'

'So there is property involved?'

'Sorry yes, I should have told you that first. The estate consists of your uncle's house which is quite a substantial property to the west of the town in a place called St Cross. It has about seven bedrooms and extensive gardens bordering on the River Itchen.'

My interest went up another notch. Property prices in Winchester were ludicrously high and the St Cross area was very exclusive. If the house also had fishing rights on the river it would worth a fortune. 'And it's all been left to me?'

'Yes but there are some caveats. You can't sell the house for at least ten years being the main one.'

My heart sank, if the place was in need of any repair then it could literally become a millstone around my neck.

Mister Simpson must have read my thoughts. 'Don't worry about that Anthony. There is also a large sum of capital to go with the house which will be yours whatever happens.'

He mentioned a figure that made my hair stand on end. 'Say that again.' I said.

So he did. 'Of course, you will need to come down here as soon as you can to sort out the paperwork and we need to go through the will in detail. There are a few minor bequests and few specific instructions for you but I assure you they are not onerous in any way.'

'Just one thing Mister Simpson,' I said. 'Knowing the town as I do, I can guess as to the worth of the property but can you please give your absolute assurance that the financial bequest is as firm as you say and that there are no other strings attached.'

'My dear boy, I can confirm that the figure is correct and is the net value after all taxes have been paid. I could pay the amount into an account of you choosing this very day if you should so wish. However, it would be far more sensible for you to come to my office so we can go through the detail and talk about the other minor bequests. Also, I would strongly suggest you get hold of an accountant to advise you on how to manage the whole estate. I can recommend several.'

'Yes, that all sounds fine. Look, I need some sleep and I will have to go into the office to sort some things out but I will be down tomorrow morning. Would ten o'clock be alright?'

'Perfect, I will see you then.'

I put the phone down and found myself automatically making coffee without even thinking about what I was doing.

Suddenly, the phone rang again. This time it was my boss, Chief Inspector Frank Cosgrove. A pompous self-serving prat. He had joined our section two months ago and had successfully alienated just about everyone in the team. First, he reorganised everything and everybody before he had even had time to see how we worked together. Then when everyone was still trying to work out what their new duties were, he started handing out bollockings for our shortcomings. He had taken a particular dislike to me as his deputy but that was alright because I had taken an even larger dislike to him.

'Peterson, I know you've only just come off shift but tough. My office now.' And the phone went dead.

Cursing under my breath, I grabbed my jacket and headed back out the door. As I walked down to the tube station I mentally reviewed my terms of employment. I had paid off my degree in terms of the number of years I had served. I was pensionable but not in any large way and if I did what I was thinking of doing then I would lose that. But what the hell, it would be worth it.

As I went into the large outer office several of the boys gave me a sympathetic look. I could easily work out why and wasn't disappointed when I went into Cosgrove's inner office.

'Shut the door, don't sit down,' was all he said without looking up and he continued to read something on his desk.

Bollocks to that. I pulled up a chair and sat, staring at him and daring him to say something.

He looked up when he heard the chair scrape but only frowned. He placed the pen he had been holding down next to the file he had been looking at and stared at me. Frank Cosgrove was old for his rank. His lank hair was receding severely and turning grey. He clearly didn't look after himself and his large belly slopped over his suit trousers. The office scuttlebutt was that it was his last chance at promotion and he was trying to play the new broom and the tough boss to make an impression on those upstairs. It wasn't going to work on me.

'What the fuck happened last night?' he asked in his surprisingly high pitched voice.

'Nothing, as I'm sure you already know.' I answered giving him no more than I needed.

'Why the fuck not?' His voice had already started to rise in tone as he was clearly working himself up to something. 'This whole operation was based on information supplied by your informant and they were meant to have moved by the end of the week.'

I thought of all the responses I could have made. Like the information had not been that precise and I had made that very clear at the start. Like any policeman worth his salt would have known that anyway. But frankly, I was tired, fed up with this posturing idiot and after the phone call this morning had no reason to want to explain anything to him.

'Do you know what Frank,' I said. 'I've just about had it with you and your fucking tantrums. We both know that you were stupid enough to tell the Superintendent that we would have an arrest by now, even though I told you it was fifty fifty at best.'

His face began to turn a rather interesting shade of purple. Good. 'So here's the deal,' and I threw my warrant card and building pass onto his desk. 'I quit. I know that means I lose my pension rights and any gratuities for my service. I don't give a toss about that. What it does mean is that I don't have to put up with you for another moment longer. No, don't get up. Goodbye.' I turned my back on him and walked to the door.

Just for once, he was speechless. I opened the door but as I went out into the main office it was quite clear that everyone had heard our little conversation. The walls were very thin and we hadn't exactly been keeping our voices down.

'Sorry to let you down guys but I have better things to do with my life.' I said to the room before anyone could say anything. The door opened behind me and all heads turned towards it except mine. Before anyone else could speak, someone started clapping. Soon everyone in the room had started to clap as well, everyone except the man behind me. I walked away shaking a few hands as I did so.

As I walked out of New Scotland Yard for the last time, I smiled to myself. The air felt clean and fresh. I had thrown my career away and a new life beckoned. I had no idea what was to come, all I knew was that it was going to be a great deal more interesting than what I was leaving behind. I was happy, as happy as only a newly minted multi-millionaire could be.

Chapter 3

The next few months were strange, almost as strange as what was to follow but more of that later.

The next morning, I was sitting in the solicitor's office as he read the will to me. It was exactly as he said over the phone. The whole estate came to me. There was a small bequest to a couple who had looked after the house for him and there was also a small parcel and letter, which I was to open when I had gone to the house. And that was it. I was rich and would never need to lift a finger again for the rest of my life. I wasn't actually too sure about that thought. The stories of lottery winners having their lives ruined came to mind. What the hell, I was going to find out for myself.

Once the paperwork was signed, I was given several sets of keys. Some were for the house and a couple were keys for the two cars that were apparently in the garage. They looked quite old. I was intrigued to see what sort of vehicles they would fit. Mister Simpson drove me down to the house as I had come down by train and actually didn't own a car. Working in central London made car ownership a waste of time and money.

The house sat behind a large Laurel hedge so little could be seen from the road. As we drove in I could see that it looked in good order. The garden was neat and it looked like the lawn had been recently cut.

I turned to Simpson. 'It seems that my uncle's staff have stayed busy. Everything looks really well looked after.'

'Yes, Emily and Mike Graham. He employed them part time, they live further down the road. She does the house and he does the garden. It seems they have kept up with the work. You'll have to negotiate some sort of arrangement with them. It's up to you of course but I believe they have been here some time.'

One more thing to think about but my thoughts then turned to the house. It was built, like many in the city, of dark red brick intermingled with grey flint. The roof was grey slate. The front door was covered over by a porch. It looked old, respectable and quite inviting. We got out of the car and I went up to the front door and tried several of the keys until I found one that worked. Inside the hall was spacious with black and white tile flooring. An imposing staircase dominated the hall with rooms off to either side. I took some time looking around the ground floor. The place was meticulously clean but it had an air of melancholy about it. The furniture in the dining room and front living room was distinctly old fashioned as if the owner had given up purchasing anything for years. The kitchen was fairly modern and again it was spotless. I got the impression the place was hardly lived in but bearing in mind it had been owned and occupied by one man maybe there were more personal spaces somewhere else. The rooms upstairs were very much the same. Clean and old fashioned, all except for one. This had obviously been my uncle's bedroom. Although there were few personal artefacts around it had a much more lived in air.

'There is one more room you must see Anthony,' Mister Simpson said. 'Come with me.'

He led me to the back of the main first floor landing where there was dark, leather bound door. It had clearly been in regular use as the leather itself was worn almost away around the door handle, presumably where the owner had pushed it open. We went inside. What a contrast to the rest of the house. It was enormous and overflowing with books, papers and furniture. To the left side, where there was a long picture window, there was a massive oak desk almost completely covered with documents, writing implements and all sorts of bric a brac. The walls were covered in paintings, some looked quite old. Many seemed to have a military theme although quite a few were landscapes of places I had never seen. At the opposite end of the room from the desk was a television and two large very comfortable looking leather button down sofas. In the middle of the far wall was a large fireplace with two more arm chairs and a long table set out before it. Next to it for some unaccountable reason was a full length mirror in a guilt frame. There was also another small door which, when I opened it, led to a small staircase that seemed to go to the back of the house. Despite its size, the place felt cosy and lived in. I also realised it wasn't my place, the whole character of the room was based around that of my departed uncle. I felt like an interloper. Quite what I was going to do with everything here, I had no idea.

'Well I must be going now Anthony,' Mister Simpson said. 'I presume you will wish to stay. Would you like me to pop round to the Graham's house and ask Emily to do some shopping for you and maybe arrange some meals.'

For a second I couldn't work out who he was talking about but then realised it must be one of the couple who had been employed to look after the house.

'Yes, that would be most helpful. You know I hadn't quite realised the size of the task ahead of me. There's so much to sort out. I'm not sure I have a clue where to start.'

'Might I suggest you look at that letter and parcel,' Simpson replied. 'If I was a guessing man I think you might find it's there to help.'

'What? Oh yes good idea,' I had completely forgotten that I was still holding them.

Simpson let himself out and I went over to one of the sofas and sat down. The letter was very short. It simply said that all would be explained if I watched the film and that he wished me joy in my inheritance. Slightly non-plussed, I opened the little parcel to find an old VHS tape. I looked around and sure enough underneath the old massive television was a player. I fiddled with the controls for a minute before a flap opened on the top of the machine and I was able to insert the tape. There were two remote controls so I was able to turn on the TV and found that tape was already starting to play. I had missed the first few seconds so I hit the rewind and sat back as it started again from the beginning. It had obviously been shot in this room with my uncle behind his desk. The first thing I realised was that he looked remarkably like my father. If it hadn't been for the large handlebar moustache it could have been my dad. He started to talk to the camera.

'Tony my boy. If you are watching this then I've passed on and you are now my heir. I wish you all the joy it may bring. I suspect you have a thousand questions, I will try to answer as many as I can. We only met once when you were about three so I don't suppose you remember me at all. That has been the regret of my life and I will explain why. However, I have followed your life and career and know that you are a fine young man. I feel honoured to be able to pass my wealth on to you.

You may see a resemblance between me and your father. That is because we were twins. Not identical but pretty close. However, we chose different paths in life. He went into business, I joined the

Royal Marines. That didn't stop us both falling in love with the same girl. In fact, in nineteen eighty one, your mother had agreed to marry me. Fate played its hand then and early the next year, I was one of many called to sail down south and fight in the Falklands. When I said I was in the Royal Marines, I was also a member of the Special Boat Squadron the Navy's answer to the SAS. You may have heard of us. Whilst most of us went to liberate the islands, myself and a small team were smuggled onto the mainland. I won't go into our mission except to say it went horribly wrong. My team were wiped out and I was captured. I spent eighteen months in captivity. When I was eventually released and got home I discovered that I had been reported as dead and your parents had married. I will let you work out the timings but there is every chance that I am actually your father. When I confronted your mother she was adamant that it wasn't so and I was in no position to argue. My life was a nightmare. When you're declared dead it's not much fun convincing the authorities that it isn't actually the case, even when you are standing right in front of them. A year later, I called around to see you and to cut a long story short, had a terrible row with both your parents. Things were said that shouldn't have been and we severed all contact. I don't know what you were told, if anything. However, in the end, I outlasted them both but now I've been told I only have a few months left as well so I'm making this tape in the hope that you will forgive me and accept my gift to you.

I bought the house with money the military gave me as back pay and severance although it was in a hell of mess then and I did most of the restoration myself. You may wonder how I came about my money. You will find that out in due course. I have no doubt.

What I would really love you to do now is chuck out all my old rubbish. Anything you don't want, please don't feel you have to keep it but maybe keep a few things for yourself. I know there are some things in the garage that you probably will want to consider. I suggest you go and have a look as one of your first priorities. If you think I am being a bit enigmatic about some issues you are absolutely correct and that is deliberate on my part. There are some things you must find out for yourself. Well, one thing actually and it will make far more sense if you discover it on your own. It's a reflection of all that's happened to me over the last three decades.

I'm stopping this now before I get too maudlin. Good luck son or nephew or whatever. I wish you a long and fruitful life.' The tape turned to static.

Bloody hell. I sat back and wondered just what more surprises were in store. I replayed the tape several times letting the whole story sink in.

I went out onto the landing. The house was eerily quiet. Then I remembered what my uncle had said about the garage. As he had been so specific I decided to go and have a look. It took me some time to find it as it was actually a separate building around the back of the main house. I had the bunch of keys still with me and soon found one for the large up and over door. I pulled it up and stared inside. Uncle Peter had obviously known something about me.

Chapter 4

The next few months flew by. The first thing I had to do was attend the funeral. Uncle Peter had arranged it all in advance. He had been in a hospice for the last few months of his life and had taken it on himself to arrange his own send off. I wondered why he had not contacted me after my parents had gone or even in his last few weeks. All I could imagine was he felt a sense of guilt for not being part of my life much earlier. When I met the Grahams they said that he had been away very often although they never knew where he went. However, when he came back he always spoke of me. It was almost as though he had treated the old couple like family. In the end, the only people at the funeral were myself, the Grahams and Peter Simpson the solicitor. It was a sad affair. I wondered why the old man didn't seem to have any friends. Maybe they had all preceded him.

After that, I threw myself into sorting out the house with the help of the Grahams. They were both more than happy to see the place modernised. They had been nagging my uncle to do something about it for years but as he was away so often nothing ever got done. So I employed an architect and interior designer and gutted the place. It took months before the builders moved out and the new furniture was delivered but when it was finished it was modern airy and bright. The only part of the house I left unchanged was the study. It took me ages to go through all the paperwork and clutter, not that in the end there was much to it. Just the dross of a man's life from bank accounts to letters to tradesmen. One thing that was odd and I couldn't get my head around, was where all his money had come from. Regular and large payments went into various savings accounts and investments but the source was never made clear. I found out who his accountant had been and took him on to continue to manage the accounts. Even he had no idea where the money originated although he was adamant there was nothing underhand. Once cleared out, I bought a decent television, sound system and installed broadband and a decent computer. I left the rest unchanged. I kept all the furniture and paintings and turned it into my man cave.

While all this was happening, I was still grappling with the momentous changes in my life. At least with the house being rebuilt and the estate to sort out, I was able to keep busy but I realised that fairly soon it would all be completed and then what the hell was I going to do? I had heard stories of people retiring from active life and losing the plot completely, unable to cope with the pressure of inactivity. I was beginning to wonder just how true the stories were of lottery winners becoming desperately unhappy.

I had looked up a few old friends and that seemed to go well to a degree but they all had their lives to live and work to occupy them. Meeting up for a few beers and reminiscing could only go so far.

Then I met Carrie and nearly everything changed. She came into my life like a bright whirlwind. Even so, after our first meeting that had gone far too fast, far too quickly we both took a step back. It was almost as if we had scared ourselves with the intensity of our feelings for each other. She had a flat in a large old Victorian house not far away, she also had a demanding job so we started to see each other regularly but agreed to keep it at a less intense level until we could at least see if it was going to last. We had both had had relationships in the past that had turned sour and neither of us wanted that to happen again.

One thing we did that we both loved was to explore the city. Much had changed while I had been away but the core of the place was the same. The beautiful water meadows and Winchester College grounds. There was the cathedral with its own extensive grounds as well. She took me around to my old school. There was a great deal of new building but the old, original, Victorian school building was still in use as it had been in my day.

Something else Carrie loved was what I had discovered in the garage. Despite not owning a car when living in London I did have a passion for motor vehicles, particularly old classics. It seemed that my dear departed uncle did too. In the garage was an old Bentley that I knew was worth a fortune and an Aston Martin DB5. Both had clearly been well loved and Carrie and I had great fun tearing around the countryside in both, particularly the Aston.

Despite all this, I was still fretting about what to do with my life. Carrie had some great ideas all of which included both of us disappearing off to a remote sunny island somewhere. I knew she was only half serious. She loved her job and to be frank I had loved working for the police. I even considered whether I could apply to the local force. However, only two months after I had met Carrie and the house was finished everything changed once again.

It was a wet Wednesday and I was on my own. The Grahams weren't around and Carrie was at work. I was bored. Sitting behind the large desk, I was looking through some old documents in the last box to be investigated. It was very uninteresting, basically bills and cheque stubs. I had realised early on that my uncle was a bit of a hoarder. Still, this was the last of a great deal of dross. For the umpteenth time, I wondered about what my uncle had been alluding to in his video. 'Something I would have to find out myself'. Well, with the demise of this box of paper, there was nothing else to discover as far as I could see. I sat briefly back in my chair and looked over the room. The mirror caught my eye as it often did. The desk almost faced it and as it was the full height of the room it gave a reflection of myself sitting facing it. I saw a man in his thirties, of middle height with brown hair. Carrie called me handsome and who was I to argue, although it seemed clear to me that I needed to exercise more. I vowed to dig out my jogging gear. After all, there were plenty of beautiful runs along the banks of the Itchen only yards away from the house. Then the phone rang again for the third time.

Something I had been meaning to do for some time was to get an extension lead so the damn thing could sit on my desk. For some reason my uncle had it sitting on a small table between the fireplace and the mirror. Even better, I could get one of those cordless ones and not have to worry about where to put it. With a sigh, I got up to answer it praying that it wasn't yet another nuisance call from India telling me my computer account needed unblocking or asking whether I had done anything about the car accident I hadn't actually had last week.

I didn't make it to the phone. Or rather I did but went straight past it. There was an old rug in front of the fireplace and it had rucked up in one corner which I had totally failed to notice. As I stomped towards the phone, my foot caught the edge of the rug and before I knew it I was making a fairly good attempt at a swan dive straight towards that bloody mirror. There was only one thing I could do. I put my hands out to protect my head before it smashed into the glass. It didn't work. To my horror and surprise, my hands and then the whole length of my arms seemed to disappear into the glass. I braced myself for the impact on my head and nothing happened. It was like sliding through a curtain of water except that I didn't get wet. I was so bloody surprised that I failed to see the floor coming up towards me and that did hurt as I head butted it. I lay there stunned for a moment wondering what the hell had just happened. The first thing I realised was that the phone had stopped ringing and then, as I looked up, I could see I was still in the study. The weird thing was that I was now facing my desk as if I had turned through one hundred and eighty degrees somehow. I groggily got to my knees and looked around.

I immediately realised that something was really wrong. The desk was covered in papers again, otherwise it looked very much the same except that my computer was nowhere to be seen and the large, expensive television and sound bar that I had bought had been replaced by what looked like a nineteen fifties television made out of wood.

'What the fuck,' I muttered to myself as I got to my feet. My forehead was throbbing. I knew there were some paracetamol in the bathroom in my new en suite bathroom. When I went out onto the landing things became even weirder. The house looked like it had been before I had the builders in. No, it looked even older. The wallpaper was a horrible embossed design and there were no carpets. I went to where my bedroom should have been and although it was still a bedroom it looked like something out of a film set. There was a massive mahogany bed and an old fashioned dressing table. There was even a pitcher of water and bowl on a stand where the sink should be. The radiator was massive great cast iron affair under the single sash window, no double glazing in sight anywhere.

I went over to the window and looked out. The garden looked the same although the tarmac drive had been replaced with gravel. Then I realised that the telegraph pole that brought power and telephone to my house was missing. I looked at the ceiling and there was a light in a large ornate light fitting and there was a switch by the door. When I operated it the light came on so there was obviously power to the house.

Getting more disoriented by the minute I went down to the hall. The floor tiles were the same but that was about it. I was suddenly overcome with a sense of panic. This just couldn't be happening. I ran back up to the study slammed the door behind me and closed my eyes. When I opened them again nothing had changed. Was I having some sort of concussion?

Chapter 5

I took a deep breath and forced myself to think. I had tripped over the rug and fallen towards the mirror. Was this the thing that my uncle said I had to discover myself? If so it made no sense. Maybe I should look at the video again. Without thinking I went over to where the television should be and looked at the box that was sat there. It certainly looked like a television, albeit one from a museum. I then notice an envelope on the top. It was addressed to me. I opened it and pulled out several sheets of paper covered in typing. I collapsed into one of the sofas and started to read.

Anthony,

Apologies that this is typed but you probably couldn't read my hand writing, dammit even I can't do that and there are no video tapes in this world so I can't leave you a visual message. If you are reading this you must have come through the mirror.

I stopped and looked back at the large glass mirror. What on earth did he mean by coming through it? The bloody thing was made of glass – wasn't it? I carried on reading.

When I bought the house, the mirror was already there. I was going to get rid of it when I accidentally put my hand through the glass. As you will now have realised it is a door to another world. I wasn't sure if it would work for you as I've done some experiments and no one else I know can use it. That gave rise to some odd comments from my acquaintances when I asked them to touch it as you can imagine. However, I have some reason to believe that it is tuned (if that is the right description) to people of my close family and anyway if you are reading this then it obviously did work.

The world you are now in is fundamentally different to the one we were born in. Please go out and look around if you haven't done so already. I have put a history book on the shelf by my desk. I strongly suggest that you read it all before you do anything.

21

I looked over at the shelf and sure enough, I could see a large leather bound book.

The key difference between the two worlds seems to be that here, the first and second World Wars never happened, at least not in the way we remember. The assassination of the heir to the Austrian Empire never took place. Consequently, nothing happened in 1914. But nothing is that simple as you can imagine. The Russian revolution did take place but in 1920 and when it did, the Germans took the side of the white Russians and helped suppress it. The result is a German Russian empire that takes in half of Europe, Russia and large parts of the Far East. Nominally it is shared by the current Kaiser and the Tsar, in reality it is dominated by the Germans.

Of course, the British Empire never had to bear the costs of the two wars and is still largely intact although a move away from colonialism to a shared commonwealth is well underway. America had never managed to flex its muscles as it had in our time and although wealthy, is not really a world power. China is a basket case still and coming more and more under the influence of Japan not the least because that gives it some protection from the predation of the Germano Russian alliance. So as you can see world politics are very different. This is just a brief summary you really need to study the book I have left you.

Sorry for the brief history lesson but you need it to understand the world you find yourself in. Imagine what it was like for me when I first crossed over. Society is similar to that of Britain in the fifties at least in part. Technology is very different. Without the spur of two major wars, it took far longer to develop things that you and I take for granted. For example the jet engine has only just been developed.

Enough! This was madness. I must be having some sort of waking dream. I must be sitting at the desk asleep. The best way to get out of this was to go back. I stood up and now that I knew I was dreaming it was a simple matter to walk back through the mirror. I was so sure I would then wake up at the desk that I almost stumbled and fell over again when I found myself back in my study but facing the desk instead of waking up in my chair. Looking around, I could see that at least I was home again.

Something rustled in my hand and I realised I was still holding my uncle's letter. I almost dropped it in astonishment. No, surely I had been dreaming? I went over to the booze shelf and poured myself a large whisky. It might only be ten in the morning but I really needed one. My hand was shaking as I poured the scotch into the glass. I managed to gulp some as I sat down.

I stared at the window for some time trying to work out what the sodding hell had just happened and then remembered the letter. I was still clutching the papers in my left hand. I smoothed them out and started to read again.

There's nothing like our digital technology, don't try and use a mobile phone for example.

You are going to have to work this out for yourself just as I did. I did consider trying to explain it to you face to face but I wasn't sure the mirror would work for you in my presence and then you would never have believed me. As to how and why it works, I have absolutely no idea. I did try and do some research into multiple universe theories but that's all they are, theories. All I can conclude is that the two wars were such cataclysmic events for humanity that somehow a second world was created to provide an alternative. Frankly, that's as good an explanation as I can come up with. Maybe you will achieve a better understanding than I ever managed.

But all that aside, it is a fantastic opportunity. Go and explore, it's a much gentler society in many ways although many of the prejudices that we got rid of still linger on. You have probably wondered how I made all my money. I'm afraid you will have to rightly accuse me of being guilty of insider trading. Watching the stock market and investing in companies that are developing technologies that I know will work, has proved very lucrative. At the end of the letter are some addresses you will need, including my banker, my solicitor and my stockbroker. They all have letters from me identifying you as my heir as well as some others to ensure there are no questions when you turn up. The only practical way to bring wealth across the portal is in the form of gold, they still use sovereigns so I have also included the name of a man I use to sell it on to in our world. I'm sure he thinks I'm a crook and I know he is but it works and of course, I have not actually been committing a crime, well not one recognised by either government.

When I first went through, the house on the other side was derelict much like it had been when I originally bought it. Once I had got my head around what was going on I managed to take enough gold across and buy it. Property prices, indeed all prices are far lower. It appears that without wars, inflation is much less.

I have arranged for notice of my death to be telegraphed to my solicitor and you are the named heir to my estate in my will. It will say that I was abroad in South America and that I was buried there. It will be quite believable. Also, there is much less needed to prove identity and I have ensured that my solicitor has all the necessary paperwork to prove you are a bona fide citizen of the British Empire.

There are couple of servants looking after the place rather like the Grahams. They live in a house down the lane just like in our world, their names are Michael and Mavis Thompson. I have told them about you and they are expecting you some time.

One final point. Some people are the same in both worlds. It's not surprising I suppose although they will have been brought up in a totally different way but it can be quite disconcerting to bump into an old acquaintance from your world and then find him in this one. They won't know who you are though, it seems we are unique.

I could write more but this should be the start you need. Trust me, it's far more than I had. I know it will take some time for all this to make sense. Frankly, after thirty years, it still amazes me. Please study the history book I've left you and go and see the people I've listed starting with the solicitor. But more than that go and explore, take advantage of this unique gift.

Your Uncle

Peter

I threw the papers down again and stared at the wall. The whisky was at least calming me down a little. I've no recollection as to how long I sat there thinking strange thoughts. Eventually, I got up and went for a walk along the river. It was a beautiful spring day and the gentle atmosphere of the meadows calmed my thoughts. By the time I returned to the house I had convinced myself that it had never happened and that when I went up to my study all would be back to normal. And so it was, except for several typed sheets of paper lying on my desk.

I strengthened my resolve. The only way to prove that this had been some sort of waking nightmare was to punch that damned mirror, maybe the pain on my knuckles would break me out of what was obviously some sort of psychotic episode.

I went and stood in front of the glass. The reflection was exactly what I would expect to see. I raised my fist and gritted my teeth for the pain to come and smashed it forward. There was no pain and I put so much momentum into the blow I followed my fist through the glass. A second later I was back in the other study.

Fuck.

Chapter 6

The next week was the most confusing of my life. I came to terms with the situation, what else could I do? It was real, there was no doubt about that. Knowing what I had been told by my uncle and at least accepting it in part, I decided I must really go and see this new world for myself.

So on that first day, I steeled myself and simply walked through the glass. I then left the house and walked out onto the main road behind it. The road was quite narrow and there were no white lines on it. Within a few seconds, if I needed confirmation that this world was something strange, I got it. A lorry approached. It looked like something out of the fifties except there was a cloud of white vapour behind it. It chugged past me, the driver giving me a cheerful wave. Bloody hell, was that a steam powered lorry? Soon afterwards, a car came the other way. At least this one seemed powered by some sort of internal combustion engine but I had never seen the design before although the name Morris on the back was at least familiar even if the dated design wasn't.

It was about a mile to the centre of town. In retrospect, I suppose I should have checked the garage. Uncle Peter was bound to have had a car in there. I idly wondered whether there was a bus service but then realised I didn't have any of the local money. It was then that I walked past a couple who were on the other side of the road. I gave them a cheery good morning but all I got in return was a surprised stare. Unsure why, I suddenly realised that my clothing probably looked quite odd. The man was wearing a hat of some sort and dressed in a jacket and tie and his partner a long flowery dress. I, on the other hand, was wearing chinos, a pair of trainers and an open necked polo shirt.

Having gone less than a quarter of a mile I decided to beat a hasty retreat. When I got back to the house, the door opened before I could touch it and a middle aged man wearing a black waistcoat and cravat stood there.

'Ah, you must be Master Anthony. Mister Peterson did say you would probably drop in unexpectedly. I'm sorry I wasn't here to greet you but we didn't know when you would arrive,' he said, giving me a discrete appraisal from my toes to my head. 'I am

Michael. I understand that you've come from abroad, from one of the colonies no doubt.'

'Er yes,' I replied. 'It seems I am going to need some help with your customs here.'

'Indeed Sir. The master left quite specific instructions. 'By the way, do you know when he will be returning?'

How the hell was I going to answer that? I decided to take the bull by the horns 'I'm terribly sorry and I hate to tell you but he will not be returning. As I'm sure you know he goes away quite regularly and he was with me some weeks ago and caught a fever. Unfortunately, he passed away.' I responded.

The news didn't seem to be much of a surprise. 'Yes Sir, we knew he had been unwell for some time. Will there be a funeral?'

'I'm afraid it's already happened. We were abroad you see and it didn't seem necessary to return the body.'

Michael maintained his stoic demeanour despite the news. 'Indeed Sir. Might I suggest you come in and we can sort out some suitable attire? I take your luggage will be following on.'

This was all getting a bit awkward. 'Michael you must know that Mister Peterson was not quite the usual sort of person.'

'Yes Sir, he had his strange ways but we have grown used to them over the years.'

Just then a rather florid, plump woman came in looking upset. 'Oh dear I'm so sorry, did I hear that the master has gone.'

'My dear, you know we were expecting it now so don't fret. This is the master's nephew. I take it you will be staying here Sir. And I'm sorry but this is Mavis my wife. We look after the place together.'

'Yes, my uncle told me about you. And look don't worry. I have every intention of maintaining your employment. But I am really going to need your help. I am very definitely a newcomer to these shores and will be looking to you both to guide me. Also, my luggage seems to have gone missing so if you could help me settle in and stop me making a fool of myself I would be extremely grateful.'

After that things went much more smoothly. Quite what the couple actually thought about my uncle and his nephew, they never even gave the slightest hint that they thought the situation was unusual. I suspected that they knew far more than they were letting on.

I spent a day reading the book my Uncle had left for me and was very glad I did. It was quite superficial but there was a lot of context I needed as well as an understanding of what technology was available. I also tried an experiment and went and retrieved my phone. I shot a few digital photographs and video and then took them back to my world. They didn't survive the trip. In fact, neither did the phone, it was completely wiped. It seemed alright in the new world but clearly didn't like being taken back through the mirror. So much for gathering detailed proof of my experience. I decided not to take my laptop over.

The day after that, dressed appropriately in a tweed jacket, shirt and tie, Michael drove me into town in the Aston Martin. It was very definitely not the same sort of car that I had in the other world. It looked more like an early Rolls Royce with a button down leather interior and the chauffer sitting in a separate cockpit at the front. When I told Michael I was quite capable of driving, he looked quite put out and said that it would never do to allow a gentleman to drive. In fact, I was quite glad that I had been banished to the back seat because there didn't seem to be many traffic rules at all and very few traffic lights. I would probably have had an accident within minutes.

We had deliberately left early for my appointment with the solicitor because I wanted to look at the city. It was really strange. It was the same but also it was very different. The Broadway at the bottom of the high street was still dominated by the giant statue of King Alfred and the city Guildhall. However, the high street itself was open to two way traffic unlike in my world where it had all been pedestrianised. What was worse was the surface was cobbled which made my teeth rattle as the primitive suspension of the car spectacularly failed to cope with the bumps.

'Why on earth does this part of the city still have cobbles?' I asked Michael as we rattled up past the odd ornamental, little stone tower called the Buttercross for some reason. I had never found out how it had got its name.

'City fathers Sir, they want to keep the town as original as they can. There's been debate about it for years. They don't like change,' he replied.

'*Ha*,' I thought to myself. '*Just like the lot in my world.*' Mind you, back there, the High Street was also cobbled but that was because the area was now a pedestrian precinct. The overall impression I got was the whole place felt smaller although I couldn't really say why. Maybe it was the lack of new buildings which made the medieval side of the town more real.

'What does the city do for industry Michael?' I asked. 'Does much get done here?'

'No Sir, most people seem to work in London and just come here to live. We have two train lines and it takes less than an hour to get to Waterloo from either of them.'

Yet another similarity to my world then although over there, there was only one line.

One thing that really surprised me was just how much was going on in the main streets. The shops were all doing a thriving business, from butchers and greengrocers to several large department stores. It almost felt like I was in an outdoor shopping mall. Then I realised that must be exactly where I was. When I asked about out of town shopping, Michael obviously hadn't a clue what I was talking about. It seemed that in this world, the High Street was still the centre of enterprise instead of nothing more than rows of designer outlets, restaurants and mobile phone shops. I have to say it was a great improvement. I was also quite surprised at the way people dressed. It seemed there was some sort of demographic divide here. Most older people were wearing what I would call conventional but old fashioned clothing. Suits, jackets and ties, even bowler hats for the men and long flowery dresses for the women. However, many of the younger people seemed to have thrown away that convention. Jeans, much longer hair and polo necks were common, certainly no ties.

When I mentioned this to Michael, he gave a grunt of disapproval. 'Indeed Sir, the younger generation seem to want to be different these days. Most even refuse to wear a tie as I am sure you can see. Standards are falling I'm afraid, who knows where it all will end.'

The way he spoke made me think he felt the end of the world was coming. I wondered what he would make of the fashions of my world. Luckily, he would never find out or he might have a coronary.

We arrived at our first appointment, Uncle Peter had clearly set things up very well. The solicitor had a photo of me and it seemed that that was all that was needed to confirm my provenance. As with his other will, I was the main beneficiary although there was a provision for the Thompsons which made Michael more than happy. It seemed the solicitor thought I was a very wealthy man although the estate only ran to just over half a million. Obviously I was going to have to come to terms with very different values in this world.

My accountant was very much of the same opinion and we spent some time going over the accounts which all seemed in order.

My final appointment was with the stockbroker. A man of about my own age. His name was Julian Fletcher and I took an instant liking to him. Sandy haired and wiry he had an air of nervous energy. He was very keen to see me and subtly tried to pump me for information. I made it clear that I would have some ideas for him in due course but was still too upset over the death of my Uncle to try and get to grips with the stock market. We then moved on to talk about more generalities.

'Have you decided how you are going to cope with all your invitations yet?' He asked with a twinkle in his eye.

'Eh, what on earth do you mean?' I asked, surprised at the question.

'Oh come, on, a good looking young man, heir to a great fortune and with an air of mystery around him. All the mothers in the city will want you around for drinks and to parade their unmarried daughters in front of you. And that's just the so called polite society, don't forget we live in modern times and there are endless opportunities to meet people in the clubs and bars in the town. I'm sure your presence will also have come to their notice. The city grapevine is pretty good you know.'

He must have seen the bemused look on my face. His words had caught me completely by surprise. It was an angle to this situation I hadn't even considered, not for a moment. I suddenly realised that I had been caught up so much in this wave of change that I hadn't actually considered my future. Did I really even want to be part of this world? Even though I knew it existed, it didn't need me. I could go home and just get on with my life. After all, I was rich and had a girlfriend there. A girl who, if things continued to develop, could be more than that. But would I be able to ignore what I was experiencing now? Would I be able to resist the temptation? Jesus, this was not going to be easy.

Julian broke into my contemplation. 'Actually, I've got an idea that might help. Your uncle was not that well known to be honest. He kept himself to himself. I think it would help greatly if you put yourself out a little more.'

'What on earth do you mean by that?' I asked.

'Well, your Uncle was buried overseas but why not have a wake for him and then you can invite everyone important. You can decide who you really like and everyone can make their minds up about you. Look, I know you're a stranger to our shores but I could arrange it for you. I know most people in the city, those that count anyway. Let's face it, the cost isn't an issue, you can afford it. What do you say?'

I could see that the idea clearly had merit and he was obviously very keen to be involved. A cynic might suggest he wanted to keep in my good graces in case I proved to be the gold mine my Uncle had been but he seemed genuinely keen to help. And why not? If nothing else it could be fun.

'Alright, that sounds a really good idea, let's do it.'

Chapter 7

Julian was true to his word and three days later a large Marquee had been set up on the lawn next to my house. Both the Thompsons were drafted in to help as well as several staff that Julian engaged. Invitations had been sent all over the city and nearly all had been accepted. It seemed that he was right and everyone wanted to come and meet the man of mystery. Luckily, the weather stayed fine as forecast. The Marquee was certainly not big enough to get all those who had accepted my invitation to take cover if it had rained.

The invitation had made it clear that although the party was to celebrate the life and death of my Uncle it was not to be a sad affair. Black clothing was not required. When the local vicar heard about it, he volunteered to give a reading which seemed appropriate and I would then give a eulogy. After that, the bar would be open and let battle commence.

Julian's assessment that I would be seen as fair game for every single female in the city also appeared correct. As soon as my eulogy was over I was besieged by women, both matrons with young daughters in tow and also girls on their own. I was amazed at how young some of them seemed to be, especially the ones chaperoned by their mothers. At one point I felt like I was trapped in some sort of Jane Austen novel. Despite the fact that many of the girls were very pretty, the whole thing became a real pain in the arse. Eventually, I was able to escape and made my way over to a knot of men who were all clustered around the bar.

When they saw me coming they moved aside and seemed to want to make me welcome.

'Ah, it's our esteemed host,' a voice said and my hand was vigorously shaken by all and sundry. At least by being next to the bar I was able to snaffle a drink. My first one having evaporated under the heat of all that female admiration.

Conversation was focused on questions about my intentions and less than subtle enquiries about my business and fortune. I managed not to be drawn on either subject and kept to platitudes.

Suddenly from behind me there came a booming voice. 'Let a bobby see the bar there's a good chap. Oh sorry, you must be our host. I do apologise it's just that I'm dying of thirst in this heat, don't you know.'

I felt the hairs rise on the back of my neck. I knew that voice only too well. How the hell could he be here? I turned and looked right into the rather bloodshot eyes of Chief Inspector, Frank, bloody, Cosgrove. Except it couldn't be him, not here. And although the voice was the same, the man looked quite different. His hair was almost completely gone and rather than being at least two stone overweight, it was more like three or even four. He was wearing a suit with a bright yellow waistcoat that was putting up with a great deal of strain to its buttons.

He had his hand out to me and I automatically shook it. I know my uncle had warned me that I might meet people I knew from home in this world but I hadn't really expected it, especially with someone I had a strong personal and professional dislike of. All that said, there was something about this version of Frank that wasn't the same. Instead of the almost permanent frown and angry look, this version looked more content and full of bonhomie.

'Welcome to the lovely City of Winchester,' he said with a wide grin. 'And don't be worried about anything, the Winchester Bobbies keep the place well guarded.'

He must have seen my non plussed look. 'Sorry, you probably don't know but I am the senior policeman here. Chief Inspector of the Winchester force no less.'

For a second I was quite taken aback. Not that this version of Frank was a policeman, more for the intelligent and lively look in his eyes. They may have the same name and looks but this was definitely not the same man.

'Well that's good to know,' I said. 'I shall sleep well in my bed knowing that I am well guarded.'

'So Mister Peterson. I hear you've been living abroad and were with your uncle when he died. It must have been a sad time for you. We never really got to know your uncle he was always off somewhere,'

'Oh please call me Tony,' I said. 'Yes, he was a strange man in many ways.'

'And where exactly where you both when he met his end? If you don't mind me asking?'

33

Shit, I knew this was going to come up. I had been able to prevaricate up until now but his man seemed far more eager to hear more and determined to get an answer. Several days ago I had realised that I would need to understand much more about this world. Uncle's book has given me a head start but I was still a babe in arms when it came to the social world of contemporary society. I had spent several evenings watching the television, which to my surprise had been in colour. The dated design had me convinced it would be black and white. The programmes weren't hard to understand and consisted mainly of quiz shows and music programmes with the odd thriller thrown in. Much like home in fact, although the way people spoke seemed very old fashioned. The music was a revelation. The standard three guitars and a drum was fairly common but the variety was enormous. It seemed that they had had their music revolution in the sixties just like us. However, the newsreaders still wore dinner jackets and spoke as though they had a plum in their mouths. Still, I had caught up on some of the news. There were several on-going small wars in central Europe. It seemed that not everyone there liked being ruled by the Kaiser. The British Empire was also undergoing profound change and there had been several bloody uprisings especially in Africa although all seemed peaceful at the moment. It had seemed that my safest bet if asked, was to say that I had been with my uncle in South America. In Argentina to be precise. It was a country with strong ties to Britain but still independent. It was also a place that was popular with the British for holidays.

'We were on holiday in Buenos Aires,' I said. 'I'll be honest, my uncle knew he had an incurable disease and he decided to take one last break. Unfortunately, he caught a chill and that seemed to accelerate the process. Luckily, I had joined him by then and at least I was there when he departed.'

Frank gave me an odd stare. Had I said something wrong?

'That's very sad but I would like to talk some more maybe in a few day's time if you are available? This is neither the time nor the place.'

It may have come out as a request but I got the strong feeling that it was one I really ought to comply with. The last thing I wanted was to get on the wrong side of the law within a few days of arriving here. Of course, I could always simply disappear but there was so much about this new world that I wanted to discover.

'I would be delighted,' I replied.

He slapped me on the back. 'Excellent, I'll be in touch.' He moved off into the throng like a dreadnought ploughing through a stormy sea.

I notice Julian approaching. 'I see you've met our esteemed Bobby. He's quite a force of nature isn't he?'

'Yes, you could say that. He wants to meet up in a few days. I got the impression it wasn't a request.'

Julian nodded. 'Don't worry, he's well known for being a bit nosy but a good copper by all accounts. Anyway, have you met every eligible female in the city yet?'

'If not, then I've made good inroads,' I replied as I snagged another drink from the tray of a passing waiter. 'How long do we let this go on for? I'll be honest it's all starting to get a bit wearing.'

'Oh, another hour or so should be sufficient. Just gird your loins and then you will have done your duty.'

'You know Julian, I'm really grateful for your help in all this. I wouldn't have even know where to start without your help.'

'You're welcome. There really aren't enough single men of our standing left in this place and it's nice to have a kindred spirit. Mind you, I may soon be joining the ranks of the downtrodden married masses soon if I'm not careful.'

I felt he really meant what he said but couldn't help adding, 'and no doubt some investment advice will do no harm.'

He laughed. 'Absolutely old chap. Now I need to introduce you to these lovely people over here.'

I was dragged back into the scrum for more platitudes and sly glances.

Once everyone had gone and the place had been cleaned up, I went to sit by the banks of the river. I own a good two hundred yards of riverbank at the bottom of the main garden. It was a wonderful evening. The sun was setting behind me and shining a golden light on the slopes of the old Stone Age fort of Saint Catherines hill in the distance. The river was flowing gently over its gravel and weed bed and I could see brown trout hovering amongst the green fronds. I sat on the gentle bank with a glass of wine in my hand and realised I was more than a little pissed. I lay back and looked up at the sky and tried to make some sense of what had happened to me. Could anyone have experienced such a change to their life? I had been a successful policeman with early promotion and a good career ahead of me. Within weeks, I had left that all behind. I was rich and apparently the sole human capable of travelling between two completely different worlds. And I had absolutely no idea what to do next. This world seemed much gentler in many ways. The people here had been spared the horror of two dreadful wars. That didn't mean the place was perfect that was quite clear. But in some ways, life here looked preferable to my own world. There was no sign of real mass communication or the digital toys that we all seem to need every moment of our lives at home, yet life seemed to go on pretty well.

Then I realised there was actually one thing this world lacked and suddenly it seemed to me that it was the deciding factor. There was an overriding reason I couldn't make a life here even had I decided it was what I wanted to do. It was all down to a Ponytail and bright sparkling brown eyes that turned me to jelly every time they   looked   into   mine.

Chapter 8

It's funny how minor things can make such a major change to one's life. When I went to bed that night it was in my world. I had crossed over and immediately rang Carrie but she said she was snowed under marking homework. I considered going back but then remembered that the bedroom over there lacked an en suite and far more importantly the bed lacked a duvet. It had sheets and heavy blankets and I'm pretty sure the mattress was made of old cart springs, literally. There was no reason to use it at all I realised. My mind set really needed to change. I had been sleeping in the thing for days now when I didn't need to at all. However, I made a mental note to deliberately disturb the bed the next morning otherwise Mavis would no doubt want to know where on earth I had been. I wondered how Uncle Peter had managed these silly minor issues. Silly they may have been but I really didn't want my secret discovered for no other reason than no one would believe me and God knows what would happen then.

One thing I did need to do urgently was to go to the new world and do some research. If that nosy version of Frank wanted to dig into my past I needed plenty of background to keep him happy. The South American story was quite a good one. The solicitor had told me that he had received a copy of a death certificate from there, which showed that Uncle Peter had been thinking well ahead. In addition, I had picked up that Argentina was a popular holiday destination when watching some adverts on the television. But I also needed a story about my past because he was bound to ask.

So the next morning I went back over, jumped onto the horrible bed and mucked up the sheets making a mental note to get rid of the damned thing as soon as possible. In fact, there was no reason why I couldn't remodel the whole house, after all, I had already done it once.

Much to Michael's annoyance, I then insisted on taking the car myself into town. I think he didn't rate me as capable of driving it and to be fair he wasn't far wrong. I quickly discovered that the foot pedals were in different places. It seemed that in this world they had standardised on a different layout. The throttle was in the middle, the clutch to the left and the brake on the right. After a couple of abortive attempts to get moving, I got the hang of it and gave him a cheery wave as I drove out of the gate in an almost controlled fashion.

I headed to the City library. I was hoping it had a reading room, it certainly had one when I was a kid although I hadn't been in my one since I returned. It also had a large car park at the back which was handy.

Having survived the drive, I parked up and made my way through the double doors and into the large space. Off to my left was the reading area as I had hoped and in front of me was the main desk. I hadn't been looking carefully at the desk as I approached, as I was looking around the room. So when I reached it to ask where I might find the periodicals which were going to be my first line of research, I really, really wasn't expecting what happened next.

As I asked my question the girl behind the desk who had been looking down at something lifted her head.

I was looking straight into the eyes of Carrie.

My first reaction was shock. What the hell was she doing here? How the hell did she get here? Then I realised she was wearing clothes that were definitely not her style. I would never expect to see her in a cardigan. Her hair was wrong too. She had a page boy cut and she told me she hated short hair. I also noticed a ring on her left hand.

I must have been gawping because she frowned at me and spoke in a frosty tone. 'Yes Sir, can I help you?'

My brain finally caught up with events and belatedly I realised that she must be like the policeman, the same person but of this world not mine. Oh shit, this could get complicated.

When I didn't immediately answer she spoke again. 'Are you alright Sir? You look like you've seen a ghost.'

'No, no sorry. It's just that you look just like someone I used to know. But that was a long way from here.'

I could immediately tell that she thought it was some sort of chat up line and wasn't impressed. 'Yes Sir, well, what can I do for you?' She asked in a frosty voice.

Oh bloody hell what did I want? For a moment I couldn't remember. I needed to get away and think. 'Er where can I read the latest magazines please?'

'Over there Sir,' she said sharply and pointed. 'To your left.'

I muttered some sort of thanks or was it an apology? And made a hasty exit. The magazines and even copies of the day's newspapers were on racks and I was able to take a sample and sit down. My mind was no longer on my mission at all. I pretended to read but in reality, I used the magazines as a cover to study Carrie. There was no doubt in my mind that it was her. Except that of course it wasn't. This was so confusing. She had the same small mole on her left cheek and even her mannerisms were the same. When she was looking down and concentrating on something she twirled her hair by her left ear with her finger. It was something I actually found rather irritating, not that I had ever said anything about it to her.

But of course, this version knew nothing about me. So why was I even concerned? My Carrie was safely teaching history a billion miles away. The two of them could never meet. At that point, I realised that it could even be possible that there was a version of me somewhere in this universe. I needed to think this through and sitting spying on this girl was not the way to do it. I put the magazines down, nodded my thanks to Carrie and left. I headed home and told Michael I would be in the study all day and must not be disturbed.

I spent the afternoon in my study in the new world looking again at uncle's book with the television on in the background but spectacularly failed to maintain any concentration. After a couple of hours, I decided I was wasting my time and would go back through and insist that my Carrie and I spend the evening together. That was the exact moment when the phone rang. Over here it was an ugly Bakelite thing with a rotary dial although I had seen push button ones elsewhere.

It was Julian. 'Hello sport, doing anything tonight? Only I've got an invite to a really top hole jazz club that's just opened in town and wondered if you wanted to join me?'

Damn, I was looking forward to a dose of sanity but could I say no? Julian had been so helpful and I really owed him for everything he had done recently. Well, my Carrie was not actually expecting me so there was no real reason not to accept.

'Alright Julian. Where and when?'

The club was at the bottom of the high street. I got Michael to drive me there and before he did that I asked for advice on what to wear. At first, he was reluctant to help, saying that it was not the sort of place he had ever patronised. After insisting that he must know something he eventually relented and suggested some slacks and polo neck sweater. As I had already noticed it was the sort of casual clothing younger people liked these days and very definitely not up to the standards that Michael expected.

When we got there I told him I would get a taxi home. As he left, he gave me a look that seemed as though he thought I was selling my soul to the devil. I just grinned back at him. I was looking forward to seeing how they let their hair down in this universe.

As I walked in, the smell hit me between the eyes. My policeman's hackles rose immediately, the aroma was unmistakable. Oh God, was I in the sort of place that could get me arrested by just being there? What the hell was Julian thinking?

The man himself was already there propping up the bar. The place looked like a cross between an English pub and a dance hall, albeit with a very small dance floor. At least Michael had been reasonably accurate about what people wore and I didn't feel out of place at all. That said, Julian was wearing a collarless shirt and waistcoat which seemed almost too casual compared to others. Still, what did I know?

'Ah there you are,' he called as I came over. 'What's your poison?'

'Julian, what the hell is going on in here?' I asked as I looked around and could see dozens of people smoking but it clearly wasn't tobacco.

'Eh, nothing old chap just people relaxing and having a good time.'

'But they're all smoking.'

Julian looked non plussed. 'It's only H old chap nothing wrong there.'

'H, what the hell do you mean by that?'

'Hemp, you know, fun weed, soothing smoke. What's the problem? Don't they use it where you come from?'

'Well yes but not legally. Jesus Julian, we could get arrested.'

'What are you on about old chap? It's all legal, has been for years, just like alcohol. They tried to ban that many years ago as well and that was a waste of time. Now if you were talking about tobacco that would be a different thing. That's just bloody dangerous and highly addictive. Thank goodness that was banned. I don't think there's a country around the world that now allows it.'

For a moment I couldn't think of anything to say. Over here tobacco was the illegal drug and Marijuana was perfectly acceptable. As I thought about it, it made a great deal of sense. Mind you I couldn't see it working back at home.

'Sorry Julian,' I said. 'It's not in wide use at home and anyway I'm a straight booze man. So what have we got?'

I looked at the bar. Many of the labels looked odd but some were familiar. 'A large Scotch if I may.' I said. At least that was pretty generic and I had a good idea about what I would get.

'So how are you settling in?' Julian asked as he relaxed back against the bar. 'Any of the beauties of Winchester caught your eye yet? There were plenty to choose from the other day.'

'Sorry Julian,' I replied. 'It's far too early to even contemplate such a thing. I've only been here a short while.'

He laughed. 'Well, tonight should be a little different. No stuffy old parents to oversee the ladies. I think you'll find things a little freer and easier here.'

He wasn't wrong, what with the Scotch starting to hit the right spot and the amount of chemicals in the air I was starting to relax whether I wanted to or not.

The band appeared on the stage. I have to say that when they started I was quite impressed. They had an odd mixture of instruments ranging from an electric guitar of sorts to a double base and clarinet. However, the music was really good. A sort of mixture between jazz and rock. I idly wondered if I could introduce some of the classics from my world but it was yet another of those ideas that I realised would have to wait for some time. For whether I decided just how I was going to fit into this place in the future.

I have to say I did enjoy the first part of the evening. In some ways, it had the same sort of atmosphere that I remembered from my younger days. The music was loud but good, there were plenty of pretty girls all who seemed more than willing to go onto the dance floor. The scotch was slipping down quite well and I was really starting to relax and get into the mood.

I had noticed that Julian was looking pensively at his watch occasionally. 'What's the matter old chap have you been stood up?'

It was clear he didn't understand the expression. 'Sorry, are you expecting someone?'

'Yes but she's always late. I don't know why I should be so surprised. She said she couldn't get here before nine but it's almost ten now.'

Suddenly, his face lit up as he must have seen someone come in through the entrance. I turned to follow his gaze and immediately cursed under my breath. There, looking as lovely as ever was Carrie. She was accompanied by another striking girl with long blonde hair but I hardly noticed. Damn but this was going to be awkward.

Julian stood and so did I as they approached. 'Girls, this is my new friend Tony, he's the chap I told you about with the big house. Tony, this is Carrie Parks my fiancé and Elaine Smith her partner in crime.'

We shook hands. Carrie gave me a strange look but we all sat down as Julian went off to the bar to get the girls their drinks.

'Sorry we couldn't make your big party the other day,' Elaine said. 'But we were both working that afternoon and couldn't get the time off at short notice.'

'What? Oh that's alright. It was Julian's idea so that I could meet some of the locals or maybe so that they could meet me.'

'Yes,' Carrie said. 'Your uncle was a mysterious man by all accounts. Julian said he thought it would be a good idea for you to become more known in society.'

'Well, I suppose it worked,' I said. 'Look, sorry about the awkward meeting today but you really do look like someone I know and it caught me by surprise that's all.'

Elaine turned to us both and raised an eyebrow in amused enquiry.

'Tony came into the library today,' Carrie explained. 'I think I might have been a little rude, please accept my apology.'

'No need,' I said. 'A simple misunderstanding that's all.'

Just then, we were rescued from more awkward conversation by the arrival of Julian with a tray of drinks.

After that, the evening became slightly surreal. Seeing Carrie with another man was strange and even a little upsetting. I repeatedly had to remind myself that she wasn't my Carrie. The conversation slipped past me on many occasions partly because I often hadn't the slightest idea what they were talking about and didn't want to display my ignorance and partly because I couldn't concentrate. Elaine must have been rather put out by my lack of attention to her but she was very good at hiding it. Maybe she put it down to my reputation as a man of mystery. Either way, I soon realised that I needed to escape. So as soon as I could, without appearing rude, I made my excuses and departed. I went straight home and without hesitation left the place for my own comfortable bedroom in my own comfortable world, jumped into bed and pulled the warm comfortable duvet over my head.

Chapter 9

When I woke the next morning I decided that I needed a break from the madness of an alternative reality, containing an alternative of the girl I was falling in love with. I needed to do something completely different. I needed to make some serious decisions. Things could just not go on as they were at the moment.

It was a Friday and Carrie and I were meant to be having a quiet weekend. I decided that was not a good idea. I spent the morning making alternative arrangements.

I rang her at lunchtime when I knew she would be out of class and have her phone turned back on. 'Can you get Monday off?' I asked when she picked up.

'Why?' she asked.

'A surprise but can you?'

'I have a few days owing and it's not my busiest of days. Yes probably.'

'Good, pack some things for a weekend away. Make sure you have some nice evening clothes and no, before you ask, I'm not saying anything more. It's a surprise remember.'

That evening we flew to Paris from Southampton airport in a chartered private jet. Dammit, I had all this money now so why not splash some cash and make the weekend something to remember?

I hadn't told Carrie where we were going but she soon got the message when she saw a few famous landmarks outside the window as the aircraft banked to land.

'Paris, that's lovely Tony but come on, what's this all about?'

'Quite simple really. I can afford it, I wanted to surprise you and it could be fun.'

'She gave me an odd look and leant over and kissed me. 'Thank you, let's make sure it is fun.'

I grinned back as I had a fairly good idea what she meant. Once on the ground, it didn't take long to hail a taxi and get clear of the airport. Our hotel was on the Champs Elyse itself and the room was spectacular. Mind you, it should have been, the amount it was costing. I still wasn't used to the millionaire lifestyle it seemed.

Carrie was enchanted by it and spent several minutes minutely inspecting every inch before turning back to me. 'What have you got planned for this evening?'

'Simple,' I answered. 'Dinner at one of the best restaurants in the city. Tomorrow and Sunday we can do anything you want but I have a few ideas for evening entertainment. We fly back midday on Monday.'

'And what time is the table booked for tonight?' She asked as she came up to me and put her arm around my waist.

I looked into her lovely brown eyes and inhaled her scent. 'In about two hours.'

We almost made our table on time. We were only half an hour late.

The rest of the weekend was magic. That's the only way I can describe it. We did most of the corny tourist things. We went to the top of the Eiffel Tower and spent some time in the Louvre. We walked along the south bank looking at all the bookstalls and painters vying to paint our portraits. We also spent quite a lot of time in bed. As I said it was magic. I also made an important decision. It was something I had been thinking about for some time and so on Saturday afternoon, I managed to sneak away for a couple of hours to do some shopping.

Despite all this, all the time, in the back of my mind was the problem about what to do about the other world and that bloody mirror. So I made my second important decision of the weekend while I was out at the shops.

Our last evening was in the hotel restaurant. It had a lovely veranda overlooking the heart of the city.

'I don't know about you Tony,' Carrie said, 'But I'm exhausted, we must have walked miles over the last few days. But it has been absolutely wonderful thank you so much.'

'Good, I'm glad it worked out so well. It was a spur of a moment thing.' I suddenly found my pulse racing. Now was definitely the right time. 'But I'm so glad we did do it. It's helped me make up my mind about several things.'

'Oh? You have seemed a little preoccupied on occasions. Is there something worrying you?'

'Not worrying as such, more how to solve a rather odd problem. I'll tell you more later but first, there is something else I need to ask you.'

She looked over at me smiling and raised an eyebrow. We had just finished our meal and the table only held coffee cups and two liqueurs. I reached over and put my hand over hers. 'You've been the best thing that's ever happened to me Carrie, you must know that.' She was about to speak so I forestalled her. 'I know it's only been a relatively short time but I can't think of my life without you. I fell in love with you that day on the High Street you know. So Carrie, it's a simple question. Will you marry me?' I pulled a small box out of my pocket and opened it showing her the results of my shopping expedition the previous day. A rather large solitaire diamond set in a gold band.

I don't think she had been expecting the question because the look on her face seemed to be of genuine surprise. *'Oh God,'* I thought. *'She's going to say no and I'll look a complete idiot.'*

Her hand squeezed mine. 'I did wonder if you had something like this in mind,' she said. 'And what girl could turn down an offer in such a romantic setting. You know that I've always had a crush on you, right from our childhood. It hasn't gone away. Yes, of course I'll marry you.'

Neither of us had noticed what was going on in the rest of the room but clearly the other diners had seen me hold the ring out to her. When she held out her hand and I slipped it on her finger there was a round of applause from all around us. Embarrassing or what? Even worse, the Maître D then came over and offered us a glass of champagne. We had to acknowledge everyone's smiles but then both decided that a hasty retreat was in order.

When we got back to our room there seemed only one thing to do. It wasn't as if we hadn't been practicing all weekend.

Later that evening we were both lying side by side on a rather rumpled bed. Carrie leant over and prodded my chest. 'I seem to remember you said you had a rather odd problem to solve. So what is that all about?'

I lay back and looked at the ceiling. I had wondered why Uncle Peter had kept his involvement in the other world so low key. He seemed to have only used it to make shrewd investments and add to his fortune in this world. I was beginning to understand why he had done it that way. One of the other things I had decided that weekend was that I was going to do something similar. There was no way I could live a double life in two separate universes especially with another Carrie over there. However, I had to accept that now I knew of it, there was no way I could simply ignore it. On top of all that, having decided to ask Carrie to marry me I knew I couldn't keep it a secret from her. The real problem then was how on earth I could tell her and how on earth I could convince her I wasn't barking mad. Otherwise, it could be a very short engagement.

'Carrie I'm going to tell you a secret. It's a very, very strange story and its one I still have trouble accepting myself. As you know, when my uncle died he left his entire estate to me. However, there was more to it than money and a house. I'm going to tell you more when we get home and I will hopefully be able to convince you that I'm not barking mad. But without a practical demonstration, you will never be able to believe me. If that all sounds weird, well that's exactly what it is.'

She looked me in the eye. 'Wow, I wasn't expecting that. Alright, you show me what it is tomorrow when we get back. But it better be good after all that.'

'Oh, it will be, trust me.'

We got back home mid afternoon. Carrie was starting to get cross with me because I wasn't being very forthcoming about my strange story. I wanted to tell her more but really felt that doing it in the right place would help my credibility. When we got home I made us both a cup of tea and we headed up to my study.

'Goodness, this is the first time I've actually been in here. It really is a man cave,' she said looking around at the old fashioned furniture and modern electronic devices.

'It's the only room in the house that I've left completely unchanged,' I said. 'Apart from chucking out what seemed like several tons of paperwork. My uncle was a real hoarder. And I suppose that 'man cave' is a pretty good description. Now Carrie, grab a seat we need to talk.'

We plonked down in the two old leather sofas and I started to tell my story. I showed her the video that Uncle Peter had left me and all went well. I then asked her to come with me to look at the mirror. I asked her to put her hand on the glass, half expecting that it might work for her too but no such luck. Now was going to be the difficult part. I didn't want to demonstrate anything until she knew at least part of the rest of the story.

'Carrie please trust me now. Some time ago I tripped over that rug there and fell into the mirror. I went through it to somewhere else.' I stopped and looked at her.

'Say that again Tony, I thought you just said you went through a solid pane of glass.' She had an odd smile on her face.

'Carrie on the other side of that mirror is another world.' I saw she was going to say something. 'No, let me finish. It's a world like ours, the only difference is that the two World Wars never happened so things have developed differently. My uncle discovered it and that is how he made all his money. Look, here is a letter he left for me in a room almost identical to this one.' I handed her the creased pages from the desk where I had left them. 'Please, before you say anything just read it.'

She read silently for several minutes and looked up at the mirror occasionally. When she had finished she looked back up to me. 'No Tony, this is nonsense. How can you expect me to believe such rubbish?'

I could see she was starting to get angry. Frankly, I didn't blame her.

'I completely understand Carrie. Watch.' I stepped through the mirror. My study on the other side was just as I had left it before the weekend. I had told the Thompsons that I didn't want them to go in there at all and always locked the door from the inside. They weren't surprised as my uncle had given them exactly the same instructions. I decided to wait a few minutes so grabbed the book my uncle had left for me to read about the new world and then stepped back.

The look of utter shock on Carrie's face was actually quite funny, even if the situation was far from it. 'What did you just see?' I asked.

'You, you just disappeared. It was like you walked through the glass. Do it again.'

So I did but came straight back this time. 'Carrie, sit down, we need to talk a lot more and I've got some reading material for you as well.'

If everything had been difficult for me to accept, at least I had had the evidence of my own two eyes. Everything I told Carrie was second hand apart from my disappearing act. We spent the rest of the afternoon going through my uncle's book and with me explaining my adventures over there in between. In the end, she seemed to accept it all. The evidence was pretty overwhelming. Then she started asking awkward questions like were there other versions of ourselves over there and shouldn't I consider telling the authorities what I had discovered. For the first question, I said it could be possible but I hadn't come across anyone like that yet and prayed she wouldn't pursue it further. Luckily she didn't. For the second, we both agreed that it could quickly become a nightmare for both of us.

One thing I really wanted to reassure her about though was what it would mean for our relationship. 'Carrie I have no intention of doing anything more than what my uncle did. They are way behind us in most technologies although in some areas like medicine they may be a little ahead. I haven't had time to investigate in any depth. So, all I intend to do is visit occasionally and deal with my stockbroker, he's a really good guy.'

She seemed to accept this. I just prayed that it didn't become an unresolvable issue between us. I would do everything I could to make sure it didn't. It was almost dark and I realised we had spent all afternoon and well into the evening talking.

'Carrie let's stop. This isn't going to go away any time soon. Why don't we nip down to the pub for a late supper?'

'Goodness is that the time,' she said, looking at her watch. 'Right, yes, we need to take a break and then I need to go home, some of us still have to work.'

As she said it something occurred to me. There were a couple of the latest newspaper in my other study that I had picked up after my trip to the library. I didn't really want my book leaving home but Carrie could take those away with her and get rid of them when she wanted.

'Hang on just a second,' I said. 'I've got something you can take with you that'll give you some really good background.'

I went over to the mirror and stepped through. I rummaged around for a few minutes looking for the newspapers and anything else I could grab. Then for a second, I couldn't work out what was going on. There were lights flashing outside, dammit they were blue lights. I assumed they meant the same thing over here as they did at home. Before I could react, the study door was smashed open and a policeman appeared followed a few seconds later by the bulk of Inspector Frank Cosgrove.

'Ah, found you at last. Your people said you weren't at home, it seems they were wrong. I shall be having words with them about that. Anthony Peterson you are under arrest.'

'What,' I cried out. 'What the hell are you on about?'

'You are under arrest for the murder of Mister Julian Fletcher. You will now accompany me to the police station.'

Chapter 10

My immediate reaction was to bolt for the mirror. It was only feet away. Maybe I should have done just that but two things stopped me. Firstly, how would I ever explain my return at some later time? Secondly, something the Inspector had said didn't ring true but if Julian had been murdered, then despite our fairly brief acquaintance, I owed it to him to try to help.

Those few seconds of dithering made my mind up for me. A burly constable grabbed me by my arm and I was hustled out of the room. As I looked behind me I was grateful to see that the police were not tearing the place apart, yet another indication to me that there was more to this than met the eye. I was taken downstairs and put in the back of a large van of some sort. It had windows so I could see where I was going. The constable had climbed in with me but refused any of my attempts at conversation. It was soon quite clear where we were going. The police stations in both worlds were obviously in the same place. It was the same brick, Victorian building but the décor was definitely not the same. The van pulled up at the rear and I was hustled down a corridor covered in institutional green tiles to a large metal door which the constable opened with a large key. The room inside was bare except for a wooden table and two very uncomfortable looking wooden chairs. It was lit by a single unshaded light bulb. It almost reminded me of a stage set from a bad television production, except this was real. In my day there would have been a tape recorder and almost certainly a one way mirror in one wall for the interview to be observed.

I took one chair and settled in to wait. As someone who had conducted countless interviews over the years, I was pretty sure I knew most of the tricks of the trade. The first one being to make the interviewee stew for a while. I passed the time wondering what Carrie would now be doing. Hopefully, she would realise that something had detained me and just go home. Somehow I didn't think she would do that at all but there was always hope.

Cosgrove only gave me fifteen minutes of stewing time before the door opened and in he came, all bonhomie and smiles.

'Mister Peterson, let's keep this simple shall we?' He said as he seated his bulk on the chair on the other side of the table away from me. I had deliberately chosen the chair that backed against the door. It would normally be the one used by the interrogator but I had spoiled his gambit. He didn't let it show.

'It's quite simple, we want to know what you had to do with the murder of Mister Fletcher.' He looked hard at me still with the smile that never reached his eyes.

I simply stared back.

'Are you going to tell?' Me he asked.

'I will when you get round to actually asking me a question,' I replied.

He sighed. 'Very well, did you murder Julian Fletcher?'

'No.'

It was clear I was not responding in the manner he wanted so he tried a different tack. 'Where were you this afternoon between four and six in the afternoon?'

I suppose I could have said I was in another universe trying to tell an unbelievable story to my fiancé. I was sorely tempted to do just that for a moment, just to see the look on his face. Common sense prevailed.

'You don't want to know that at all do you?' I replied. 'This has very little to do with this murder you are going on about. You're fishing for something.'

The smile slipped from Frank's face for a second. 'Now listen to me, you are in a great deal of trouble so I strongly suggest you cooperate for your own good.'

'Bollocks,' I said. 'You have absolutely no evidence to link me with this murder. When you arrested me you failed to read me my rights, this interview is illegal as there is no independent witness, you haven't even offered me the right to legal representation. Do you want me to go on?' I was fairly sure that I was on solid ground with these points as they had been enshrined in police procedures for many years and I considered it highly unlikely that things were that different here.

Frank looked at me for several moments without saying a word. Eventually, the smile returned and my gamble was proved correct. 'Fair enough but your reply at least helps me with some of my issues. You clearly have some experience in legal matters. So I really have only one question. Who exactly are you? Before you answer, let me tell you what the problem I have with you is. Firstly, your uncle was a very private man. He was extremely inconspicuous and never caused the slightest trouble. However, it was quite clear he was a very shrewd investor and so if for no other reason was of general interest to me. That said, I never had any reason to look at him in any detail. Then you appear on the scene and seem to want to take a much larger part in the city's social life. Yes, I know that's hardly a crime but out of curiosity, I decided to do a quick background check. Your solicitor has a birth certificate for you. You were born in Australia to British parents. Those parents are registered at Somerset house as is their child along with his death certificate. I have come across this trick before Mister Peterson where the identity of a dead child is used to build a new identity. I have telegraphed Australia asking them to tell me what records they have about you. What do you think they will come back with?'

I looked him in the eye. 'Absolutely nothing. What's more, if you try to do any more investigating in this country you will find a complete blank as well.' I had idly considered that this scenario might happen at some time and so had already come up with the bones of a plan. I was going to have to flesh it out now as I talked.

'I would also suggest that if you are foolish enough to continue to investigate, it could be bad for your career. Do you follow me?'

Frank's eyes narrowed. 'You're saying, I take it, that you are employed as a member of His Majesty's Government? So tell me at least what kind of work you are involved in, in this little back water city. I think I should at least know if there is trouble brewing on my patch.'

'Good question. But you are using the wrong tense. I did undertake certain work for an organisation that doesn't exist but no more. If you must know, I was rather like you, a sort of policeman. However, circumstances changed and when my uncle died and I inherited, I decided to take early retirement.' Of course, all this was true in one sense. I find that even when telling bare faced lies, using as much of the truth as possible can really help your plausibility.

'So, there is nothing happening on your patch,' I said. 'Apart from this murder you talk about. I take it that it's real?'

'Oh yes and you have to admit that there is at least a link between Mister Fletcher and yourself. He was your uncle's stockbroker and I assume was also going to do work for you?'

'Yes and we had already become friends. The party the other week was his idea. I'm beginning to wonder if it was actually that good a one.'

Frank had clearly made a decision. 'Mister Peterson, I'm still not sure that I believe what you've said to me although the complete lack of any history actually lends some credence to your story. I did wonder if something like this might be the explanation. However, you're not off the hook yet. You say you were a policeman so I'm going to suggest that you accompany me to the crime scene and tell me what you can deduce. I might then at least be able to make some assessment of your skills.'

'Fair enough,' I said, grateful that for at least the moment, he was accepting my story. 'There is one condition though.'

'Oh and what would that be.'

'You lot pay for the repairs to my study door.'

'Yes sorry about that, we had been waiting for you to arrive and then one of my men saw movement against your study window and rather jumped the gun. Mind you, you must tell me sometime how you managed to get into the house without us seeing you arrive.'

'Ah,' I said. 'I have a secret tunnel. Or if you had bothered to check you would have found out that the house has a rear entrance and stairs to my study.'

Chapter 11

It was getting late by now but it didn't take long to get to Julian's house which was apparently where the crime had been committed. The property was in a typical suburban road not far from my house but closer to the city centre. I knew that he had inherited the place along with the business from his father who had died several years ago. I wasn't quite prepared for how grand the house was. I wondered just how much my uncle's input had been in generating the wealth that was on display here.

We drove up a short drive, the house was set back slightly from the road and just like my place and most of the other houses in the area was constructed of brick and flint. There were two police cars already parked by the front door but no sign of anyone except for one constable seemingly guarding the front door.

Frank had been remarkably reticent during the drive over and I didn't push him. He had already said that he wanted to know what I made of the scene. I also desperately wanted to know what had prompted him to decide that I needed to be taken into his custody. Especially as he now admitted that I was not actually a suspect.

We climbed out of the car and past the constable into a large entrance hall.

'His girlfriend discovered him,' Frank said. 'She's in the drawing room over there but I want you to see the crime scene for yourself first.'

'Do you mean Carrie?' I asked. 'He introduced me to his girlfriend the other night.'

'That's right Carrie Parks. It'll help that you know each other.'

I refrained from any comment.

'Come with me,' he said as he strode up the main staircase. 'You probably know that he had an office in the High Street. What you probably don't know is that he also seems to have done quite a lot of business from home. This was his study or office, whatever you want to call it.' He indicated a door. 'Before we go in you should know that the body has been moved but the rest of the crime scene remains undisturbed. He was found seated in his chair with his head resting on the desk. I assume you are aware of the precautions needed under these circumstances?'

I assured him that I did but also noted that there was no protective clothing available apart for a pair of rubber gloves which he handed me. I was pretty sure that DNA had not been discovered here yet and so supposed it didn't matter that much.

The room was dark. Heavy blinds covered the bay window at one end. I blinked as Frank turned on the lights and illuminated the scene. There was a large wooden desk and a large comfortable looking chair behind it. The desk was covered in papers, some of which had spilled onto the floor. I looked around carefully and couldn't see any other signs of disturbance.

It was clear that the scene had been very thoroughly investigated. Markers had been placed in various places, Frank assured me that extensive photographs had been taken. There was white powder everywhere where it was clear that fingerprints were likely. It seemed that the police here knew their business.

'The body has been taken for a post mortem examination but everything else had been undisturbed,' he said.

I turned to him. 'Any sign of a break in anywhere in the house?'

'No nothing,' he replied.

I went over to the desk and looked carefully at it. There was a coffee mug to one side but I quickly realised why Frank thought I was something to do with this. There was a photograph of me, clearly taken at my party the other day and some hand written notes which were all about me and my uncle. There also appeared to be financial records but whatever had happened here they had been scattered everywhere.

'So tell me about the body,' I said as I continued to look around. There was no sign of blood or any other violence. 'What was the cause of death?'

'Stabbed,' Frank said. 'One wound in the left side of the chest just below the armpit and straight into the heart. At least that's what it looks like. We will need the post mortem to confirm it. There was almost no blood which I have to say is unusual so there may be more to it.'

I didn't say anything but I had seen something like this once before. I decided to keep my powder dry.

'So any thoughts?' Frank asked.

I didn't answer that directly. 'I take it that you decided to pull me in because of the subject matter on his desk?' I said as I studied it as closely as I could. 'It seems that Julian was doing his own research. Do we know if it was disturbed by someone looking through it all? Because to me it seems to have been scattered in some sort of struggle rather than having been rifled through and examined?'

'Yes, that's what we think too. It may well have been him struggling as the killer struck. We will take it all in and check for prints but I wanted you to see it first.'

'That seems sensible,' I said. 'But from what I can see it's just records of Julian's and my uncle's investments. There's nothing secret about any of that. I'm more worried about how he was murdered rather than why at this stage.'

'Go on,' Frank said.

'Bear in mind that this is early days. But to me, it would seem the killer was known to Julian. You said there was no sign of a break in, so he either had a key or Julian had left the place unlocked. More importantly, if someone not known to him had come in, why would he have remained seated?'

The victim's chair had obviously been moved to facilitate removing the body. 'I take it the chair was in its normal place where these scuff marks are on the carpet?' I asked, indicating where the carpet was worn.

'Yes, as I said, his head was touching the desk top as he fell forward.'

'So how would the killer have been able to stab him in his chest? The desk would have been in the way,' I said as I continued to think things through. 'You say the wound was off to one side?'

'Off to the left,' Frank said. 'What are you thinking?'

'Someone standing behind him could have reached around and delivered the blow, especially if Julian was relaxed and not expecting anything. If the blow was on the left, that indicates to me that the assailant was left handed. Reaching around from the right would have been too obvious. The post mortem should give us more information about that, especially the direction the blade went in.'

'That will all have to wait until tomorrow I'm afraid,' Frank said. 'But you seem to be competent in your appraisals, I'll give you that. I'd like you to come to the station tomorrow and we'll see where it goes from there.'

It was phrased like a request but was clearly yet another instruction. Once again the need to be able to come to this world in the future drove my reasoning. I could go home but that would not be sensible. However, I did need to go back to Carrie. God knows what she was thinking by now, it was almost midnight.

Just then, there was a commotion at the door and the other Carrie burst through. 'Inspector, when am I going to be allowed to go home?' She shouted at Frank. 'I've been here for hours.'

Frank looked embarrassed.' Sorry Miss, yes of course you can go now unless you have any questions for Mister Peterson.'

His question caught both me and Carrie off guard. She reacted first. 'What has Tony got to do with any of this? Why is he even here?'

I looked over at Frank who was watching us both. I was pretty sure what he was up to and decided not to play his game.

'The good Inspector is stuck for suspects, you found the body and there are papers all about me on the desk. He wanted us to meet to see if there was any reaction between us that might help him decide if we had anything to do with this.' I turned to Frank. 'Correct?'

He had the decency to look slightly embarrassed. 'It was worth a try. Mister Peterson you've played these games before. And you're right, at this stage, there is very little to go on.' He turned to Carrie. 'Yes, of course you can go home my dear. I will get one of my constables to drive you home.'

'And me?' I asked.

'Well you still haven't given me an alibi, now have you?'

'I haven't got one I'm afraid. I was out for a walk and when I got home I went upstairs to my study by the back stairs. I often do that as it saves having to tramp through the house with muddy feet. You haven't met my housekeeper. Believe me, doing that is really not worth it. But come on, why on earth would I want Julian dead? I have no motive and assuming the house was locked, no means of getting in without doing some damage.'

Frank sighed. 'No, you're right I suppose but I would still like to know more about your background. Alright, you can go too but as I said, I would like to see you first thing in the morning. There is much more to this than meets the eye and we need to talk further.'

When I got downstairs, the police car with Carrie in it was also waiting for me. As I lived closer, the driver took me to my place first.

'I'm so sorry Carrie,' I said to her as we pulled away from the house. 'I know you and Julian were a couple but do you have any idea who would want to do that to him?'

She didn't say anything for a moment and just let out a sob and put her head on my shoulder. 'No, he was liked by everyone. Who would want to do that? We had plans you know, Oh God this is so awful.'

It felt really peculiar to have her crying on my shoulder but I had to put emotion aside just as I always did when on a police case at home. We spoke a little more between the sobs and there didn't seem to be anything more to be gleaned from her. If didn't take long to reach my place and it was time to go home, literally. Carrie said she was alright to go on to her place on her own so I got out wondering just what I was going to say to the same girl a million miles away.

Chapter 12

I didn't have to wait long to find out. I went in up the back stairs and straight through the mirror. Carrie was lying on one of my sofas fast asleep but woke up as soon as she heard my footsteps as I appeared.

'What the hell happened Tony? You said you would only be a few moments.' She was clearly quite upset.

I went and sat beside her and explained what had happened.

'So this chap Julian was murdered? But did you know him that well?'

'Not really, he was my uncle's stockbroker and I had every intention of using him as well. The thing is, I really liked him. It was Julian who arranged a party for me to meet the locals and we even met one evening for a drink. But that's not the real problem. As I said before I had decided to do the same as my uncle and keep the whole world at arm's length but now I've got this nosey policeman on my case I'm a bit stuck. If I simply disappear by staying over here for a while, then I can never really go back without raising all sorts of questions. Don't forget there are amazing opportunities to make money as my uncle did. Now that I know about the place, the temptation will always be there to visit. And anyway, once a policeman always a policeman, I want to know who did this and why.'

She didn't look too happy with the answer.

'Look, I can't just let this go, but once it's over, that will be it. Just you and me OK?' Then I had an idea. 'You could be of great help you know. You teach history and you told me your degree concentrated on the last century. How about doing some research for me while I'm stuck with this. You've already got the book that my uncle left me. Tomorrow I'll stop off at a bookshop and see what else I can get hold of. Think of it, you'll be researching a completely original history.'

I could see the idea had taken hold. 'Look, let's sleep on it. I need to go back tomorrow and you need to get back to work. We can regroup in a couple of days. If nothing else it will give you more time to get to come to terms with the whole situation. Believe me, it took me more than a day.'

It was getting quite late now and we both agreed sleep was becoming a necessity. So with many things left to resolve we hit the sack.

Neither of us slept that well and by six we were both awake.

'Did I have a weird dream last night?' Carrie asked as she rolled over to look at me.

'No love, sorry but you didn't. Everything I told you and showed you was true. Look, that book is there on the dressing table.'

'This is just crazy you know. It can't be real.' She said and buried her face in my shoulder.

'Sorry but it is and there is no way of ignoring it. Look, it's a fantastic opportunity for you as a historian and for me to build on our fortunes but I've got to resolve this murder first otherwise we might just as well give up on the whole thing.'

We couldn't sleep so I got up and made us some breakfast. Luckily, when I had gone over the previous evening I had been wearing simple slacks and a jersey which would pass muster in both worlds. However, I decided that this time I would need to dress properly for the occasion and that meant raiding my wardrobe in my other bedroom. So straight after we had eaten, I reluctantly said goodbye to Carrie and promised to be back in a couple of days at the latest and laden down with reading material for her. I really didn't want to leave her but there was no way I could leave things as they were.

As soon as I had crossed over I went to my room and got changed. This time it was a tweed jacket, cavalry twill trousers, brogues and the most important item, the tie. Mavis must have heard me moving around because as soon as I went downstairs she ushered me into the dining room for my second breakfast of the morning. I could hardly say no, not the least because she would give me her 'look' if I had attempted to leave the house without eating.

Michael then insisted on driving me into town. I told him to drop me off at the Police Station. To his credit, he didn't ask why, although I would have bet my bottom dollar he knew all about the police visit the previous night. I would have to come up with an explanation at some time but now wasn't it.

As soon as I went inside, it was clear that the whole place was on full alert. I idly wondered when there had last been a murder in the city. Looking at the way everyone was diligently rushing about I suspected it must have been some time ago. The desk Sergeant directed me to Frank's office and said that I was expected.

Frank was sitting behind his desk in an oasis of calm. His outer office was full of policemen talking on phones or scribbling furiously away at their desks.

'Good morning, Mister Peterson,' he called cheerfully. 'Would you like a cup of tea?'

By now my back teeth were awash with the stuff and I politely declined. 'Any progress?' I asked.

'Not really,' Frank replied. 'My people are doing background checks and door to door enquiries but nothing so far. The last time we had anything as serious as this was four years ago and it's a bit of a wake up call for all of us. In fact, I'm rather stretched at the moment and wonder if you could do me a favour?'

'Of course,' I replied. 'More than happy to help.'

'We've asked Somerset House for all their records on Mister Fletcher, you know the usual, birth certificates, family details and all that. Usually, we would wait for them to be posted or I would send one of my men up to collect them but they're all busy at the moment. If you could take the morning express to Waterloo I would be really obliged. As I'm sure you know Somerset House is just over the bridge from there. You could be back by lunchtime.'

Was this some sort of test I wondered? Then I realised I hadn't seen anything even like a fax machine so far, maybe they did need to rely on the postal service to get the documents they needed. Even so, I was going to take anything this man asked me to do with a degree of suspicion.

'Of course,' I replied. 'When's the next train?'

'Oh, they go every half hour. I'll get one of my men to run you up to the station. Here take this,' he handed me a slip of paper. 'This is my authorisation for you to collect the files and a warrant for the ticket.'

Slightly bemused I let a constable drive me up to the station. The next few hours proved to be more of a revelation about this new world than I could possibly have imagined.

The station looked as I expected from the outside but once I was on the platform nothing was the same. The décor was quite modern looking with advertising hoardings along the walls. The rail track was weird. The rails were almost twice as wide as normal and U shaped. Along the centre was a continuous metal plate about eighteen inches high. Then the train appeared. It caught me by surprise as there was almost no noise at all.

I gasped in surprise. The engine, at least that was what I assumed it was, was shaped like a bullet with a large fin at the rear. The carriages behind had a similar shape. It was almost silent, all I could hear was a faint hissing noise. The metal plate in the centre of the track seemed to fit into a slot in the centre of the engine and presumable the carriages as well. The really weird thing was that there were no wheels. At least none that I could see.

'Magnificent isn't it?' A voice said to one side of me.

I turned and saw a middle aged man with a red beard. He was wearing a dark suit and had a bowler hat perched on his head.

'A Parsons Electric Levitator. No one else in the world has them. A triumph of British engineering.' He said it with obvious pride in his voice.

'Excuse me?' I said.

'The train,' he replied. 'A Parsons steam turbine, generating electricity to suspend the train on magnetic repulsion and drive it forward with induction motors. Virtually no moving parts, smooth as silk and very fast. British innovation to lead the world.'

For a moment I didn't know what to say. I didn't want to appear ignorant. 'Yes I'd heard about them but this is the first time I've seen one in the flesh. Very impressive.'

As I said that the train stopped and a door slid open automatically in front of me. The man gestured me ahead of him and I climbed aboard. We both sat in comfortable chairs opposite each other. The carriage was open like modern ones in my world but with plenty of room.

'Robin McGregor,' the man said and offered his hand.

I shook it back. 'Tony Peterson. I take it you are a bit of an expert on these trains then.'

'Oh, not just trains but all modern technology. It's a fascinating world we live in is it not?'

I had to agree. He then went on to explain how the train used a steam turbine to drive a generator which powered not just the propulsion but also the magnets that suspended the whole train. My attention was taken from his explanation when we started to move. I hardly felt a thing as it accelerated out of the station. Unlike trains I was used to it was utterly smooth and just kept steadily accelerating until the countryside outside was a blur.

'Jesus, just how fast is this thing?' I asked.

McGregor laughed. 'Oh, this is a slow one. As it's the express it won't stop now until Waterloo but will have to slow down past Clapham. Still, we will probably reach at least two twenty. That's nothing though, the east coast mainline expresses can manage three hundred and seventy five. I believe the record is now just over four hundred.'

I was amazed. Here was a world with cars out of the fifties, no sign of even a basic computer and yet they had trains that did four hundred miles an hour. I realised I was going to have to re-think my assessment of the whole place.

It got even weirder a few minutes later. Suddenly, in the distance, I saw something massive in the sky. It didn't take long to realise what it was. However, unlike the airships I had seen in the old black and white films this one was blue and sleek. There appeared to be engines integrated into the long cabin underneath the balloon itself. Also on the nose was a massive emblem of a stylised eagle. Painted in black it had only one head but two coats of arms on its chest.

McGregor must have seen where I was looking. 'Bloody Germans love those things but it took the Russians to make them work properly. I hate to say it but the Russians produce some fine engineering, almost as good as us.'

I simply nodded. My head was full of questions but I didn't want my ignorance to show. If I had the scale of the thing right, then it seemed to be heading towards where Gatwick was in my world. In fact, looking into the distance I could see two more of the massive machines but at almost ground level. I was becoming increasingly aware of my ignorance. If the British didn't use these things and from McGregor's dismissive tone, I assumed they didn't, then what the hell did they use? When I got to London I was going to get some books on technology for me as well as detailed recent history for Carrie.

Before I had time to settle down, the train was slowing and to my amazement, we pulled into Waterloo only half an hour after leaving Winchester. No wonder they didn't worry about cars if the trains were that good. Mister McGregor bade me a polite goodbye and I left my seat still in a slight daze.

Apart from the platforms themselves, this Waterloo was very similar to mine. The famous clock was there although the board with the train arrivals and departures was still made of analogue signs, not an electronic panel anywhere. Although there were taxis waiting in a line at the exit I was pretty sure I knew the way and decided to walk. It wasn't far.

Waterloo Bridge looked different. I remembered that it had been the only bridge damaged during the Second World War so maybe that accounted for it. I was also surprised by the amount of shipping still in the river. Looking downriver I could see that there were still a large amount of the commercial docks in use. However, if anything were needed to convince me that this was a different world altogether it was the skyline. Having spent many years in the Met, I was totally familiar with the look of the city. Winchester city centre could have been the same place give or take some minor difference, not so with London. St Pauls was there and looking the other way, so was Westminster and the tower of Big Ben. But otherwise, the place was almost alien. It was partly that many buildings were standing that I didn't recognise at all, presumably those that had survived the wars. However, all the tall skyscrapers and modern designs just weren't there. In fact, St Pauls was the tallest building. This was very definitely not my city.

Forcing myself to get a grip, I walked over the bridge to Somerset House which was just on the right hand side on the northern bank. I went in the main doors and presented my credentials to one of the men manning the massive reception desk. He told me to wait briefly and went behind the desk through a side door and reappeared a few minutes later with a large package wrapped in brown paper and addressed to Inspector Frank Cosgrove. I was asked to sign for it and that was it. I looked at my watch, it was only just past ten thirty. Over an hour ago I had been in Winchester, I still had trouble believing it. I suddenly realised that I really didn't want to go back just yet but I had promised to return as soon as I could so was rather honour bound to do so. As I walked out and looked up along the Strand I caught a glimpse of red hair. Suddenly, all my old police instincts came to the fore. Someone was playing games and I was pretty sure who it was and why they were doing it. Time for me to play back.

Chapter 13

The red hair was disappearing in the distance which meant he had waited for me to come out of the building so he could hand me over to someone else. I didn't want to start looking around or do anything unusual so I decided to cross the road. This would give me ample opportunity to look both ways. Unlike Winchester, the traffic in the Strand was quite heavy and there didn't seem to be any pedestrian crossings in sight so I took my life in my hands and made a dash for it. Luckily, nothing was moving that fast and I made it across in one piece. It was clear that pollution from the cars was not considered an issue in this world and I was coughing from the exhaust smoke by the time I regained safety.

Pretending that I was worse than I was, allowed me to look back into the traffic and sure enough, about fifty yards down a man in a brown suit had also made it across. Good, let the fun begin.

I was hoping that a certain back street I knew would still be here because they specialised in book shops and I could kill two birds with one stone. Taking my time, I turned right up past the Old Bailey and then left into Covent Garden. Instead of a mass of designer bars and restaurants, this was still a flower and vegetable market and very crowded. I made my way across but made sure that I took my time so that Brown Suit didn't lose sight of me. Once clear of the crush, I walked across to Charing Cross Road and once again took my life in my hands crossing to get into Irvine Street. Sure enough, there was a row of book shops. It was clear that some things had a degree of permanency. Making sure that Brown Suit saw me, I went into one shop that seemed to have what I wanted.

The place was empty when I entered. A little bell rang above my head and a bespectacled man appeared behind the counter. 'Can I help you Sir or do you just wish to peruse?'

'Er, actually you might save me some time. I'm looking for some books for my girlfriend. She loves history, in fact she teaches the subject in my home town. A couple of volumes of World and British history of the last century would be just right.'

The man was far too polite to ask whether buying books on history were a suitable present for a young woman. 'Just a moment Sir, I'm sure I have just what you want.'

He disappeared into the bowels of the shop and so I went and looked at some shelves I had spotted marked 'Engineering'. There were several books that were just what I wanted. I might even get to find out what a Parsons Turbine actually was. I chose two and took them to the counter.

The proprietor reappeared with a selection of histories and I chose a couple of those and added them to my own pile. They were all neatly wrapped for me and I was offered a large bag which was quite useful as it also had room for Frank's documents. I paid a quite substantial sum without query and then went on to the next part of the plan.

Looking out of the front window, I turned to the proprietor. 'Oh dear, you know I said the history books were a present for my girlfriend? Well, I've just caught a glimpse of her walking down the street. We weren't meant to meet until lunchtime. I don't suppose you have a rear entrance so I could avoid a possibly awkward meeting?'

Without batting an eyelid he showed me to the back of the shop and through a door into a storeroom. At the back was another door that opened onto a back alley.

'You can only turn right Sir, it leads to Leicester Square, I'm sure you will not be noticed.'

Muttering my thanks, I made my departure. However, once in Leicester square I doubled back and sure enough, there was Brown Suit dithering around near the book shop. To give him his due he was making quite a good fist of it but it was clear he was getting worried. Eventually, after a few minutes, he made a decision and entered the shop.

While he was having his conversation with the owner I needed to change my appearance. As the day was quite warm I removed my jacket and stuffed it into the bag and it was followed by the tie. It was the best I could do at short notice but should change my appearance enough. I then went back to the end of the alley to wait. Sure enough, Brown Suit appeared looking angry. I had taken cover behind a parked taxi and it was clear that he had decided I had long gone. Without any effort to look around him he strode off towards the city. We backtracked across Covent Garden, past Somerset House and towards Aldwych. Just as I was wondering where he was going, he stopped and went up the steps of a plain building which fronted the main road. There was nothing on the outside to say who or what occupied the place and I realised there was no more I could do. I made a mental note of the location, turned and headed back towards Waterloo deep in thought.

The journey back to Winchester was as exciting as the one up to London and it seemed that in no time at all I was back. I didn't even have time to start digging into my books. Time for a head to head with the good Inspector.

It was just past Midday when I arrived back at the Police Station. Apparently, Frank had gone out for lunch and so I handed over his dossier to the duty Sergeant and went in search of him.

The Bird in Hand was a pub a few hundred yards down the road. In my world, this whole area had been demolished and replaced with blocks of flats. Here it was just an old row of terraced houses with the pub at the far end.

The pub had that distinctive aroma of beer and people. Being lunchtime it was quite crowded but I soon saw my quarry sitting at the back of the main bar in a little booth. We both saw each other at the same time and he waved me over. I could see his glass was almost empty so made hand motions to ask if he wanted another. I took his cheery wave as agreement.

Another similarity in both worlds seemed to be breweries and I was glad to see that the Wadworths brewery existed and was brewing here. I ordered two pints of 6X and took them over to Frank's table.

'Got the parcel then?' he asked, as he sipped the top off his pint.

'Gave it to the duty Sergeant, your chaps should be going through it now.'

'Thanks for that and thanks for the pint Mister Peterson. You really did do me a favour you know.'

'I think we can dispense with the Mister now, don't you? Why not call me Tony, all my friends do.'

He gave me an odd look. 'So we're friends now are we Tony? Well, you'd better call me Frank, even my enemies do that.'

There was something about this version of Frank Cosgrove that I was actually starting to warm to. His doppelganger was a mean and angry man. I had heard stories of a failed marriage and a run in with a senior officer. Both men had a core of steel to them but this version didn't seem to have the same bitterness and anger. If anything, there was a dry humour overlaying his whole outlook. That didn't mean I was going to trust him. So far his questions and been far too pointed and difficult to answer. Anyway, I now wanted some answers but I would take my time.

'So, is there a Mrs Frank somewhere?' I asked.

The question seemed to hit some sort of mark. 'There used to be but I'm afraid the flu epidemic of eighty eight got her. No, don't worry about asking, many of us were in the same situation. They say they can vaccinate against it now. Shame it came too late.'

I winced inwardly. I really felt the need for more detailed background information, it seemed I could trip up on almost anything.

'Sorry I asked Frank, I was merely trying to make conversation.'

'I understand. What about you? Is there a significant other somewhere in the world?'

Once again the truth or as close as I could get seemed the best idea. 'Yes there is but she's a long way away at the moment. I've had a couple of close calls over the years but this time it looks like it's the real thing. I've just got to get things settled here first. This murder hasn't helped.'

'That I can understand. By the way, I'm paying a visit to the morgue this afternoon, you are welcome to come along.'

'Thanks Frank but first I have something to ask.'

He looked surprised. 'Of course, if I can help I will.'

'Robin McGregor. One of yours I take it?'

Frank was either a very good actor or really didn't know what I was talking about. I had deliberately sprung the name on him in the hope of getting at least some sort of reaction. There was none.

'Sorry Tony, you've lost me there.'

'I met this chap at the train station. Well dressed, middle aged, with red hair.'

'So?'

'He chatted to me all the way to Waterloo and seemed to be fishing a little. When I left Somerset House I saw him and then, when I went to do a quick bit of shopping, I was followed by another man in a brown suit. Ring any bells?'

Frank sat back and looked at me. 'You think I put someone up to trying to pump you for information and then follow you around London?' He let out a chuckle. 'Come on old chap even if I had the manpower which I don't, I can think of plenty of better ways of getting information about you. I've already done that to some extent. I thought we had a truce at the moment.'

Dammit, if Frank hadn't been responsible then who had? 'Actually, I managed to turn the tables on the chap following me and followed him back to a place near Aldwych. If I gave you the address, could you see who owns the place?'

'I suppose so but are you sure you're not just being a little paranoid here. There could be a perfectly innocent explanation after all.'

'Frank, I told you I used to be a policeman, trust me I know when I'm being followed. Someone wanted to know why I was in London.'

'Alright I'll look into that address but come on it's lunch time now and they do a really good steak pie here. Let's drop all this for the moment and have a bite to eat.'

Chapter 14

The morgue was a dismal building but there again I've never visited one that wasn't. Frank and I had chatted amiably over lunch although it was quite clear we were still circling around each other just a little. It was also clear that the ethos of my time, of eating a sandwich at your desk and getting on with the job, was missing here. By the time we left I reckon that most of the station had been in for several pints. It seemed quite the norm and my head was buzzing from unaccustomed lunchtime drinking.

Once inside, we were met by quite a young man in a white coat. He was introduced as Doctor Smith. He was quite chatty and took us through into the autopsy room.

'The cause of death was a single stab wound to the heart,' he said as he pulled the white sheet clear of the body. 'Otherwise, there were no other signs of a struggle. He was a fit man and quite healthy. I estimate time of death to between five and ten in the evening.'

'No defensive marks anywhere?' Frank asked.

'Some very slight signs of bruising around the mouth but they don't seem significant. The knife entered the heart very precisely which is why there was very little bleeding. Whoever did this knew exactly what they were doing.'

'And the weapon itself, are there any indications as to what it was?' I asked.

'Good question. The blade was nine inches long and there was some sort of guard at the end. If you look at the entry point there is slight bruising where it stopped the blade going in further. Also, if you look at the shape of the wound I would say that the blade was double edged and had a slightly diamond shape to it.'

I looked at the two men. Neither seemed to have come to a conclusion about that. But I had seen this before. I was pretty sure I knew exactly what the weapon had been. I decided that now was not the time to tell them. I wanted to find out more before I came to any conclusions. If Frank was half the detective I thought he was, he would work this out for himself.

'No toxicology?' I asked and then prayed that the word meant the same here. Luckily it seemed that it did.

Smith answered. 'No alcohol and only residual traces of H. Otherwise completely clean.'

'Thank you Doctor,' Frank said. 'If I could have the full report in due course and obviously contact me if anything else comes up.'

'Er there was one thing,' the doctor said. 'It's not really in my bailiwick but he was wearing a signet ring.'

'So what,' Frank said. 'Many people do, I've got one on now.'

'It's not the ring its what's engraved on it,' Smith went over to a tray and picked up the ring and handed it to Frank.

He studied it for a few seconds then handed it to me. 'Recognise the symbol?'

Deeply engraved into the face of the ring was an animal of some sort. It looked like some mythical beast because it had the wings and head of an eagle attached to what looked like the body of a lion. It meant nothing to me and I said so.

'It's a Griffin,' Frank said. 'There is no inscription with it which is odd. Normally a family motto would be included.' He turned to the doctor. 'Thank you Smith. I'll take this as evidence although of what, I have no idea at the moment.'

There was another strange thing about the ring but as neither man mentioned it I decided to keep it to myself.

We left the gloomy building and out into brilliant sunshine. I blinked to clear my eyes and then turned to Frank. 'If you don't need me any more, I've got some shopping to do and then I need to get home.'

'No, that's fine. If you think of anything let me know. You've got my number.'

We parted our ways. I did indeed want to do some shopping which I did on the High Street. I went to a newsagent and bought just about every magazine and newspaper I could and added them to my bag of books. I then decided to walk past the cathedral and along the water meadows to get home. I had a great deal to think about which kept me fully occupied for the whole walk.

When I got home I fully intended to go straight to the study and go back through the mirror. Carrie would still be at work but I could get all her reading material ready for her as well as maybe making a start on my own.

It wasn't to be. As soon as I let myself in the front door Mavis was there to greet me. 'You have a visitor Sir. I've put her in the drawing room.'

'Thank you Mavis, who is it?'

'She said her name was Parks. She's very pretty. Would you like me to make some tea?'

It was clear that Mavis was dying to know more and I wasn't going to give her the satisfaction. 'Yes that would be lovely Mavis,' I said as I turned and went to the door of the grandly titled drawing room, which in my world was simply the living room.

Carrie was sitting on one of the horribly uncomfortable looking sofas. I made a mental reminder to myself that I needed to strip this house out and start again, preferably with comfortable furniture and decent decoration. I dumped my rather large bag by the door.

'Hello Carrie, is there something I can do for you?'

It was clear she had been crying, her eyes were red and puffy. She also looked quite determined, even angry. 'Yes, there is. I've been thinking all night and can't understand what was done to Julian. The one thing I do know is that his desk was covered in papers about you and your uncle. It's clear to me that you must have had something to do with it.' She said it with a defiant, look on her face.

'I agree but that doesn't mean I know why it happened.' I replied. In fact, that was one of the issues that I had been grappling with ever since I had been to the murder scene.

'But you must know something,' she said defiantly.

I could see she was working herself up into a state. She had probably not slept at all and was looking to lash out at someone and I was the closest and a damned good candidate.

We were saved by the door opening and Mavis coming in with a trolley. On the top was a large teapot and cups. Underneath was a large plate of sandwiches, what looked like scones, jam and some cream and even a large Victoria sponge. Mavis thought we needing feeding up.

'Thank you Mavis,' I said as this trolley of calories came to a stop by my chair. 'It's all right I'll be mother. It all looks wonderful.'

She gave Carrie an odd conspiratory smile and then bobbed her head to me.

As the door closed I put two cups in their saucers. 'Tea?' I queried.

Carrie nodded. 'Just milk please.'

'What about some sandwiches, scones and cake? I could then be arrested for murder for trying to give you a heart attack.'

She gave a little laugh as she took her cup. I took mine and sat back. 'Carrie, I honestly don't know what this is about alright? Look, I've done some police work in the past and I have no intention of just letting the local bobbies follow this up. It seems to me that you need to go home and get a decent night's sleep. I promise that anything I discover I will share with you.'

She sipped at her tea and I could see she was trying to fight back tears. 'Alright but there is something not right about this whole situation. Your uncle was a very strange man by all accounts and I'm sure there is more to this than you are prepared to tell me. Julian was very keen to make friends with you. He told me that he and his father had made a great deal of money out of your uncle and the investments they made. He also told me that your uncle used to disappear regularly for long periods of time and no one could get in contact with him. No one knew where he went. You already seem to have the same habit.'

What could I say? There was no way I could tell her the truth and not just because she was effectively the girl I was going to marry. She might be the same person in some ways but she had had a totally different upbringing, in a world I was only just beginning to understand.

'Carrie I can't answer for my uncle and yes, I am a fairly private person and I do have significant interests away from here. You are just going to have to accept that. But I promise you that I will not cut you out of this situation. I want to know what Julian's murder was all about just as much as you do. It's even possible that whoever did this will be interested in me next. So I would rather get to the bottom of it before I get involved even more.'

She looked up at that last remark. 'Oh God, do you think you are in danger as well?'

'Who knows, I'm certainly not going to take any risks. Now look, I'll get Michael to drive you home and you get some sleep. And I promise that anything I learn I will share with you, alright?'

She nodded and as she finished her tea, I went out and found Michael in the kitchen with Mavis. I asked him to get the car and run my guest home. I also thanked Mavis for the tea but explained that my guest really hadn't been that hungry. She didn't seem upset and I expect the contents of the trolley would be put to good use.

Eventually, the house was quiet and I retrieved my bag and went up to the study. Before going through, I looked around and took some simple precautions. Then it was time to go home.

Chapter 15

Getting back to my real study and my world was such a relief. On the other side, there may have been murderers and suspicious policemen. Here there was none of that. I was so tempted to just walk away. I wondered if there was any way of smashing that bloody mirror. I supposed that at worst I could cut it free of the wall and chuck it into the sea or encase it in concrete. Then, as I dumped my bag on the desk, common sense prevailed. One of the newspapers flopped out and I read the headline 'King in plans to visit India.' A whole new world to explore and understand. Dammit they had trains that did four hundred miles an hour. I would never forgive myself if I cut myself off from that.

Luckily, that was when there was a knock on the door and Carrie let herself in. I was so surprised and happy to see the real her, I went over and gave her a hug.

'Ok you can put me down now,' she said after a few seconds. 'What brought that on?'

'Oh nothing really, just glad to see the girl I am going to spend the rest of my life with.'

She gave me a funny look and then her gaze went over to the table. 'Been shopping I see?'

'Yes,' I said and opened up the bag. 'Here you are, two detailed histories of the last one hundred years or so, also a large selection of magazines and papers. That should keep you busy for a while.'

She started leafing through the papers while I started to tell her about the events of the day.

'So, you're pretty sure someone was following you when you were in London? She asked.

'More than that,' I said. 'I'm pretty sure that the chap on the train was fishing for information as well.'

'Have you got the address of the place in London you saw the chap in the suit go into?'

'Yes but why would you want that?'

'Who knows, maybe it's being used the same way here.' She said. 'I can use google maps and a quick internet search to see if anything interesting comes up.'

My computer was on the desk and I gave her my password. She frowned in concentration as she clicked away at the keyboard.

'Got it,' she said. 'It's the headquarters of the Honourable Guild of Traders whatever that is. Hold on I'll look them up.' She studied the computer again.

I went over and looked over her shoulder. She had got up the home page of a web site. My heart leapt. The first thing I saw was the logo at the top of the page, a Griffin.

She started reading from the text. 'Founded in the seventeen hundreds, they were a simple guild for many years and are now an organisation to promote British trade world wide.' She turned to me. 'Sound pretty innocuous. There are loads of these legacy organisations. Many have become charities some are still fairly active like the Freemasons.'

'Over here maybe but over there it may be very different. Is there any connection with Winchester in their literature?'

'Hang on. Nope, no mention of anywhere else but London but as you say that doesn't mean anything if the histories have been diverging for over a hundred years.'

I stopped and looked at Carrie. Her eyes were alive with speculation, she even seemed more interested in the situation than I was and I said so.

She sat back in my desk chair. 'I've been thinking hard about this Tony. I would have dismissed it out of hand had I not seen you simply disappear several times. I'm dying to start getting into all those books and magazines. It's as you said before, a once in a lifetime opportunity for a historian.'

'You realise that you may never be able to tell anyone about this, don't you? Partly because you would probably never be believed but also because no one would ever believe you.'

She laughed. 'I know but I would believe it and who knows what we might find out in the future. I would like to investigate the history of this house for instance and why the mirror only works for you. Maybe one day we could get it to work for me as well.'

I had no answer to that and had a flash of what it would be like for the two girls to meet. I would need to be a long way away I decided.

'Let's just stick with the basics for the moment,' I said. 'There are a couple of other things I've discovered and haven't told the police about yet.'

We talked for an hour or so and then Carrie made a very good point. 'And there is something else you could do that would really help.'

'Oh, what cunning plan have you come up with now?'

'Remember you told me that if you take anything digital over and bring it back it gets wiped?'

'Yes I tried to take some photos on my phone and it got trashed when I came back.'

'So why not an old fashioned camera or cine camera even?'

'Oh bloody hell, why didn't I think of that?' I said. 'But where would you get one these days?'

'Ebay would be the obvious place or you could buy one over there and get it developed and bring back the prints and films.'

'Not sure the format for film would be the same so we might not be able to play them over here. Photos should be alright though. I tell you what, you have a look out for a small cine camera and projector and I'll buy a camera over there.'

'That makes sense,' and then she thought for a second. 'Also maybe there are other things you could bring over here that would help, especially in a police investigation. For example, you could get DNA samples and as a minimum, check for family relationships or rule people out, even if you couldn't identify them.'

'Good point,' I conceded. 'Mind you, I'm not sure they would understand if I went around asking to put swabs in people's mouths. And I would still need an analysis done over here. I guess several people owe me favours in the Met. Let's just see what comes out in the wash.'

'What about the victim. Have you or the police investigated his background, you know his family, girlfriends and the like?'

It was a good question up to a certain point which I certainly would not be discussing with her. 'That was in my mind to do next time I go back. Frankly, a motive is the most difficult thing to establish at the moment. Means and opportunity are fairly clear but I've absolutely no idea why anyone would want to kill him.'

I could see that Carrie was getting itchy fingers to start looking through all the magazines and books but frankly I was longing for a bit of normality. I suggested we go for a walk and end up at the pub.

She agreed but looked longingly at the pile of books and magazines as we left the study. We didn't go far, just up the lane to the main road where the Green Man was waiting for us. It was a private house in the other world but here it had been a pub for all the years I could remember. We got some drinks and I ordered food and then went out the back and sat in the beer garden. It was a lovely evening and we could see over the meadows to the regular shape of St Catherines hill in the distance as once again, it was catching the last of the evening sun.

'So what do you want me to concentrate on Tony?' Carrie asked as she admired the view.

'Good question. Their technology isn't anything like as backward as I thought. They just seem to have gone off in different directions. I'll look into that but anything you can come up with would be fine. I guess I'm really after how their society works and what was different after nineteen fourteen. The two main power blocks seem to be the British Empire or whatever it is that it's turned into and this European block of Germany and Russia which I assume includes Austria but I've no idea of what other countries. At first glance, it looks like a pretty unstable arrangement but it's lasted for over a century so there must be some stabilising mechanism at work. I just wish there was some form of database we could dig into.'

'Well, there will be,' she said with a smile. 'You'll just have to order a set.'

'Eh? What do you mean?'

'Don't you remember the good old Encyclopaedia Britannica that everyone used to have in their houses? I'll bet there is a pretty good version over there.'

'I hadn't thought of that,' I said. 'I guess we're so used to just going online and getting the answers we want that I'd forgotten about what we used to do. I'll see what I can do. But we also need to talk about the next few weeks. I think I'm going to have to spend the majority of my time over there. I don't want people thinking I can just disappear, literally that is, even if that is actually what I can do. Once this murder business is sorted then I will just try to blend into the background like my uncle did. In hindsight, that party was probably not a good idea.'

To my surprise, she didn't seem too upset about the idea, probably because of all the reading she was looking forward to. 'Alright, I understand but how are we going to stay in touch?'

'Whenever I get the opportunity I'll pop over and send you a text. That will only take a few minutes. I'll leave my new phone charged on my desk. You're more than welcome to use the study so you might even be in when I can make it. How does that sound?'

'Fair enough. Are you going to take anything across, like a laptop?'

'No, I don't want anything unusual to be found and I couldn't bring it back anyway. Also, they don't use 240 volts. For some reason, it's 150 over there and so I'm not even sure I could charge it. Let's keep it simple. I can always nip across when I need to.'

Chapter 16

After supper, we went home and went to bed. Carrie already had keys to the house and as soon as this affair was all over I was going to suggest that she give up her flat and moved in permanently with me. However, that would just have to wait. There were things I urgently needed to investigate in the other world. So much so that I was up at six in the morning. I gave a sleepy Carrie a goodbye kiss, grabbed the books on engineering and went through the mirror.

In my other bedroom, I jumped into bed and gave it a good work out so that Mavis would have something to make later in the morning and then dressed and went back to the study.

Time to check my traps. The rear stairs were steep and dark and whoever it was had not seen the light dusting of talcum powder. Sure enough, I had a couple of good footprints to examine. The tread looked quite normal but the foot size was surprisingly large. The back door showed no sign of being forced so whoever had opened it knew how to pick a lock. Back upstairs the hairs I had put on the desk drawers were all missing. Someone had made a cursory attempt to open my safe in the corner but that was never going to happen. You would need explosives to get into that. It was quite clear that the room had been very professionally and thoroughly searched. I was glad that my decision to keep any of my technology out of the study had proved to be the right one. However, I now felt that the safe would be secure enough if I did want to have things to hand.

I went back down the rear stairs and into the little courtyard and the back of the house. The yard held the house's dustbins and a woodshed to one side. I went past the bins to the back gate which led onto the lane. The verge was wet but there were no signs of tyre tracks, not that I expected to find any.

I went back inside to think. It wasn't long before I heard the bustle of Mavis downstairs in the kitchen. As I sat down to yet another heart attack special, I asked Mavis whether she or Michael had seen anyone approach the house that evening or night.

She looked worried when I asked. 'No Sir, has there been a problem?'

'No, not at all Mavis. I thought I heard someone during the night. It must have been my imagination or a really good dream.'

When she had left I decided on priorities. There were no databases for me over here. I had no staff working for me to do the groundwork. At some point, I might well turn to Frank and his people but first I wanted to find out as much as I could myself. Even finding out someone's phone number and address was a chore. There was a copy of the phone book by the phone in the hall. I thumbed through it but Carrie wasn't listed. A trip to the library would be needed. I decided to walk as it was a pleasant day. It only took twenty minutes and once again I was struck by one major difference. Over here they seem to have buried all the wires. It was only when I looked and noticed that there were no telegraph poles or power lines that the reality struck home. Most cities in my world seemed to be held together by wires. It was yet another example of how fundamentally different the two worlds were.

Not surprisingly Carrie was not at the front desk of the library but her friend Elaine was. I just hoped she wasn't too pissed off with me after the way I had all but ignored her the other night.

'Hello Elaine,' I said as I came up to the desk.

She looked up and clearly remembered me. 'What can I do for you?' she asked in a very professional and not very friendly tone.

'Look, I'm sorry about the other night. I had something rather important on my mind.'

'What? Oh, I'd completely forgotten about that. Carrie has told me everything you know. We share a flat and we've been friends for ages.'

'I'm sure she has but please believe me, I'm in just as much a quandary as she is. I didn't know Julian that well but I'm still determined to find out what happened.'

'Shouldn't that be police business?' she asked, still not looking mollified.

'Yes of course but I used to be a policeman as well and I seem to have been implicated in some of what happened. All I want is to talk to Carrie, now that she has hopefully had a good night's sleep and find out a few more things about Julian.'

'You can ask me you know. I used to go out with him before Carrie did.'

'Oh, I didn't know that.' I said in some surprise.

'No, I don't suppose you did. Don't worry, the break up was a mutual thing. I found someone else and we parted as friends. Look,

I can't talk now. My break is in about an hour you can buy me a coffee.'

I spent the time reading the papers and trying to make sense of the news. When she became free, we went over the road to a café next to the Catholic church. I ordered two coffees and we sat down.

'So you knew Julian for a long time?' I asked.

'We were at school at the same time. He was at Peter Symonds Grammar I was at the girl's County High School down the road. We never got together in those days but we moved in the same circles. I only really got to know him when he came back when his father became ill. He worked for his father in the short time before he died and decided to stay on and keep the business going.'

'What was he doing between school and coming home? I asked. 'That must have been quite a long time.'

'Yes, nine years. He was in the Royal Marines. He left them to look after his father and the business. He didn't talk much about it but I knew he'd done some operations overseas.'

One piece of the puzzle clicked in to place as she said it. 'What about family, is there anyone else?'

'His mother died years ago but he's got a brother who will presumably inherit. He is in the Marines as well.'

'What, still serving?'

'As far as I know. I expect the police will know. Presumably, they will have contacted him as next of kin.'

'What about Julian himself? I got the impression that although he was a prominent businessman in the city he also was a bit of a rebel. He clearly favoured the more modern styles of dress and behaviour.'

Elaine laughed at that. 'That pretty much sums him up. He was caught between needing to stick to convention. A stockbroker is there to do a client's bidding after all and most of them were of the old establishment. But I think his time in the Marines had given him a pretty low regard for convention. I know he was looking forward to working with you. Your uncle had been very good for the firm and he was hoping you would follow his lead.'

'I don't suppose Carrie mentioned that his desk was covered in paperwork about my uncle and myself for that matter.'

'Yes, she mentioned it. Why? Was it important?'

'I don't know. It could just have been what he was looking at when he was attacked or it could be why. I've really no idea at this stage.'

'So what are you going to do now?' She asked.

That was a good question. It didn't seem necessary to go and talk to Carrie any more at least for now. Elaine had answered all the questions I had in mind. 'I think I'll go and talk to the Police again,' I said. 'There isn't too much I can do on my own. Please give my regards to Carrie. Tell her I'll keep her in the picture if anything comes up.'

We parted soon after and I made my way down North Walls Street, down past the Cinema which in my world was a block of flats towards the bottom of town. Looking at my watch I decided it wasn't worth going into the Police station itself. I walked past and made my way to the Bird in Hand.

Sure enough, Frank was sitting in his alcove with a pint in front of him. He looked for all the world like a plump Toby Jug. He looked just like everyone's favourite uncle, if you didn't know him for who he truly was. However, I knew that under that exterior of bonhomie was a mind like a steel trap. One thing I was not going to do was underestimate him.

I made my way to the bar and ordered two pints and then went over and plumped myself down opposite him.

He looked up as the pint appeared in his vision. It was clear he had been lost in thought.

'Ah, just the man,' he said. 'We need to talk. I think you've been keeping a few things back from me.'

'And you haven't been doing the same?' I asked.

'Fair point, you first.'

'Julian Fletcher wasn't murdered, he was executed.'

That got Frank's attention. 'Go on.'

'The murder weapon was almost certainly a commando knife. Nine inches long, double edged with a flat diamond shape profile. It's a technique taught by the Commandos to take out a sentry or someone you really don't like when you want to be silent and not leave a load of blood behind. The knife goes in below the third rib and punctures the left hand side of the heart, stopping it instantly. You hold it there for at least a minute to let the blood pressure drop and then you can scarper without leaving blood everywhere. The knife has a small guard at the end of the blade the exact shape of the bruise we saw on the corpse. The bruising around the mouth was almost certainly because the killer put his hand there to stop Julian crying out.'

'And you know this how?'

'I used to be in the Marines as well. I only served a few years as I was shot in the ankle. Although it has almost no effect on my mobility it was enough for them to invalid me out.' I didn't tell him that it was probably a very different sort of marines and the bullet was fired in Afghanistan. He would definitely not have understood.

'Why didn't you say this at the time yesterday?'

'I wanted to see if you would work it out. Did you?'

Frank sighed. 'Not exactly, although I had thought it was something like that.'

'And did you know that Julian was an ex-Marine and his brother is also serving?'

'Yes we did. We've been in contact with the brother. He was in Scotland on exercise. He'll be here later today. Anything else?'

'That ring. The doctor called it a signet ring and you didn't contradict him but it wasn't. Signet rings have the engraving done in a mirror image and cut deeply so they can be used to imprint sealing wax. That ring had a normal picture engraved on it. It was something else entirely.'

'Go on.'

'I haven't had a chance to check it out yet but I've been told of a society called the Guild of Traders that use the Griffin as their symbol. Have you heard of them?'

He dodged the question. 'So I was right to take you along with me wasn't I? But of course, none of this actually helps discover a motive, even if whoever did it had the means and opportunity.'

'When's the brother arriving? Do we know?'

'Tomorrow I believe but before you go there he has a cast iron alibi.'

I decided that was enough from me. 'So what about that building in London did you find out anything?'

'To be honest I haven't had time to look into that yet but how about we go and consult our Oracle after lunch. It shouldn't take long. We have a full system in the station.'

I realised I had absolutely no idea what he was talking about and didn't want to appear ignorant so just agreed. The conversation drifted then and once again we had lunch. I was going to have to go on a diet after this or I would end up looking just like him. But what the hell was an 'Oracle'?

Chapter 17

Three pints later I was vowing to myself to become teetotal. Drinking at lunchtime only gave me a headache at tea time. Not that half the Winchester police seemed to have a problem with it. Frank and I went back up the road and into the cop shop. Instead of going down the corridor to his office, he led me down a set of steps behind the reception desk.

'I don't know why you didn't do this at the Library,' Frank said. 'You said you were there this morning. Theirs is almost as good as ours and probably gets updated as often. Records of this building would be bound to be in their system as well.'

What the hell was he talking about? It almost sounded like he was talking about a modern database of some sort. I made non-committal remark about assuming the Police system would be better and we came to a door with the words 'Oracle Winchester Police' written on it.

Inside, the room was quite large, clearly a basement that stretched under the whole of the building upstairs. In front of us was a counter with an odd looking device on top. The room was full of what looked like filing cabinets with an odd system of what looked like rails and tubes above them all. I had no idea what on earth it was. Off to one side, there was a man in a brown coat who was fiddling with something.

'Ah Inspector, what can I ferret out for you today?' He had horn rimmed glasses, thinning hair and a pale complexion '*Not surprising if he spent all day down here,*' I thought.

'Afternoon Derek, this is Mister Anthony Peterson he's got a query for you.' Frank turned to me with an expectant look.

Shit, what was I meant to do now? Well, this was meant to be finding out about the building in London. So I gave the address. 'I need to know who owns it and what use it is currently being put to.'

'No problem,' Derek said. He went to the big box on the counter and started tapping away at something. It sounded like a keyboard. Suddenly, something started moving over one of the filing cabinets and before I could see what was going on, a small square box dropped from the overhead rails onto the desktop device and disappeared into it.

Derek started humming to himself. 'Alright, built in seventeen sixty five by a traders guild it was used by them until nineteen thirty eight. It was then leased to an insurance company but they moved out last year. It's currently unoccupied.'

I had absolutely no idea where this information was coming from but didn't dare say so. I decided to press on. 'Who actually owns it?'

'Hmm, let me see.' Derek spent a few more seconds doing whatever it was he was doing. 'Right, the Traders lot seemed to have sold it to an offshore company who own it to this day. They're called the Venta Corporation and they're based in the Virgin Islands. That really won't help as I have no commercial records of companies based there. Sorry, that's about it. Hang on, I'll give you a print out.' There was a noise like tearing calico from off to one side and Derek disappeared for a second and then came back and handed me several sheets of printed paper. Trying not to be amazed as the speed and quality of the printing, I scanned the pages. Derek seemed to be right, this was a waste of time.

I turned to Frank. 'Looks like a dead end then, dammit. It may be unoccupied but that doesn't mean that it's not being used. I need to find out more about this Venta Corporation.

'You'll be lucky,' Frank said. 'The Virgins are notorious for guarding their secrets. It's why so many rich people hide their wealth there. Sorry, that's about all we're going to get.'

'One last question Derek,' I said. 'What do you have on the guild that built the building? For example, do they have a crest and why did they disband?'

'Hold on a moment,' Derek said as he tapped away again. 'Crest was a Griffin and they were formed to promote trade within England itself rather than internationally. They disbanded when they sold the London property in thirty two. No reason seems to have been recorded. Sorry, that's all there is.'

'Thanks Derek, it looks like we've hit a brick wall. I might as well go home now unless you've anything else for me Frank?'

Frank gave me an odd look which I chose to ignore. 'I agree, the whole investigation seems stuck at the moment. I'm just hoping that the house to house comes up with something. And if you do stumble across something please don't wait this time please.'

I nodded. 'Yes well, we've both got to learn to trust each other I guess. Anyway thanks very much.' Of course, I still hadn't told him that my study had been broken into and searched last night so I almost felt guilty about that but not completely. I would bet my bottom dollar that good old Frank had not told me everything either.

We parted company and I decided that another trip to the library would be in order. There was a young man on duty this time. I asked if I could use the library's Oracle whatever it was.

He asked for a fee of one pound and told me I could have half an hour and if I wanted anything printed it was a penny a page. He then took me through a door to a small room with a desk a chair and some sort of terminal. I assumed it was similar to the one in the police station. Presumably, all those storage devices were not on show in here.

'Er, sorry to ask but I've lived abroad up until now. Can you tell me how to use this?' I asked.

'Really? I thought everyone would know that. Did you live on the South Pole or something,' he asked in a condescending tone.

'Just humour please.'

'Use the keyboard to type in your query. Make sure the keyword is the first thing you type and any additional search words to follow after.'

I thanked him and he left closing the door behind him.

The first word I typed was 'Oracle' and then 'Design'.

The screen I was looking at was rather like my television but with a green screen. Within seconds there was a quiet click and information started flooding the screen. It was all very technical but Oracle appeared to be a very sophisticated system similar to the old microfiche readers I remembered from the past. However, it appeared that the information was far more compressed as the sheets were tiny in comparison to those I remembered. The terminal I was using was definitely a computer of some sort but used an analogue system which included some incredibly detailed and sophisticated mechanical devices as well as electronics that used transistors as the main processing logic devices. Frankly, most of it was way above my head but one thing was quite clear. This world may not have digital processing like mine but that didn't mean it wasn't incredibly sophisticated. This computer, because that is what it was, was as effective in its own way as anything we had. Mind you it did need a large room to store its data rather than a microchip. I also discovered that there was a nationwide distribution system for information that updated each Oracle in the country on a daily basis. It might not have been the internet but every citizen could query it if they wanted.

I sat back and contemplated just how out of my depth I probably was. The more I stayed here, the more I realised how little I knew. Looking at my watch I had one last question to ask. I queried Winchester and what names it was known by previously. It only took a few moments to discover the link between the Traders Guild, the Venta Corporation and this city. I wondered whether Frank had come up with the same idea or indeed already knew.

I needed to get home and think things through. I also needed to get into those books on engineering. If I wasn't careful it was quite clear that my complete ignorance of this world was going to land me in trouble and sooner rather than later.

It wasn't to be. I walked home still feeling fuzzy from too much beer. I was going to have to get myself a bicycle I decided, they seemed very much in fashion. Either that or a car that had the bloody pedals in the right place. Still, it didn't take too long to reach St Cross and by then I had walked off the worst of the beer. When I walked into my drive I saw a large black car parked in front of the house. As I walked up to it a large man in a black suit got out.

'Mister Peterson,' he said. 'Would you come with me please?'

I hate it when people presume on my patience. 'No, now please get that car off my drive.'

'Sorry Sir but you really do need to come with me.'

I stopped and appraised the man. He wasn't actually threatening me but it was quite clear that he would if he had to.

'Give me one good reason why I should?' I said.

He reached into his pocket and took out a small business card. I took it and studied the name and the logo.

'You only had to show me that. You didn't have to be so bloody rude.'

Maybe I would now get some answers.

Chapter 18

The car was another one like mine, where the chauffer sat up front in a separate compartment but this time there was a screen between us. Conversation was going to be non-existent. I didn't care, the business card had the logo of a Griffin on it and one word 'Venta'. Wherever I was going there would at least be someone who would enlighten me.

It soon became clear where we were going. We headed up the steep slope of Sleepers Hill and turned right at the top before turning left into Chilbolton Avenue. In my world, this was one of the more exclusive areas of the city with some magnificent houses. It seemed the same was true here. I did notice though that there were far fewer buildings with much bigger gardens. Presumably, the residents hadn't felt the need to exploit the land they owned to build yet more properties. Half way down, the car pulled in through a magnificent pair of gates and up to the front of a large Georgian mansion. My driver or was that abductor? Got out and held the door of the car open for me. I ignored him completely and went up to the front door which opened before I got there. A real classical butler, dressed in a formal suit was waiting for me.

'If you will come this way Sir,' he said and turned without waiting and headed off into the darkness of the vast hall. I hate being patronised so decided not to do anything. I just stood there and looked at the massive wooden staircase in front of me and wondered what the butler would do when he realised he was being ignored.

Strangely, he didn't come back to fetch me. He simply disappeared through a green baize door at the rear of the hall. I stood my ground.

It didn't take long before another man appeared. In his early sixties, he was slim and elegant, dressed in a casual jersey and slacks. His blonde hair was slicked back showing a large forehead below which were two piercing blue eyes.

'Mister Peterson, so glad you could make it,' he said as if nothing untoward was going on at all.

'And you are?' I asked coldly.

'Sorry, I'm forgetting my manners. I am Alec Jeffries, I own a few businesses locally. You may have heard of me?'

'Nope, not a clue who you are,' I said in as offhand a way as I could. 'Oh and I didn't like the threatening manner the way I was invited to come here or the attitude of your butler for that matter. So why don't you just say what you have to and then your thug can give me a lift home.' I didn't think for a minute that he would do that. I was wanted here for a reason but I wasn't going to put up with any further arrogance or bullying.

'Oh dear, yes I do apologise,' he said. 'My people can sometimes be a little over zealous. Look, why don't you come and join me and my friends for a drink and I can explain what this is all about.'

I reluctantly let myself be led across the hall and through the door. The room the other side was breath taking. It was like a cross between a baronial hall and a ball room. There was even a minstrel's gallery along the right hand wall. It was partly filled with a long, highly polished table and a dozen or so chairs. At the far end were two large doors which were open and I could see a gathering of men outside with drinks in their hands. They were standing on a patio and admiring something in the distance.

I followed my host onto the patio and everyone turned to look at us and all the conversation stopped.

'Gentlemen may I introduce Mister Anthony Peterson, the nephew of our old friend Peter Peterson who as we all know passed away recently.'

There were about twenty people present plus a young girl who was serving drinks. They all nodded and smiled at me. The waitress came over and offered me a glass what looked like champagne from a tray. I took the proffered glass and took a sip. It was very good. I realised what everyone had been looking at. The patio was higher than the surrounding garden and not too far away I could see the Royal Winchester golf course. A green, very close to the boundary of the garden could easily be seen. Four players were just leaving.

'You'll have to excuse us,' my host said. 'Watching the variable standard of putting has become a bit of a pastime for us. I believe some of us even have the odd wager on the results.' He then turned to the crowd. 'Right, everyone, time for business, let's all go inside.'

At that point, I was very tempted to just turn round and walk out. The arrogance of these people was starting to get on my nerves. However, the need to hear what they had to say overrode my irritation.

Inside, everyone sat down around the table. I was offered a seat at the far end, my host sat at the other. As this was going on I had time to study the people around me. One thing was quite clear, everyone here had money. Apart from the quality of their clothing which ranged from suits to casual wear, it was in their bearing. These were men who knew their place in society and it was at the top.

Suddenly, the lights dimmed and Alec Jefferies stood up. 'Welcome everyone to our extraordinary meeting and welcome Mister Peterson. The purpose of getting together today is to explain to Mister Peterson about us and discuss the future.'

'Before you carry on,' I rudely interrupted. 'I know exactly who you are. This is the board of the Venta Corporation. The name comes from the old name of Winchester, Venta Belgarum which later became Venta Caester and then over the years became Winchester. You were formed out of the old Traders Guild but for some reason decided to drop out of sight in the thirties and move here from London.'

'Well done Miser Peterson,' Jeffries said in an ironic tone. 'You've clearly been doing your homework. I assume you worked most of that out from the crest on poor Julian's ring and yes, before you ask, he was a member of this group. Although I might add that we call ourselves a Society not a Corporation.'

'That and being followed by a man in London who led me to a certain house in Aldwych,' I responded. I saw surprised and some concerned looks around the table at this remark but only from certain people which was odd..

Even Jeffries looked a little discomforted. 'I think it might be better if you let me continue, if you wouldn't mind. We can then discuss all these issues afterwards.'

I decided to let him have his say, after all it was why I was here.

Jeffries nodded towards the far end of the room and a large white screen dropped down over the wall. A projected slide appeared on it. If I hadn't known better I would have thought it was PowerPoint. The slide was the Griffin logo.

'The Traders Guild was started formally in the seventeen hundreds although earlier organisations can be traced back more than four hundred years before that. There are similarities with the Free Masons in that regard. The aim of the guild was to best look after trade within the city of London. At that time foreign trade was developing as the engine of the British economy but the Guild wanted to protect internal trade as well.'

'*And no doubt fix prices and act as a cartel for its members,*' I thought cynically.

'The guild continued until the thirties but by then London was losing its premier position as a trade centre to places like Liverpool, Manchester and Birmingham. The Stock market crash of thirty seven saw many of its members bankrupted. However, a few members had seen what was coming especially after the conflict in the Far East and had moved their wealth off shore. The Guild effectively collapsed and the remaining members decided to relocate here. We still have the same basic aims as the original guild but are now more interested in this City and the local area. You could say we are a pale shadow of the original guild but that said, we believe we serve a useful function.'

I refrained from comment. Who knows, maybe they did do more than line their own pockets and anyway it was clear that Uncle Peter had dealings of some sort with them.

A few more slides were shown, detailing the group's activities and to be fair they did seem to have some philanthropic activities. They sponsored a children's home and paid for a complete wing at the city hospital. I decided to stop being too judgemental.

'One of the things that has given us so much commercial success in the past,' Jeffries said with a wry smile. 'Was our relationship with your uncle. He seemed to be very much a man to keep his distance and although we did meet on rare occasions, his dealings with Julian and his father before him had proved to be very beneficial to us all.'

'And you want to know if that is going to continue with me?' I asked.

'Something like that. You seem be happier to have a higher profile than your uncle. Several of us came to your party the other day but there were so many guests you may not remember who came.'

I had thought some faces looked familiar now I knew why.

'Then the murder of Julian not only caught us by surprise but made us realise that we would need to speak to you directly, hence this meeting.'

'Which we could have handled a little better, especially if we are looking for this man's good will,' an old looking man in a business suit off to the right of the table said, looking sternly at Jeffries

'Yes, fair point and I have already apologised to Mister Peterson,' Jeffries said looking put out at the interruption.

It seemed to me that he very much thought of himself as the top dog of this group and didn't relish being criticised. I parked that thought away for future contemplation. However, the fact was that I probably needed these people if I was going to continue to follow my uncle's lead and invest in this world made me keep my counsel, at least until I had the full picture.

Jeffries turned to me. 'Your thoughts Mister Peterson?'

'Well firstly if I do continue to invest and provide investment advice we will both need a new stock broker. As I understand it, Julian's brother is still serving in the Royal Marines so I don't expect he will be taking up the reins even if he wanted to.' Secondly, I need to put some thought into what I do next. In principle, I have no problem with continuing with an investment policy but I would like to see Julian's murder resolved first. So please just bear with me until then.'

My answer seemed to satisfy everyone and soon after that the meeting broke up and more drinks were served. I mingled for a while and was introduced properly to all the members and tried to memorise all the names.

In a quiet moment, Jeffries pulled me aside. 'Mister Peterson, please don't take this the wrong way but it's been clear to us for some time that your uncle was something more than he seemed. Not the least that when he was away he literally disappeared, I mean totally. We were more than happy to live with this after all it was none of our business.'

I cut him off before he could continue. 'But you might want to investigate further if I decide not to be so cooperative?'

'You could put it that way I suppose. Let's just stick with the status quo.'

My hackles were up again. 'Mister Jeffries I don't like being leant on. Please understand that. As you say my uncle was mysterious. Believe me, you have no idea what you might find if you push me and I include searching my study last night as an example of pushing me too far.'

'What? No, I have no knowledge of that at all.' Jeffries actually looked quite startled and hid his surprise quite well but I wasn't fooled for a minute. He wanted to lean on me a little and such a covert action was exactly the sort of thing I would expect him to do.

'And it was clear to me that some of your members were surprised when I mentioned Aldwych.' I said, deciding to turn the screw the other way. 'I don't know your secrets and have no desire to find them out but it's quite clear you have your fair share.'

'Touché Mister Peterson,' he said with a wry smile. 'Would you like me to get my man to take you home?'

'If you would be so kind.'

Chapter 19

When I got home Mavis had laid out a salad for me which I took up to the study. I quickly popped over through the mirror and sent Carrie a text simply saying I had discovered the elusive Ventas but that we needed to talk. I did contemplate calling her and getting her to come over but decided I needed to do some research of my own. Tomorrow would be fine I said I would be there about six.

I then went back and sat in one of my sofas and started to brush up on my engineering. It immediately became clear that despite no digital technology to speak of, this world had come up with some pretty amazing achievements. The proper name for an Oracle was an 'Oracle Engine' which seemed to hark back to the Victorian era when Charles Babbage produced his famous mechanical computers called 'Difference Engines'. They seemed to be in common use worldwide. Of course, they no longer used gears and rods. The electronics were there but all seemed to work in a different way. I had to remind myself that we got to the moon with similar levels of sophistication in the sixties. No wonder Frank looked strangely at me when he first suggested using it. I already knew about trains so I had a good look at aviation and got the shock of my life. It seemed that the Germano Russian Empire had specialised heavily in Zeppelins as they were also called here. The modern ones were something quite different from the ones I knew about from the First World War. There didn't seem to have been an equivalent of the Hindenburg disaster but they were all filled with helium these days and had a staggering lift capacity.

It also became clear that the tension between the two empires was reflected in the technology in use. The British seemed to have decided to ignore air ships and concentrate on aircraft. There was one massive machine that looked uncannily like the failed Brabazon airliner from my world. There were also flying boats galore and then something caught my eye. It was a picture of a machine that looked like nothing I had ever seen before. As I read, I discovered it was called a WIGE, which stood for Wing in Ground Effect, although unsurprisingly that had been turned into Wiggy in popular parlance. In essence, it was an aircraft with tiny wings that flew at about fifty feet using the aerodynamic lift provided by being so close to the surface. Apparently, they were excellent for long ocean crossings because they were fast and could safely fly through just about any weather. Aircraft here, without the jet engine, just couldn't fly high enough to go over the weather. The WIGE could just plough through it quite happily and if anything went wrong it could safely land on the sea. There were still transatlantic liners but just like at home it seemed that their heyday was long over. When they could only do thirty miles an hour and the Wiggy could do three hundred there was no competition

By now I was getting tired and went to bed. I had a plan for the next day and just for once it had nothing to do with policemen, murders or secret societies. I was up early and even made a valiant attempt at the breakfast Mavis had produced. I made a mental note to see if this world was aware of the dangers of cholesterol. Then I pinched the car and drove into town. During all the small talk yesterday I had been given some good steers as to where I should go. My first stop was a bedding emporium. Not only did they have comfortable looking beds and mattresses but they also had a massive selection of things to go on top which, halleluiah, included duvets. My other plan to drag some across through the mirror was not necessary. Mind you, I still had to convince Mavis that they were not the devil's work. She was very much a hospital corners, heavy blankets and eiderdown sort of person. Tough, she would just have to get used to these new-fangled things from the continent.

I then made my way to an office above one of the shops in the High Street. The architects firm of Crombie and Spencer had been highly recommended. They didn't disappoint. Even though I had not made an appointment they welcomed me in, gave me coffee and listened attentively to what I wanted done to the house. I suspect that someone from the previous day may well have tipped them off that I wanted to spend some serious money. We spoke about my ideas in outline and then made an appointment for that afternoon so that someone could come around and measure up with a view of drafting some plans for me. I didn't mention that I already knew exactly what I wanted not the least because building regulations and concepts could be different here. Anyway, I didn't want an exact clone of my other house, it wouldn't be in keeping in this society.

Morning chores complete I considered going around to see my friend Frank but in the end decided that I couldn't face more lunchtime beer. It would take several more days for the routine work to finish up and not a great deal could be done until it was. So I went home again and warned the Thompsons that there were going to be some changes to the house in the near future. However, my courage failed me and I'm afraid I chickened out about telling Mavis about the bedding. That could wait until she was confronted with the delivery which should be the next day. I spent the rest of the afternoon in the garden as the weather was so warm continuing my studies. Actually, despite the lack of lunchtime beer I fell asleep and only woke up when Mavis brought me a cup of tea at four o'clock. Soon it was time to nip over and spend the evening with Carrie. I would come back later, just in case something came up with the investigation but I was really feeling the need for a dose of reality now. This universe was stranger than it looked on so many levels.

When I stepped through, Carrie was sitting at my desk with a book in front of her, a pen in her hand a notebook to her side.

Her smile, as she saw me magically appear, blew all my misgivings away. 'Hello, Darling she said. 'How was Narnia?'

'You've no idea, you really haven't,' I said. 'I just wish I could show you in person.' I went around the desk and gave her a kiss. 'So come on, what have you discovered?'

'Before I answer that here's a little present.' She handed a small camera.

'It's an old eight millimetre cine camera. It's even got instructions and there are two reels of film. As you said, ebay came up trumps. I've found someone in town who can develop the films and it also came with a projector.' She pointed towards a side table where an old fashioned projector was sitting.

'Well done,' I said. 'I'll take it across with me. And I guess I'd better buy that camera as well. Anyway, what has your research discovered?'

She didn't answer me directly. 'Tony, do you know what exactly your uncle invested in over there?'

The question caught me by surprise. 'Vaguely, he primarily put money into small, start up companies. Some were pharmaceutical I believe and some were in modern engineering or medicine. I think he was looking for areas where we were ahead that could yield beneficial results. Why on earth do you want to know that?'

'Bear with me. Do you intend to do something similar?'

'I guess so. As I said in my text yesterday, I've made contact with this Venta organisation. Basically, they're a group of rich Winchester businessmen who want me to continue doing things along the same lines. It seems they all made money out of his investment recommendations. Come on Carrie, why are you asking me this?'

'You can't do it Tony,' she said looking worried. 'There's a real danger you could set off a catastrophe. Your uncle should have known better.'

'Carrie, you're going to have to explain that.'

'I know. Look how much do you know about how the First World War started here?'

'Er, the heir to the Austrian empire was assassinated in Serbia. Austria demanded outrageous compensation in reparation but Serbia was allied to Russia. Russia mobilised and Germany was so paranoid about being attacked on two fronts, if the French and British also mobilised, that they decided to strike first. It was called the Schlieffen plan if I remember my history.'

'Very good Tony and although it was the spark, the kindling was already in place. Britain was arming like mad. They had a policy that for every Dreadnought battleship the Germans built, they would build two. The Germans were led by a slightly deranged idiot who was also paranoid and was trying to build his own Empire. The Austro Hungarian Empire was collapsing but still powerful and the Russians, whilst a basket case politically were also in a very aggressive mood. In your new world over there, the assassination didn't take place and things rumbled on until nineteen twenty when finally the Russian people had had enough and started a revolution. Unlike in this world though, the Kaiser was still on his throne and he supported the Romanovs. Oddly, that little war settled things down and the big confrontation between Germany and us never happened. After the First War over here, the Allies placed ridiculously overbearing restriction on Germany at the peace of Versailles and that led to the extremism that gave rise to the Nazis. Over there that didn't happen and also the Americans never had to get involved and bail us all out whilst at the same time making us enormously in their debt.'

'OK I've got all that but what does it have to do with my potential investments?'

'Tony, your world is now effectively back in the scenario we saw here in nineteen fourteen. Over the century, the two empires have expanded but there is no room left now. America has built a trading block with most of its southern neighbours but Canada is still British. So they are contained. Africa is mainly British but Germany along with its other ally, Italy, has most of the African states north of the Sahara in its pocket with the exception of Egypt. The Middle East countries are nominally independent but heavily under British control as is India. However, Germany has a controlling presence in the Far East except for Japan and China. Those two countries have been at each other's throats for so long now they are both just about bankrupt. This is all secondary though, it's the social tensions that are the real problem. The two empires hate each other and that's been a problem building over the years.'

'Yes, I've seen symptoms of that with the technology,' I said. 'The Germans use airships, while the Brits refuse to contemplate them and rely on various forms of aircraft and vice versa. So you think that tensions are high enough for them to start fighting?' Then a thought occurred to me. 'Oh bloody hell, do we know if they have nuclear weapons?'

'Well you might know better than me but thankfully I've seen no sign of them in my histories. I'm sure that if they had been developed it would be well known. You can hardly test an atomic bomb in secret.'

'Good point and I agree. I've seen no evidence either, thank goodness.'

'Yes but you know the carnage caused by our two world wars. Imagine what it would be like in that world. Two global spanning empires going toe to toe with all the technology they have. It would be a catastrophe.'

I sat back and contemplated Carrie's words. 'Shit and I'm guessing that what you are saying is that interfering with their development, especially on one side could tip the balance?'

'Absolutely, I'm not saying it will but how would we feel if we gave this British Empire enough confidence to try something on?'

I sat back and thought about what Carrie was saying. I had already caught whiffs of the tension between the two empires in the press and from various throw away comments people had made. I knew that Uncle Peter had been very low key with his investment recommendations and I realised I would need to look at them in much more detail now. Which could be problematical as the documentation was all held by the police as evidence. However, Carrie was right. It was not my world and I had no right to interfere and possibly upset the balance of power. Clearly, I couldn't give the same advice to a German stockbroker at the same time as I did it in Britain. It was not as if Carrie and I needed the money, there was more than enough for us both to live well on for the rest of our lives. Not for the first time, I contemplated smashing that damned mirror and leaving them all to their own fates. But once again the policeman in me needed to resolve this murder. Maybe afterwards.

'You're right Carrie.' I said and wondered just how my new friends of the Venta Society were going to take the news.

Chapter 20

Carrie and I spent the rest of the evening together. We talked things through a little more and then took the conversation to the bedroom which proved to be far more fun. However, I did still want to spend the night in my other bed just in case something happened. Whatever the future held I still had a case to solve. I wanted to have a look at those investment papers that had been on Julian's desk. However, there was no rush to tell the great and good of Winchester that their golden goose was going to do a runner. So about eleven, I gave Carrie a last kiss, went to the study, pocketed the cine camera and slipped across to my old fashioned uncomfortable bed. Mind you, hopefully, that would be for the last time.

The next morning, just as I was waking up I heard the telephone ring downstairs in the hall. Why the hell my uncle hadn't had an extension put in upstairs I'll never know. There wasn't even one in the study. I made a mental note to add it to the list. I quickly grabbed my dressing gown and went downstairs.

'Yes,' I said rather curtly, it was before half eight after all. 'This is Tony Peterson, how can I help?'

Once again the voice at the other end caught me by surprise. 'Tony its Carrie. Can I come over and talk again? I need to ask you a favour.'

'Of course Carrie, any time, you know that but don't you have to go to work?'

'No, I'm taking a couple of week's holiday. Can I come over now? I'll be about half an hour.'

'I'm not going anywhere. Can I ask what it's about?'

'I'd rather wait until I get there if that's alright?'

'Ok, see you then,' I put the phone down. She sounded quite worried about something but clearly it would have to wait. I went upstairs and quickly got dressed. When I get back down, Mavis was already there making me a heart attack special. It told her I would be having a guest for breakfast and when I told her who it was her eyes lit up.

'It's all to do with that dreadful murder the other day,' I explained. I got the feeling she wasn't convinced. Just then the front doorbell rang and I went to answer it.

Carrie was there looking much better than the last time I had seen her. Even so, she looked worried and upset. 'Come on in, my housekeeper is making us breakfast if you haven't had some already?'

She shook her head. 'Not hungry but you go ahead.'

We went into the dining room where Mavis was just laying out enough food on the sideboard to feed an army and fatally clog their arteries at the same time. She smiled at Carrie and gave me a knowing grin before leaving. I really was going to have to have a word with her and sooner rather than later.

Despite saying she wasn't hungry Carrie took a plate and helped herself. I did the same and we sat down. I poured us both some tea. I had given up on getting Mavis to make decent coffee.

'So what's this all about Carrie?' I asked around a mouthful of scrambled egg and toast.

She put down her knife and fork. 'David Fletcher got down here yesterday. After he called on the police, he came around to my place.'

'I take it that David is Julian's brother?'

'Sorry, yes he is. He had just come down from Scotland apparently. He's not a nice person.' She said it with feeling and a frown on her face.

'Why do you say that?' I asked. 'Do you know him well?'

'I've known him for some time,' she replied. 'I actually knew him before I met Julian. In fact it was when I was with him that he introduced me to his brother.'

'Was he your boyfriend?' I asked.

'Oh no nothing like that, at least not on my part. He only really came here when he was on leave. We were just friends but when he came round to see me he seemed a different person.'

'What do you mean by that Carrie?'

'He was aggressive and quite accusatory. He seemed to want to blame me to a degree simply because I discovered his brother's body. And he was very interested in you. Don't be surprised if he is your next caller. The police told him about what was on the desk. He asked a lot of questions and got quite angry when I couldn't answer most of them.'

'Hmm, was he upset about the death of his brother or was it something else?'

'That's where things took a turn for the worse. He didn't seem interested in Julian at all. His questions all seemed directed at the house and how the business had been faring, not that I knew much about either. He said he hadn't heard about your uncle dying but when I told him all about it, he started giving me a real grilling about you. When I told him to mind his own business and asked why he seemed so unconcerned over his brother's death he got really angry. I had had enough by then and told him to get out of my flat. He was in a real state by then.'

'Hmm, as I understand it, he was Julian's only living relative so I presume he inherits everything?'

'I don't know and frankly don't care. But I thought I'd better come round and warn you.'

'Why? Do you think he could be violent or something?'

'I don't know but he's a large, strong man and seemed to be quite upset.'

'Don't worry about me. I can handle myself.'

She looked at me and grinned. 'Yes, you're not exactly small either are you?'

I could see she was visibly relaxing. I suspected that what she actually needed was someone to talk to.

'And look Tony, I'm sorry about getting cross with you the other day. I was so upset I didn't know what was going on.'

'I sort of worked that out you know. It must have been pretty traumatic, especially as you found Julian's body.'

'Yes it was but I've got over the initial shock. What I want now is a friend.' She looked into my eyes and smiled.

Oh God, I knew that look. She was suddenly looking at me in a very different way, one that the girl a million miles away did quite often. There was no doubt that there could be chemistry between us and it would be dishonest of me to say I wasn't tempted. But I also knew that despite the similarities this was a different girl altogether. She dressed differently, cut her hair differently and had had a completely different upbringing. There was no way I was going to be unfaithful to my girl even if the chances of being found out were zero. On top of that, I didn't intend to spend much time over here and that would certainly curtail any relationships. I realised I needed to nip this whole thing in the bud and suddenly had an idea about how just to do that.

'Carrie, there's something you need to know about me,' I said looking her in the eye. 'When I lived abroad I was in a relationship and I still haven't got over it yet.'

'Oh dear, what happened?'

'He, died.' I let the words hang.

For a few seconds, she looked nonplussed then the penny dropped. A look of confusion and then embarrassment passed across her face. I knew that homosexuality had been decriminalised in this world but socially it was still far from accepted.

'Ah yes,' she stammered. I noticed a blush appearing on her cheeks.

'Look, don't worry about it,' I said quickly before she could say anything else. 'They see things differently in other countries but I would really appreciate it if you kept this to yourself.'

'Yes of course,' she said, still looking flustered. 'Oh dear, I've probably overstayed my welcome anyway.'

She started to get up but I put my hand over hers. 'You said you wanted a friend. I can still be that. I want to get to the bottom of why Julian was killed, possibly even more than you. Maybe we can help each other,'

To my complete surprise, she reached over and gave me a hug. 'Thank you,' she said. 'Let's do that.'

I suddenly had an idea. 'Carrie do you still have keys to Julian's house?'

'Yes but the police still have the place cordoned off. Why, do you want to look around?'

'Not particularly now that the police have stomped all over it but did he keep keys to his office there?'

'I think so.'

'How about you go over to the house. Say you left some personal effects there. I'm sure they won't mind letting you in. See if you can find those keys. We can then go and have a look around his office. Maybe there's something there to give us a clue.'

'But won't the police have done that already?' She asked.

'Possibly but they seem to move at a petty slow pace and there is no reason for them to do so. It's not the murder scene after all.'

We took the car and I dropped Carrie outside Julian's house. There was still a policeman at the door but she said something to him and disappeared inside. Five minutes later she was back with the keys.

'No problems then?' I asked.

'I know that constable,' she said. 'It's amazing what a smile can do. Here they are.' She showed me a bunch of keys.

I knew exactly what Carrie's smile could do but refrained from comment. We drove into town and I parked behind the library. It was only a short walk from there to the building which housed Julian's office. We climbed the stairs and I unlocked the front door. I remembered the neat and tidy office I had visited only a few weeks ago. This wasn't it. Papers were strewn over the floor and desk, the filing cabinets had all been opened and their contents ransacked. Someone had searched the place and had obviously been in a hell of a hurry.

Chapter 21

Carrie and I had a quick look around. There was little really to see and we had no idea if whoever had done this had found what they were looking for. One odd thing was that the safe was open and empty. It was a combination safe cleverly hidden behind a cork board on the wall. The board was covered in notes and a calendar all held in place with pins. I knew my way around these sort of safes even if the design was strange and was pretty sure that it could only have been opened in situ by someone with the combination.

'Something doesn't add up Carrie,' I said as I surveyed the mess.

'Why? It seems pretty straightforward to me,' she said. 'Someone wanted something that was in the office and presumably, they've got it.'

'Hmm, maybe but why open the safe and then ransack the room. If they knew about the safe and had the combination then presumably that's where they would have gone first. If it wasn't there it couldn't have been that important.'

'I suppose it depends on what they were looking for,' she said. 'Maybe it wasn't valuable in the normal sense.'

'Fair point,' I agreed but something about the whole scene looked wrong. It looked staged as though whoever discovered the mess was meant to think that. I decided to keep further speculation to myself.

'I suppose we'd better call the police,' Carrie said. 'I hope they won't be too angry about us being here.'

'They'd better not be,' I said. 'They should have been here days ago.' I went over to the desk and called the police station and asked to talk to Frank. He told me to wait there and would be over in a matter of minutes.

While we were waiting I had an idea. 'Carrie you work in the library so you must be quite proficient with the Oracle you have there. How about doing some research for me?'

'Of course, presumably it's to do with all this?'

'Yes but I need some background, some context. I'm missing something but I don't know what it is. Can you find out all you can about Julian's family? His parents and his brother, anything that might be relevant. Also, I need to know more about a certain Alec Jeffries, he's a local businessman and finally if you can find anything at all about a man named Robin McGregor. I bumped into him on the London train so he must have some connection to the city.'

'Hang on a second,' she said. She grabbed a pencil off the desk and wrote the names down on a scrap of paper. 'Yes I can do that but are you going to tell me why you want to know about those other people?'

'Yes I will but it might be better if you research them cold. I'll tell you what I know when you've looked into them and we can compare notes.'

'Alright, it'll take me a day or two. I'll let you know when I've got anything.'

Just then we heard steps on the stairs outside. The door opened and Frank appeared. He looked around the room with a frown on his face. 'When did this happen?'

'No idea,' I replied.

'And for that matter what are you doing here? We checked this office over two days ago. There was nothing here.'

'So you opened the safe then?' I asked.

'What safe? Oh for goodness sake.' Frank looked annoyed and embarrassed at the same time. He went over and looked in. 'Was there anything in here?'

'Not when we got here I'm afraid. I take it your people missed finding it?'

Frank grimaced. 'I'll be having words with a certain sergeant. So any idea what they were after?'

'Not really,' I replied. 'Carrie here had a key so we decided to come and have a quick look. I hadn't realised you had already been here. You didn't mention it. It seems to me that this looks rather staged. If they got the safe open why ransack the place?'

'Good point I suppose but I'll get my people back to do a proper search all the same.'

Just then a sergeant in uniform appeared and Frank took him outside. It was clear that words were being said. I turned to Carrie. 'I think we might make ourselves scarce.'

We left the office past a very red faced sergeant. 'Can I come round to your place this evening?' Frank said to me as we sidled past. 'I need to talk to you in private.'

'About half seven? I suggested and he nodded.

We then made our escape down the stairs and said goodbye outside. It was only a short walk to the library and Carrie wanted to get started on her task. I think she felt glad to have something concrete to do. I went off down the high street. There was a camera shop about half way down and I needed to make a purchase.

I bought a very nice and very simple camera and several rolls of film and spent the afternoon wandering around the town photographing anything of interest. I focused on places that were in both worlds but different over here as well as people's apparel and the cars. Hopefully, the photos would give my Carrie a more in depth feeling of what this place was really like. Having photographed just about the whole town centre, I went back to the car and drove home and took more photos of the house and surrounding meadows. I would drop the rolls of film off back at the shop tomorrow. Apparently, they would take several days to be developed. The contrast to my world where everyone snapped anything of interest all the time was yet another subtle prod to remind me of the radical differences between the two worlds.

True to his word, at exactly half past seven, a car rolled up into the drive and Frank got out. To my surprise, he actually looked a little uncomfortable. I hadn't told the Thompsons about the visit and they had already gone home so I invited Frank into the drawing room.

'Drink?' I asked. 'I've got quite a good Scotch or there's gin if you prefer.'

'A whisky would be nice,' he replied. 'No water.'

I poured us both a couple of fingers of Scotch and we sat down. I raised my glass in a toast and he did the same. I sipped my drink and leant back in my chair. 'So what's this all about Frank?' Why couldn't we chat at the station this afternoon?'

He didn't answer for a moment as he stared into his glass. Eventually, he looked up. 'You told me that if I asked around about you I would get no response and that if I tried to dig too far I might get warned off. Guess what? I did exactly what you said I shouldn't do and as you suggested ran into a completely blank wall. Not only that but no one has approached me regarding my enquiries. I even deliberately used some contacts I have in senior positions in the intelligence services and nothing, nada, zilch. So again I ask, who are you, Tony Peterson?'

I remained silent but inwardly I was cursing that I hadn't made greater efforts to keep prying fingers out of my affairs. I had learnt enough by now to realise that this Frank was a good man but with a real bulldog approach, he wouldn't let go easily.

He continued. 'Look, you can rest assured that I don't have you in the frame for this murder and I therefore suppose that I have no right to insist but there is something very odd going on here. You have an odd dress sense, the way you talk is unusual and things that are mundane seem to take you by surprise. It is clear to me that you're an experienced policeman. You know what questions to ask and how to look at things yet don't seem to understand our basic procedures.' He stopped talking and just looked at me.

It was crunch time. I suppose I could just stick to my story and ask him to leave but somehow I knew he would never give up. If I wanted to have any sort of life over here I couldn't always be dodging this man. Anyway, I really liked him. I liked him as much as I hated his doppelganger in my world. I also felt I could trust him. I made a decision.

'Come with me Frank, bring your glass and I'll bring the bottle. Believe me you're going to need it.'

I led him up the stairs to the study. 'By the way, you lot still haven't sent anyone around to fix that lock,' I said as we went in. 'I've had to have my man put a temporary bolt and padlock on it.'

'Oh just get it done and send me the bill,' he replied. 'Anyway, what's in here that's so important that it has to be kept under lock and key?'

'You've no idea,' I said grimly.

I sat Frank down in one of the leather sofas and poured him another drink. I had an idea and went to the desk and retrieved the cine camera. I plonked it on his lap. 'What's that Frank?'

He picked it up and examined it closely. 'It's a film camera but I've never seen one with this design. I've got one of my own at home but we use half inch film, this is smaller.'

'It's eight millimetre,' I said. 'In fact, you won't find another one like that anywhere in this world. I'm going to tell you a story and please give me the courtesy of listening. It's strange, ridiculous and unbelievable but for all that it's true. Now tell me, have you ever heard of a man called Gavrilo Princip?'

He shook his head but remained silent.

'In nineteen fourteen, operating in Sarajevo he assassinated the heir to the Austro Hungarian Empire. As a result of this Austria made such ridiculous reparations against Serbia that Russia stepped in. Germany, as Austria's ally, got sucked in and in order to pre-empted having to fight on two fronts, invaded Belgium and attacked France. Britain declared war on Germany and a terrible four year war of attrition ensued. Millions were killed. It cost this country a fortune most of which went to America who came in to the fight at the end of the war.'

I could see a look of incredulity growing on Frank's face.

'No, there's more. Wait please until I get to the end. Reparations on Germany were so harsh that they led to an economic collapse and the subsequent rise of one of the most vicious regimes ever to be seen in modern times. Led by a man called Adolph Hitler, a second European war broke out, except that this time Italy and Japan joined in with Germany. Hitler eventually overreached himself when he attacked Russia and he was defeated in nineteen forty five and the Japanese shortly afterwards. Once again, millions died. These were known as the two World Wars. I'm leaving out most of the detail just giving you the general picture. Britain and its empire were beggared with war debt and the empire collapsed. The world powers to emerge were America and Russia. They are to this day although China is probably coming a close third. The pressure of these wars led to massive increases in technological development. Jet engines were in use by nineteen forty five and are now used all over the world for military and commercial purposes. Computers developed to crack the German war codes were develop so that they are an integral part of modern life. We even put a man on the moon in nineteen sixty nine. You asked me where I came from, that's my world.'

Frank looked completely non plussed. He took another swig from his glass and looked at me as though I had just sprouted antlers. 'Prove it,' was all he said.

I got up and walked through the mirror.

Chapter 22

As soon as I was back in my own study, I looked around but there was no sign of Carrie and there were no messages for me on my phone. I needed some solid evidence and quickly. A four day old copy of the Times was on my desk so I grabbed that. I then had another thought. My laptop was backed up to the cloud so I could easily manage without it here until I bought a new one. I grabbed hold of that as well and walked back over to the other study.

'What the hell did you just do?' Frank was standing staring at me as I re-emerged.

'Getting some proof. You did ask.' I handed him the newspaper.

He took it and studied the front page. While he did, I put the laptop on the little table by the sofas and turned it on. 'Come and look at this,' I said as it booted up. 'This little machine holds more data and has more computer power than anything you will have ever encountered. Over there, it connects wirelessly to a network of computers around the world. We call it the Internet. It can tell you just about anything. You can watch films or television, do complex calculations, play games, the list is endless. Let me show you.' The screen had cleared and I went into my video directory and loaded a film. Out of sheer serendipity, it was 'First Man' the story of Neil Armstrong and his moon mission. The look on Frank's face was a sight to see.

'How are you doing that?' he asked as the opening credits appeared. 'The picture quality is incredible.'

'I told you Frank, we have developed this sort of technology way beyond anything here. I can't begin to tell you how it's done except to say it's commonplace in my world. You asked for proof, this is just the tip of the iceberg I'm afraid but maybe you can now start to see why I'm different.'

'But you walked through that mirror,' He got up and went over to it. He examined it carefully and pushed his hand against the glass. 'Do it again,' he said.

I did but only for a few seconds. When I was back I looked at him. 'Don't ask me why I can do that and you can't because I have no bloody idea. My uncle found it and when I inherited I discovered

I had the gift, if that's what you want to call it, as well. This was just as much a shock to me as it is now for you.'

We went back to the sofas, Frank knocked back his drink and held out the glass for a refill. 'This is just bloody marvellous,' he said. 'All my life I've been a fan of science novels and here I am now, goddamit, in a real one.'

I have to say his reaction surprised me. Unlike Carrie who had taken a great deal of convincing, Frank seemed to be drinking it in. I had an idea. 'Frank, I could spend hours trying to explain what my world is like. Why don't we watch that film together? It's actually set some time ago in the sixties but it tells the story of how we got to the moon. But also it will give you some context, probably far more than I could.'

So we did just that. We watched the film and the whisky bottle lost its contents. Frank's reaction was amazing. He never once queried the authenticity of what he was seeing, all he wanted was more information. When it was over he just sat back and looked at me. So who are you Tony? How do you fit into this?'

'As I said Frank, I inherited all this. I used to be a policeman in the London Metropolitan force but when Uncle Peter died, I quit the job and came back to Winchester.' There was no way I was going to tell him about his double back at home. 'My uncle played it pretty low key and used his inside knowledge to set up investments that he was pretty sure would succeed. He did very well out of it and so did several people over here. Julian Fletcher convinced me to have that party and raise my profile which frankly I'm beginning to regret.'

'I can understand that but it probably seemed like a good idea at the time. So what do you intend to do over the longer term? The opportunities seem almost endless.' He said, clearly fired up with all the possibilities he could see opening up.

It was time to burst that particular bubble. 'To be honest Frank, once this murder is cleared up, I intend to do very little.'

'But why? Just think of all the things the two worlds can learn from each other, to do nothing would be criminal.'

'Would it? Let's think this through. Firstly, I decided to tell you all about this because I knew you would never give up until you found out. But don't think you are in a position to tell anyone else. Would anyone believe you? Especially if I denied everything. And don't forget I can disappear completely any time I wish. You would be on a one way trip to the funny farm.'

I could see my words hitting their target. 'But that's not the real issue. Remember me mentioning a man call Princip? One man precipitated an event that resulted in millions dying in two major wars. Now look at the current political situation here. What would it take to start the ball rolling between you and the Germans? If I gave some of our technology to the British what would that do to the balance of power? Sorry but it's not going to happen.'

The look of disappointment on Frank's face would have been comical if the reality of the situation wasn't so serious.

'So what are you going to do?'

'First things first, let's solve this murder. I have no objection to using techniques from my world to help if it becomes feasible to do that but I will not bring any technology through unless it's under my tight control and all will be kept under lock and key in this room. In the longer term, I've still to make up my mind. The Venta Society want me to continue giving informed tips for investment but frankly I've decided to hold fire on even that, at least until I have a better understanding of the ramifications. Oh and on that point Inspector Cosgrove, when we talked about the Venta Society when we were querying your Oracle you gave no intimation that you knew exactly who they were and what they were all about.'

'Why do you think I would know about them?' He asked with a straight face.

'Oh come on, you know everything that goes on in this city. A group of the most prominent businessmen and city fathers who meet once a month and you deny knowledge of them. Who do you take me for? I wouldn't be at all surprised if you're a member yourself.'

At last, Frank looked a little embarrassed. 'Fair point, but I was trying to test your knowledge and I was proved right wasn't I? You'd never seen or used an Oracle before. That was bloody obvious.'

'No more secrets Frank,' was all I said. 'I've been totally honest with you and I expect you to be the same.'

He nodded and we had yet another drink. It was past two in the morning when we called it quits. I offered him a spare room but he declined. I didn't ask about drink driving rules over here and decided that it was his problem if he caused an accident or got stopped. As he was the boss of the local constabulary I was sure he could manage the situation. My last thought as my head hit the pillow was that I was not going to feel sharp tomorrow.

Chapter 23

I wasn't wrong. That bloody gorilla had been in my room again last night. He had flung all my clothes everywhere, made a total mess of the bed, hit me over the head with a baseball bat and done something unmentionable in my mouth. I groaned as I rolled over, having been woken up by the light streaming through the gap in the badly closed curtains. I vowed never to go drinking with Frank again. Putting on a dressing gown, I staggered down the corridor to the bathroom and shower. Hopefully, it wouldn't be too long before the place was ripped apart and I had a decent en suite. Oh God, today I was going to have to tell Mavis that a new bed was arriving and it would be covered in the foreign travesty of a duvet. The day was just getting better.

Thankfully, after a long shower, I was starting to feel more human. Mavis brought in breakfast and her magnificent Full English at least got me back on all cylinders again. Luckily, Carrie then rang and suggested we meet at the library as she had some information for me so I was able to escape. With a complete lack of moral courage, I failed to tell Mavis about the bed but as it was due to arrive that morning at least I would be out when the first explosion happened.

Carrie was in the seated area of the library foyer when I arrived. She had a sheaf of paper on the table in front of her. She smiled as she saw me and indicated the chair next to hers.

'Hard night last night? She asked. 'You look like a train ran over you.'

'Not a train, a certain policeman, I'll tell you about it later. Anyway, you've been quick,' I said, as I saw the pile of documents.

'Actually, most of it wasn't hard to find out, it's all on public record.'

'I take it you've not seen the brother again?'

'David? No, I've not seen him but I do have quite a lot on him and the family. Are you ready to hear about them?'

'Of course, fire away.'

'Right, well as you know the father passed away a few years back. There were actually three children. A sister called Mary was in a car accident with her mother some time ago. Apparently, neither survived. Julian's father ran the business until he got cancer and then Julian left the Marines to care for him and take over the company.'

'Yes, your friend Elaine told me about that. She didn't mention the sister though.'

'Ah, that's where it gets a bit more interesting. The sister was the oldest of the three but also a little odd. She had been in and out of psychiatric homes for half her life. The family never really mentioned her. The younger brother, David, followed Julian into the military. By all accounts, he's done well although there was some sort of tragedy on an exercise on Dartmoor three years ago. David was involved. One of the trainees died of heat exhaustion but David was exonerated.'

'So what's the interesting bit?'

'There was an inquest after the car accident but only for the mother. I can't find any record of one being done for the daughter. On top of that, Julian's father made a large endowment to a private hospital out at Sparsholt, just outside the city.'

'Are you suggesting that the daughter survived?'

'If she was in the car there appears to be no subsequent record of her at all which is very strange.'

'Hmm, I can ask Frank Cosgrove to look into the detailed records. The police must still have them on file. Anything else?'

'Yes, that other man you asked me to find out about, Robin McGregor. I've found a photo here from the Hampshire Chronicle. Is this the man?'

She showed me a black and white photograph of a man shaking hands with another older man with a large chain around his neck, presumably the Mayor. The caption was about an award for a 'Mister McGregor.'

'Yes, that's him. What did you find out?' I asked as I studied the picture which must have been taken some years ago.

'He manages an estate agent business in the city. It's quite successful by all accounts but he doesn't own it. It's owned by a chap called Alec Jeffries.'

'Why am I not surprised? Thanks Carrie, that's' all been extremely useful. Look, I'm off to see the police again. I'll see if I can get any more information about the phantom sister. I think it could be very important.'

'Is there anything else I can do?' Carrie asked. It was clear she was keen to stay involved.

'You can try.' I wrote down all the names I could remember from the meeting with the Venta crowd the other evening. 'These are the people I can remember who were with Mister Jeffries. Anything you can find out about them could be useful. Also, this address in London in Aldwych has something to do with them but it would appear to be quite a sensitive issue. See if there is anything on record. We queried the Oracle at the police station and it is apparently unoccupied at the moment but I'm pretty sure that's not the case.'

She nodded and seemed happy with what I was suggesting so I left after agreeing to see her in a day or two. I then went back down North Walls to the cop shop.

Frank was in his office this time not the pub and as soon as he saw me he motioned to me to come in and shut the door. He even had the nerve to look fresh and alert despite only a few hours sleep and doing serious damage to my stash of scotch.

'Good morning Tony,' he boomed. 'Please tell me last night wasn't a mad dream?'

'What the mad story about alternative realities or the depletion of my booze stocks?'

'Both,' he laughed. 'But you're going to have to give me some time to assimilate all we talked about.'

'I realise that but at least you seem to believe me which is a start. And we really need to get to the bottom of this murder before we get too involved in other matters,' I replied.

'Agreed. We've released the body and I've spoken to the brother. He's going to stay here until the funeral which will be on Thursday next week. He'll be staying at the family house.'

'Hmm, were you aware that he called on Julian's girlfriend? Apparently, he was quite blunt and seemed more interested in the inheritance than his brother's murder.'

'Yes I got the same impression when I spoke to him,' Frank said. 'He also seemed interested in you and your relationship with his brother.'

'Well I've been doing some digging with the help of Carrie Parks and we have come up with something. Did you know there was a sister?'

'Yes but wasn't she killed in a car accident along with her mother years ago?'

'You tell me Frank. You should have the records.' I went on to tell him all that Carrie had found out.

When I finished Frank pressed a button on the intercom on his desk and asked for the records of the police investigation to be brought up. While we were waiting I asked if it would be possible to see the papers that had been on Julian's desk.

'Well, rightfully they belong to the brother now,' Frank said but as they are still classed as evidence I don't see why you can't have a look later on.

Just then a sergeant came in and put a large, dusty, cardboard ledger on the desk.

'Right, here we are,' Frank said, as he opened the box and withdrew several files of paper. He studied them and then passed them to me. I read them in turn. There were surprisingly few for a double death in a car accident. It seemed that the car was trying to overtake another one when the driver, the mother, put a wheel on the grass verge and lost control. The mother died instantly but the daughter, who wasn't wearing a seat belt was flung clear. Then the paper trail just stopped. There was an inquest report but just as Carrie had said only for the mother for some reason. In fact, after the accident report which didn't even state whether the daughter was alive, there was no mention of her at all.

I looked at the signature on the report. 'Who was this Inspector Smith who signed this off?'

'My predecessor,' Frank said. 'I wasn't involved in this case at the time although I vaguely remember it. You say that a large endowment was made to the Sparsholt sanatorium?'

'Apparently so. I wonder if someone actually survived and they were packed away out of sight?'

'Possible I suppose. Look, I'm pretty much tied up all day. Why don't you got out there and ask around? Say you're acting with my authority. That normally gets people's cooperation around here. Oh and before you go, take these with you, they're those papers that were on Fletcher's desk. I'll need them back tomorrow.'

I thanked Frank, noting how his attitude towards me had completely changed. If nothing else we were now co-conspirators or maybe it was that he now knew he could completely trust me. Whatever it was it made our working relationship so much better.

Chapter 24

As I drove out of Winchester along the Stockbridge road I realised this was the first time I had ventured into the local area away from the city apart from my short trip to London. The roads were far quieter than I was used to and an almost complete absence of road markings kept me concentrating. I realised that if I was stopped I didn't actually have a licence over here, not that I knew what would be required to get one. I made a mental note to talk to Frank about it when I got back.

I knew the turning to Sparsholt well but the village was much smaller than I recognised and I was forced to stop at the village Post Office and ask for directions. It wasn't far and soon I was driving down a long gravel drive that lead to a large, surprisingly modern building at the end. I had been pondering about how to play this. Had I been an actual card carrying copper it would probably have been quite easy but I wasn't and so I was going to have to play this carefully. All I knew was that the girl's name was Mary Fletcher and the date she probably arrived.

In fact, it all proved very easy. There was a reception desk with a rather severe looking lady sitting behind it. I went over and put on my most engaging smile. 'Good morning, my name is Tony Peterson. I'm actually here on behalf of the Winchester police. I was wondering whether I could talk to Mary Fletcher. I believe she has been here now for over eight years.'

To my surprise, the receptionist smiled back. Maybe they were a different breed in this world. 'Yes of course. Mary will be in the garden this time of the morning. I'll get someone to escort you.' She picked up the phone and asked for a porter.

In the few minutes we had while we waited I decided to do a little more digging. 'Has anyone been to see her recently?' I asked. 'It's just that one of her immediate family has met with an accident.'

'Oh dear, that is sad. Is that the brother, Mister Julian? He's a regular here you know. He comes every week if he can. Not that Mary really knows him anymore. After the accident, she never recovered as we had hoped.'

'Yes, I'm afraid it is. Unfortunately he has died.'

'Oh that's dreadful, maybe it's better that Mary won't really understand. Are you here to tell her? I'm afraid it will probably be a waste of time.'

'Yes I'll try but tell me, is there provision for her to stay here?'

'Oh yes, her father left a trust fund for her. She'll never want for the care she needs. Ah here's John. He'll take you to see her.'

A slim man in the de rigeur white coat was striding towards me. The receptionist explained what I wanted and he led me out of the back of the building to a large and well tended garden. There were about a dozen people wandering around or sitting on benches. Several were in wheelchairs. I was led over to one where a remarkably pretty woman was sitting staring into space.

My guide grasped the wheelchair handles and wheeled her over to an empty bench so I could sit beside her.

'Please stay as long as you like,' he said. 'I'm afraid Mary probably won't respond. She has good and bad days. If you need anything just pop back into the house.'

I thanked him and sat on the bench. I could see the family resemblance to Julian immediately. They were definitely brother and sister. However, she looked gaunt and there was no spark of interest in her eyes. The phrase 'all the lights on but no one home' sprang uncharitably to mind.

'Hello Mary, my name's Tony.' I said more in hope than expectation.

To my surprise, her head turned a little and she seemed to focus on my face.

'Julian?' she asked in a voice that was almost a whisper.

'No, I'm a friend of his, my name's Tony. I'm afraid I have some bad news for you.'

I was pretty sure she hadn't registered what I had said but I ploughed on. Someone was going to have to tell her even if it didn't mean much. 'Look, I'm sorry to tell you but Julian won't be coming to see you any more. He passed away a few days ago.'

She didn't say a word, just stared at me.

'Do you understand Mary? I'm so sorry but you will still be looked after, still have this lovely place to live in.'

There was no response and I was starting to run out of things to say. This was not going as I had anticipated. For a start, I hadn't realised I was going to have to be the one to tell her about Julian. It was clear that I was not going to get any useful information from her.

'Look, your other brother is here I'm sure he will come and see you when he can.'

At the word 'brother', a spark of recognition seemed to appear on her face.

'That's right, your brother David is here and I'm sure he will come and see you soon.'

Her reaction was definitely something I wasn't expecting. She suddenly stood and let out a shriek before collapsing at my feet. I jumped up and knelt down to see what help I could offer. Luckily, one of the staff must have seen what had happened and he came running over.

Mary was muttering something under her breath as the nurse and I lifted her up back into the wheelchair. She was so light it was like lifting a child.

The nurse started talking to her, soothing her and rearranging her blanket. He turned to me. 'I think she's had enough for today Sir. I'll take her back inside.'

I nodded and let him wheel her back towards the house. As I walked back to the reception desk deep in thought, I wondered at her reaction to when I said that her other brother might visit. She only said one word, repeated over and over and it made no sense. It sounded like 'Canard', the French word for duck. What the hell did that mean?

When I reached reception there was a man in a suit waiting for me. 'Mister Peterson, you were here to see Mary Fletcher I understand?'

'Yes, sorry, have I done something wrong?'

'No, not at all but could we have a word please?'

'Of course.' I followed the man into a nearby office.

'My name is John Stanhope, I'm the senior doctor here. I understand you were here to tell Mary about what had happened to her brother.'

'Actually, that's not quite true,' I said. 'I came here to see if she even existed. I'm working with Inspector Cosgrove in Winchester and we are looking into the murder of her brother. When we discovered that Mary was not in fact killed in a car crash, we decided to see if she was still alive. As we didn't know her mental state, there was a chance she could help us with our enquiries. I told her about her brother as it seemed that no one had done so and to be honest to see if I could get a reaction.'

'And that's when she fell out of her wheelchair? I'll be honest we haven't seen that much of a reaction from her since she came here.'

'No that wasn't it. It was when I mentioned her other brother, David, who I assume will be coming to see her. That's when she had her fit or whatever it was.'

Stanhope looked surprised. 'Well you didn't know she was alive and we didn't know she had another brother. Look, she was unwell before the accident but it caused her to have a complete breakdown. She came here soon after and her father wanted the whole thing kept quiet. He paid for a lifetime of care and also made a generous donation to the hospital. There was always a hope she would recover but it was a forlorn one. I had no idea that the police were not aware of where she was.'

'No that's understood and it's quite clear she can be of no help. I'm just sorry I upset her. All I did was say that her brother David would probably visit her soon, although from what you tell me he's never been here in the past.'

'That's correct,' Stanhope said. 'So I've no idea why it sparked such a reaction.'

'She did say one thing. When I was helping pick her up she kept repeating one word over and over. It sounded French and sounded like Canard, the word for duck, which seemed very odd to me.'

Stanhope smiled. 'Did you know that Mary's mother was French? She was apparently fluent in both languages. Of all the words she has said since she came here and they haven't been many, that is her favourite. It's not Canard but Connard and there is a world of difference between the meanings. Connard, I'm afraid is a rather nasty French swear word and it means bastard or jerk, a rude epithet for someone you really, really don't like.'

As I drove back to Winchester, I pondered on the visit. I had told the doctor that it had been unfruitful and that we wouldn't need to bother Mary again. However, it had yielded one vital fact. That said, I still couldn't see how it was pertinent to the investigation. I needed to talk to Frank again.

Chapter 25

The morning had flown past and by the time I was back in the city, it was past one. I knew there was no point in going to the police station. Instead, I parked up in the pub car park. Frank was in his other office and I joined him. He raised his eyebrows when I plonked his pint on the table followed by my pint of orange juice and lemonade.

'Before you ask, I actually don't like drinking at lunchtime, it only gives me a headache by four.'

'Suit yourself,' he didn't sound convinced. 'So what did you discover? Is there a mad relative hidden in the attic?'

'Yes, she's very ill and not all there I'm afraid. It was as we guessed. The family took her there after the accident presumably to hide her away and I'm guessing the police accidentally lost the inquest report to keep it out of the papers at the time.'

'Water under the bridge now,' Frank said. 'So did you find out anything useful?'

I told him about the other brother and how he had never visited but how his name seemed to spark a reaction from his sister. He didn't seem impressed. 'I'm afraid that's not going to help, is it? I guess there must have been some bad blood between them in the past. It's hardly a motive for killing your brother. Anyway the man's alibi is gold plated. He may well have had the motive and opportunity but there was no way he could have been in Hampshire at the time of the murder. We've completed all the house to house enquiries as well and drawn a blank. I'm afraid this is going nowhere.'

I sat back and thought about what he had said and had to agree. Whoever had done this, either knew Julian or had been willingly let into the house by him. The only person with any motive was his brother who stood to inherit yet he was over five hundred miles away at the time. So it must have been someone local but there was absolutely no evidence to find him. In my world, we could have looked for DNA residue. However, over here they didn't know what that was, or did they?'

'Frank do you have any way of analysing biological residue apart from blood type and fingerprints?'

'No, that's it, although we can do chemical analysis if any residue is found like gunshot traces. Why, can your lot do better?'

'Yes we can. There is a thing called DNA, don't ask me to tell you what that stands for I can never remember but it's a residue that is completely unique to an individual. The only problem is that you need to know whose signature you are looking at. We have extensive records but even if we can't match it we can ask for samples to be taken if we have justified suspicion.'

'Bit like fingerprints then, same problem, we have loads of records but if we can't find a match there's not a lot we can do.'

'So what are you going to do next?' I asked.

'Buggered if I know but I don't give up, I'll keep digging.'

'Look there is one thing, The chap I told you about who I talked to on the way to London recently and who seemed to arrange to get me followed, works here in Winchester. I've managed to track him down. There is also that building in London that we used the Oracle to check up on. It's meant to be empty but I'm damned sure it's not. This is all tied into this Venta crowd and we know Julian was a member. Maybe there is a connection here. I want to study those documents you gave me this afternoon then have a word with Mister McGregor. After that, it might be worth going back up to London.'

Frank looked at me over his pint. 'Fine, at the moment there is no direct connection with any of that to the murder. The moment you discover anything it becomes a police matter and you must pass everything on to me, is that clear?'

'Of course Frank. I would do nothing else.'

'Now there is something else we need to talk about Tony. There is a bloody great elephant in the room and I want to know more about it.'

I knew Frank would want to know more and I had no objection but I also wanted to keep everything under tight control. At the moment, if he tried to reveal my secret he would have nothing to back it up and would be laughed out of court. However, that could quickly change it he got his hands on any solid evidence.

'Look, I have no objection to showing you more and letting you learn about my world but only at my place. I can't afford to let you have any material that could be misused. I've already explained why I think that could be a real danger. We can talk about it any time but if you want to investigate material evidence it will have to be in my presence and in my study. I hope you can live with that?'

He nodded and we chatted for another half an hour before I left. I had two things to do. I needed to look at those papers but I also wanted to talk to Mister McGregor as soon as I could. I decided that the papers were more critical as they needed to be back with the police tomorrow. I would call on McGregor after I had dropped them off.

When I got home, it felt like walking into the eye of a hurricane. The eye being the quiet bit in the middle but you know you are surrounded by violent storms. The house was quiet. I went upstairs with my papers. I was going to the study but looked into my bedroom first. As I had expected, the delivery had obviously taken place. There, in pride of place, was my new bed. Lying on top, still wrapped in plastic, was a duvet and several sheets and pillow cases. There was no sign of Mavis. I nipped over to the study and dropped off the papers and then with my heart in my mouth I went down to the kitchen.

As expected she was there fussing over the stove. 'Afternoon Mavis,' I called cheerily. 'I see my new bed has arrived. Sorry, I forgot to mention it was coming today, I've been so tied up with the police recently.'

For a moment there was no reply. 'I suppose you expect me to make it.'

Oh dear, that didn't sound good. 'Is there a problem with that Mavis? I asked.

She turned to me with an angry look. 'It's bad enough we have to cope with you and your uncle before you, disappearing all the time and never knowing when you will be back. But you could have told me about the bed. And what is that thing on top of it? How do I make that into a proper bed?'

'Look, I'm sorry Mavis,' I said. 'I've been so busy helping the police with this murder I completely forgot about it, honestly. And look, I've been used to that sort of bed all my life. I'm sorry if I upset you but this is my house after all.' I immediately realised that was the wrong thing to say so ploughed on. 'I was thinking of you as well you know,' I lied. 'They are much easier to make so it will save you a great deal of effort in the morning. Come and have a look I'll show you.'

We both went up to the bedroom and I unwrapped the duvet and found a cover. I showed her how it was really just a giant pillow and how to insert the duvet, grab the far corners and give it a shake. Then it was just a case of fitting the bottom sheet and all was done.

Mavis didn't look convinced, there was not a hospital corner in sight but as I explained making it in the morning only required the whole thing to be shaken back into place. In the end, she grudgingly seemed to accept the inevitable but left me feeling I had come close to committing a mortal sin. What the hell was I going to tell her and husband when it came time to get the builders in? Oh well, I decided to park that idea for another day.

I went and hid in the study to look at the papers. As far as I could see, they were a complete record, of the investment recommendations that my uncle had made and also the results in terms of annual profits and dividends. It immediately became clear that Uncle Peter had been very careful whilst still making a considerable fortune by either world's standards. Many of the investments were in companies looking for natural resources and were multinationals. There were a few technological recommendations but nearly all were for medical research. There was nothing to do with digital technology development although a couple were for companies that did make what this world called computers but all were analogue type devices or only used basic electronics. In other words, nothing to upset the balance between the superpowers. However, from my discussions with my Carrie, I was still of the opinion that even this could be getting too dangerous. Who knew what could tip the balance? And I definitely did not want to be the one who did. Then something caught my eye. It was on the last page I looked at and as I had been going through them chronologically it was the latest entry. It was typed, but there was an annotation in handwriting. I couldn't be sure but I suspected it was Uncle Peter's. I would ask Frank if anyone had checked. There was no date but the previous entry was some three months before my uncle had died so it must have been written round about the last time he had been here. The note was very simple, it gave the name of a company 'Digitalus' and next to it in blue ink was a name, it was hard to make out but even so I could read it. It said 'Bill Gates.'

Oh Shit.

Chapter 26

The next day, after my first really good sleep in this world, I went back into town. I had the papers in my briefcase. Before I left, I had nipped back over and grabbed my new phone. I photographed them all and put the phone into the wall safe where I had already secured the laptop. I would need yet another phone when I went back but that was a small price to pay.

I parked near the High Street and made my way to McGregor and Sons, Estate Agents. I stopped and looked in the window for a few moments. House prices were tiny compared to my world. In fact, removing a nought from our prices would seem to be the value they had over here. A pretty young girl had obviously been watching me because as soon as I entered she was there waiting to pounce.

'Good morning Sir, how can I help?' She asked with a beaming smile. 'Are you looking for a property or maybe you want to sell?'

'Sorry to disappoint you my dear,' I said. 'What I would actually like is a word with your boss, Mister McGregor,'

The girl looked crestfallen for just a second as the opportunity for a commission flew by. She then plastered the smile back on again. 'Hold on Sir. I'll see if Mister McGregor is free, please take a seat.' She indicated several comfortable looking chairs. I didn't have time to sit as a door at the rear of the office opened and McGregor came in.

'Someone asking after me Lisa?' he said. 'I overheard what you were saying.' And then he stopped when he saw me. There was a look of surprise and even annoyance on his face just for a second which he quickly covered up. But once a policeman always a policeman, I had seen it and filed it mentally away.

'Mister Peterson isn't it? We met on the train to London a while ago. How can I help? Are you looking to sell? You have a house down at St Cross I believe.'

Now how did he know that? I certainly hadn't told him. 'No, not selling, maybe we could have a word in private?'

He nodded. 'Lisa, mind the shop, please. If you would come this way please Mister Peterson?'

I followed him back through the door he had arrived from. Inside was a plush office with a desk and several chairs. This was obviously where the serious clients got entertained.

'Can I offer you a tea or a coffee?' he asked as he pointed to two seats in front of the desk.

'No thanks,' I said as I took a seat. 'I've just had breakfast.'

'So, how can I help you?' McGregor asked. 'Is this business or social?'

'Neither,' I said. 'And you can cut the polite bullshit.'

He flinched as I said the words but I carried on before he could say anything. 'You deliberately met me on that train to try and pump me for information. I know that because your boss Alec Jeffries all but admitted that to me the other day at a meeting of the Venta Society or whatever you call it. What you didn't know is that I used to be a policeman and I saw you in London. I saw you waiting for me outside Somerset House and also saw you talking to a man who subsequently tailed me while I went shopping. He wasn't very good at that and I ended up tailing him. So what is going on in the house in Aldwych? I'll find out soon enough when I get the police to raid it. Oh, I forgot to mention I am helping them with their investigation into the murder of Julian Fletcher, who I suspect you knew.'

McGregor was looking more and more uncomfortable as I spoke. When I finished he had clearly come to a conclusion. 'Look you're right, Alec did ask me to see if I could find out anything about you and see where you went. I assumed it was something to do with business. He is very thorough. You might have noticed that I have very red hair and it's hard to hide that so when you were in Somerset House I telephoned a friend and asked him to keep an eye on you. But that's all. I've no idea what the building in Aldwych is that you refer to. Look, Julian was a friend dammit we went to school together, I'm just as upset as you about the murder but honestly, if you want to know any more you will have to ask Alec.'

'So who was the friend? He went into the building and must know what's going on in there?'

McGregor looked flustered. 'I know nothing about that, honestly. You will have to ask Alec.'

'No, you said you rang him and he was your friend so who was he?'

'Look I don't want to drag him into this. He was only doing me a favour. I can't say any more.'

I didn't answer, simply stared at McGregor for a few seconds. As I let him sweat I made a decision. He was quite clearly lying through his teeth but I had no powers to force him to answer. Anyway, I was sure he would be on the telephone to Alec Jeffries the moment I left the building which was what I actually wanted anyway. Sometimes the best way to get results is to kick the ant's nest and see what crawls out.

I stood up and made to leave. 'Thank you Mister McGregor, you have been most enlightening. I suspect we will be meeting again.' I left without giving him a chance to answer.

Next stop, the cop shop. I told Frank about McGregor and what I had done and how I was expecting a reaction any time soon.

'Fair enough Tony,' he said. 'It's your play but keep me in the picture.'

We chatted for a while and I agreed he could come over that evening to watch another film on my laptop. I also wanted to quiz him on what other technologies the police had over here. Depending on what he said, I had a few ideas of some other things it might be worth having on hand. With no further progress reported I decided to head home and await any reaction from this morning's visit and in the meantime I would get the film camera and shoot some home movies for my Carrie. With any luck, the stills I had taken the other day would also be ready and I could pop over and leave them all for her. I also was developing a shopping list of items she could either get for me or I could pick up if I had time. I promised myself a night with her tomorrow but with Frank due over this evening that couldn't happen today.

However, when I got home my plans had to change. There was a strange car in the drive and when I went through the front door Michael informed me that I had a visitor and he was waiting for me in the drawing room.

David Fletcher looked nothing like his brother or his sister for that matter. Where Julian had been tall and slim. David was all muscle. He had the manner of someone who worked out regularly. He must have been well over six feet tall and instead of fair hair, his black hair was cut in a military style and he had a large black moustache to go with it. He also had a permanent scowl that seemed to match the lines on his face. Sometimes I take an almost instant dislike to someone. I was fighting not to do that now. I had never met the man before. Mind you, I did remember what Carrie had told me about him.

He stood as I came through the door and held out his hand. 'Sorry to disturb you Mister Peterson but I wondered if we could have a talk. I'm David Fletcher the brother of Julian who I believe you knew?'

I shook his hand. He was clearly one of those people who seem to think that trying to crush someone's hand is a good way of making an impression. I resisted the urge to start a hand squeezing competition and motioned for him to sit again.

'How can I help you Mister Fletcher?'

'Please call me David. I believe you did some business with Julian?'

'Not really, I only knew him for a few weeks but I might have done business with him in the future. We'll never know now.' I replied.

'But your uncle did do business with him and my father before that. Quite successfully I understand.'

'My uncle was a very good businessman David. What more can I say?' It was clear that he wanted me to open up more but I wasn't going to play that game. 'Now what is it you actually want? Carrie Parks said you visited her a few days ago and that you were quite aggressive with her. I hope you don't think you can try that tactic with me?'

He had the grace to look embarrassed at that remark. 'Yes, I'm sorry about that. I was pretty wound up at the time as you can imagine.'

'Yes but it's Carrie you should be apologising to, not me. I understand that you asked her a lot of question about Julian's business and about me and my uncle?'

'I never really took much notice of the business. Julian inherited and I just wanted to carry on with my military career. But whatever happened to Julian must have been something to do with the business surely? Carrie must have known something about it. Probably more than anyone else.'

'No you're wrong there, I don't think Julian told her much about his work at all. Why would he? Their relationship had nothing to do with stockbroking. And as for my uncle, he used your father and then Julian to manage his investments nothing more. The police have discounted any connection in that direction.' I wasn't going to tell him about the Venta Society or empty houses in London. That would only fuel his paranoia.

'Anyway, what are you going to do now?' I asked. 'Julian left the Marines when his father died are you going to do the same?'

'I doubt it,' David said. 'Business has never been my thing. I don't suppose his firm will be worth much. He has a lease on the office in town and there are no other assets. I'll keep the house though. It's where we all grew up.'

'Yes I discovered that you have a sister as well,' I said watching his reaction carefully. 'I went to see her the other day. The police asked me to. I was surprised you hadn't been there already.'

At the mention of his sister, he looked startled for a second and then his face became guarded. 'Mary has been ill for many years. I don't suppose she would even know who I was. But of course, I will be going to see her soon.'

That last sentence was spoken with such a lack of sincerity it made me wonder exactly what had passed between them previously.

It was if my mentioning the sister had helped him come to a decision. 'Thank you Mister Peterson. I really ought to be going now. The funeral will be on Thursday if you wish to attend at the church of Saint Peters in Jewry Street. Thank you for your help. I'll see myself out.'

'No please let me,' I said and I escorted him to the front door. 'Did you have a hat?' I asked as it seemed many men still wore them over here.

He looked towards the coat rack and sure enough, a grey fedora was hanging there. I reached over and took it, quickly running my finger around the leather band on the inside as I passed it to him.

When he had left, I sat back in thought. His visit had seemed almost like a performance. As if he was going through the motions of a grieving brother. I would certainly put money on him never visiting his sister. The only time I had seen any animation in his features was when I mentioned Carrie. There was definitely something much deeper going on here. I also had noted that he was left handed, something else to consider. I looked down at my hand

and there were a few strands of hair on my fingers from the inside of the fedora. At least I might now be able to clear one thing up.

Chapter 27

After David Fletcher left, I still had time to nip into town and collect the films that had been developed and also take some cine footage. When I got home it was after five but Frank wasn't due until seven so I went back home and rang Carrie on the landline. I explained I would need to get back soon but she managed to get over in less than fifteen minutes.

After a rather long hug and managing to fight off the temptation to spend the rest of our time doing unproductive but very satisfying things, I brought her up to date on progress. I also gave her the envelopes of photos and the cine film that would need developing.

'Oh and I need yet another new phone and a new laptop,' I said, as I explained why I had taken them over. 'How about we have a day or two out in London early next week?' I asked. 'I need some other things as well as those two and we could have some time to ourselves, something I've been missing rather a lot lately.'

'Me too but I'll have to square that with the school,' Carrie said. 'But I'm owed some time off. So I don't see why not.' She gave me a peck on the cheek. 'Now you'd better go back over and I want to look at these photos.'

I did as I was told and it was lucky I did because Frank was early. I updated him on my visit from David Fletcher but although he was interested, he reiterated that David was not a suspect so whatever he was up to was not his business. I had to agree but there was still something nagging at the back of my mind over his behaviour. Maybe my trip to my London would help. I told Frank that I would be away for several days and he didn't press me for my reasons. I simply said I had some business to conduct. He was far more interested in me showing him some more of my world.

With the remaining battery on my laptop, we managed to watch two films that night. One was a documentary about the Great War. He didn't say a word to me as we watched but afterwards he turned to me with a strange expression. 'All that was caused by one man assassinating the heir to the Austrian throne?'

'Yes,' I replied. 'You were so lucky over here. As you saw the slaughter was terrible. Not only that but the end of the war set up the conditions for the next one. I'll show you that some other time.'

The second film was a comedy set in modern times. It was less successful as Frank just didn't get many of the jokes but it did seem to give him a better idea of what our world was like.

'You seem to have a lot more technology but I'm not sure your world is any more pleasant a place to live in than mine,' was his first observation when it finished.

I could only agree. After that, I told him about the current political situation. And we ended up agreeing that both worlds seemed to be living on a knife edge. One thing I steered clear of was telling him about the Cold War. He really didn't need to know about nuclear weapons. At midnight, I called a halt. With the weekend coming up, I wanted to talk to Carrie tomorrow and after that, I was going home for a couple of days. Not only that but I wouldn't be waking up feeling like I had been attacked by an elephant.

So the next morning, things looked reasonably bright and I called Carrie. She agreed to meet me back at Julian's office. When we got there I explained what I wanted, she gave me a strange look but agreed to let me in. Luckily, the police hadn't cordoned the entrance so there was no problem getting in again. The place had been tidied up a little but I wasn't here for that sort of information. At the rear of the office was a small toilet area with a sink with a few toiletries on a shelf above it. Also, there was a hairbrush which I had remembered seeing from my last visit. I took out a small plastic bag, retrieved some hairs off the brush and sealed it. I now had at least one way of confirming my suspicions once I got to my London next week. Carrie was waiting for me outside.

'Did you get what you wanted?' she asked.

'Yup but don't ask me to explain why I need it. I promise I'll tell you about it later. So how about a drink?'

We went up the High Street to the little tea shop that looked out over the cathedral grounds and found a place to sit outside on the pavement. I told her about David's visit the previous day. 'He said he was sorry for being rude to you but frankly I didn't believe a word of it. It struck me that there's a nasty streak in him that he sometimes struggles to keep under control.

Carrie sighed. 'He's a Jekyll and Hyde. When I knew him years ago, he was actually quite nice but could become incredibly possessive at the drop of a hat. It was one of the reasons I never went out with him, although he tried on several occasions.'

'I can understand that. Look Carrie, I've got to go away for a few days on business next week. I'll be back by Wednesday because the funeral is the next day and I don't want to miss it.'

'Have you or the police got any further in finding out who did it? I've been told nothing and as I'm not a relative I can't really ask.'

'It's not going well, to be honest. David has a cast iron alibi and there don't seem to be any more leads at least as far as the police are concerned.'

'Then why did you get me to do all that research and drag me here today? It seems to me that you are looking into several things,' she asked.

I wasn't sure how to answer that as some of my ideas would not make sense, not here in this world anyway. 'Look Carrie, the police have to follow a process and to be fair they are being very thorough but even though I respect the good Inspector, he is constrained. I, on the other hand, am not. Also, there is one element of this that involves me directly and that is why I asked you to look into Robin McGregor and this Venta group. It may be nothing and there is no direct link to the murder except that Julian was also a member but something isn't right. The police can't do anything as there is no connection but I'm not so sure, so I have said I will look into it and pass on anything I find out.'

'So where are you going next week. Can you at least tell me that?'

For a second I didn't know how to answer that but as usual I decided that honesty was the best policy. 'I'm going to London. I've got some special shopping to do and I want to meet a couple of old friends.'

'Well, I've not got anything on as you know. Do you want any company?'

Oh dear. How could I tell her I was actually going away with her? Well sort of. 'That's very kind of you to offer Carrie,' I said thinking furiously.

Before I could say more she interrupted my train of thought. 'Don't worry I know you have a different private life to most people. I didn't mean to be intrusive,' she said.

For a second I didn't quite know how to react but then remembered my 'keep this Carrie at bay' strategy and smiled at her. 'Thank you for being so understanding,' I said with a conspiratorial smile. It always amazed me how women reacted to gay men but I wasn't going to argue with her if my ruse was working so well. I changed the subject and suggested some other areas she might research for me and then promised I would try to catch up with her the day before the funeral. After she left I stayed for a few minutes. From this little square, I had an excellent view of the front of the Cathedral and the green lawns in front of it. Couples were sitting there on the grass. It reminded me of the times I had done the same thing when I was younger, quite often with Carrie's older sister Hannah when we had been going out with each other all those years ago. I realised that I hadn't asked the Carrie of this world whether she had a sister as well, and then it struck me. If I was right my trip to London could be even more revealing than I had hoped.

Chapter 28

The trip to London that Monday couldn't have been more different than the last time I had taken a train to the city. Carrie and I were in first class. Why not? I often struggled to remember just how rich I was. Years of travelling second class had made it an automatic choice. It wasn't until Carrie pointed out how little the extra cost was that I even considered it. With second class stuffed with commuters, it was definitely the right place to be.

We were sitting in one of the little two seat tables and chatting as we rumbled and clattered our way towards Waterloo.

'You know, despite all the evidence you've shown me,' she said with a smile. 'If there was one thing that convinced me that this is all true, it was your appalling driving to the station this morning.'

I laughed slightly ruefully. On at least two occasions I had slammed on the brakes thinking it was the accelerator.

'You just get used to one thing and then have to think again. Why they decided on a different pedal layout I don't know. Having said that, apparently in the twenties it was quite common over here. Mind you, this train ride shows just how much better some things are over there.' I explained to her how the maglev trains worked and just how smooth and sophisticated they were.

'And it took less than half an hour?' she asked. 'How fast do they go?'

'On this line not as fast as you might think as there are loads of stations but apparently on the long express routes like up to the midlands and Scotland they can hit almost four hundred.'

Carrie looked stunned. 'That's almost as fast as an aircraft over here, no wonder they haven't bothered with jets.'

'Oh, they've got those apparently but they're still in the early development phase.'

'Changing the subject Tony,' Carrie said. 'What exactly are we doing going up to town? I know you said we could have some time together but I know you. You've got other reasons as well.'

'Fair enough,' I said. 'Firstly, as you know I want to do some shopping for a new laptop and some other bits and pieces but I also want to call on an old friend at New Scotland Yard. He owes me more than one favour and he might just be able to shed some light on an aspect of this murder.'

'And are you going to tell me what light that is?'

'I will but I'd rather wait until I know if you don't mind. It might be a wild goose chase.'

As I spoke, the train started to slow and we pulled in to Waterloo. A taxi ride later and we were at the hotel. I had thought of booking the Savoy but even with my new found wealth, I baulked at the price. Instead, we were staying at a small discreet hotel in Knightsbridge, it still wasn't cheap but at least it didn't cost the annual income of a small country to stay there for a couple of nights.

It was mid morning and I needed to get across town to the Yard so I suggested that Carrie go shopping and we would meet up for a late lunch. Afterwards, we could hit the Tottenham Court road for the electronics I needed. As soon as I mentioned the word 'shopping' her eyes lit up and for some reason she didn't argue with the plan. We agreed to meet at Covent Garden and I set off for darkest Westminster on the tube. It didn't take long before I was standing outside the building. It felt really strange to be back here again. I had walked away looking forward to a new life and leaving this all behind me. Yet here I was about to walk back in and all for a reason that only one other person in this world would understand.

Inside it was still the usual institutional atmosphere of most government buildings. I went over to the reception desk. There were several receptionists serving the visitors but I chose one who I recognised. He was a retired copper who had worked there for years.

He looked up and immediately recognised me. 'Inspector Peterson, you're back. Welcome. What can I do for you?'

'Not Inspector any more Mick,' I said. 'I'm one of the great unwashed now.'

'Yes, we all heard what happened. Bloody well done I say. At least someone had the guts to tell a certain person where to stick it. So what can I do for you?'

'I need to talk to John Smithson, is he still here and doing the same job?'

'Oh yes, still doing the same job. Do you want me to give him a call and say you're down here?'

'Yes please. I'll wait over there, by the chairs.'

I turned to go over to the waiting area and almost trod on the foot of the man behind me. I stood back ready to apologies and looked straight into the face of Chief Inspector Frank Bloody Cosgrove. He didn't look any better than the last time I had seen him. In fact, if anything the bags under his eyes and the wrinkles on his face had only got worse. He was clearly as surprised to see me as I was of him and he took a step backwards. It was amazing how similar and yet different he was to my friend in the other world.

'Peterson, what the hell are you doing here?' were his first words.

'Nice to see you too Frank,' I said. 'And it's none of your business.'

He didn't like that but must have also realised that I was right. He looked around and saw how busy the entrance foyer was. I could sense the gears grinding behind his eyes. He obviously still harboured a grudge. Frankly, I couldn't care less and simply walked over to the waiting area and sat down giving him a stiff ignoring in the process. He dithered for a second and then disappeared towards the lift shafts. I was actually quite glad. I didn't come here to pick a fight with him. I had other fish to fry.

I didn't have long to wait. John Smithson and I went back a long time, to when we were both new constables. We had become friends then and our careers had crossed on several occasions. Whereas I had gone into CID, John could best be described as a geek who loved forensics and all things technical.

I got up and we shook hands. 'Tony, didn't expect to see you any time soon. Are you the reason the good Chief Inspector looks like someone shoved a red hot poker up his arse?'

'I expect so,' I replied. 'I just stood on his big toe in the queue over there. He's full of his usual charm and bonhomie I noticed.'

'Hah, you leaving caused him no end of grief and he lets everyone else suffer for it. Thankfully, the rumour on the street is that he's for early retirement soon. It won't be voluntary either. Anyway, how can I help? I assume you're going to ask me for a favour?'

'Yes, sorry it's such short notice and I can't really tell you what it's about. What I can say is that I'm helping in an investigation. Not as a copper you understand so I need this to be done discreetly,'

'Need what done?' John asked.

I took out the two plastic wallets and handed them over to him. 'These are two hair samples. I need DNA done on them both. I won't say anymore because I don't want to influence the results.'

'Alright, how much time have I got?'

'Tomorrow, would that be possible?'

John looked down at the samples. 'Seeing as it's you Tony. You helped me out enough in the past but please don't make a habit of this, I do have a day job as well. How do I get hold of you?'

I gave him my mobile number. We chatted for a few more minutes and then he said he had to leave. And the last thing I wanted was Frank to come back and see us talking.

After meeting Carrie for lunch we walked up to the Tottenham court road. At the top end was a small shop managed by an Indian couple. I had shopped there often in the past. If you wanted something electronic, they had it and it wouldn't cost an arm and a leg. I was greeted like an old friend when we went in. The place was bigger inside than it looked and absolutely crammed with every sort of electronic toy under the sun. What the normal punter wouldn't see was the large back room where things could be modified in just about every way.

'What can I do for you today?' Rajid asked me as if I had only been away a day or two.

I started with a new laptop and phone which was simple. But I then moved on to the device that would need constructing. 'Rajid can you make me a transformer to take a 150 volt supply and turn it into 240 volts. I need about four output ports but only the one input and that won't even need a plug just bare wires.' I would have to fit the plug myself as it used old fashioned round pins.

Without batting an eyelid Rajid simply nodded. 'Is it only for charging devices?'

'Yes just things like laptops and phones nothing more.'

'Yes that will be quite easy, I will just modify a standard laptop converter. Is there anything else?'

I looked around the shop. There were just so many things wrapped up in their garish cardboard boxes. I was like a kid in a sweetshop. Several things caught my eye. Although I had said I didn't intend giving any of this technology to anyone over there I had thought about how some of it could give me an edge. I had a building to investigate for a start. 'How long will the converter take?' I asked.

'Only about half an hour, why don't you have a look around while I do it?'

So while Rajid went to work his magic, Carrie and I started making a list.

When we left there was just too much to carry but Rajid promised me it could all be delivered to Winchester and would be waiting by the time we got back home. So I handed over my credit card which took a rather large hit and shook hands. Some, no probably most, of what I had bought would never be needed but it was just too good an opportunity to miss.

When we got outside Carrie gave me a strange look.

'What? What did I do?' I asked.

'You're the one always giving me a hard time about women and their shopping habits. You've just proved that men are just as bad.'

What could I say?

Chapter 29

I said it the next day. We had spent the morning giving my credit card even more damage in various boutiques and decided to have lunch at a bistro just off from Covent garden.

'Now look Carrie. Yesterday I bought some electronics and stuff and you gave me a hard time about it. Now what about you?'

She put her fork down and gave me a look of pure innocence. 'What do you mean?'

'Look, if I had shopped yesterday like you did this morning I would have looked at the stuff I wanted in Rajid's place and then gone down to every other shop in the road to see what they had before going back hours later and buying the original stuff from him. That's the difference between men and women.'

I could see her working up a suitable retort but luckily for me, before I could dig an even bigger hole for myself, my phone chose that moment to ring. I looked at the screen but didn't recognise the number.

'Hello? Oh, John it's you.' I listened for a while and simply said 'Yes, I'll see you there at two.'

'Was that your man at the cop shop?' Carrie asked.

'Yes he's got the DNA results I've been waiting for but there's been a snag.' I said. 'He won't say but needs to see me. There's been some complication or other.'

I finished lunch and was back in the Yard in good time. When I got to the building reception desk I was immediately directed to a small visitor's room off to one side.

John was sitting there waiting. He stood up and shook my hand as I came in. I felt something in his hand as he did so and transferred it into my grip and then into my pocket. He gave me a conspiratorial smile. 'I'm not meant to let any paperwork out and one of those samples is from someone who's very much on our radar. That's his photo and the details of the analysis are on the back. I hope it will help.'

That did sound interesting. 'And are they related? That's the first thing I need to know.'

'Absolutely but only on the mother's side. They have different fathers.'

'That sort of confirms what I was thinking,' I said. 'So who is this person on the database?'

'He's big time scum. We've been after him for some time now. He appeared in London recently just after you left. He had been operating in Manchester up until then. He's a complete head case and into most unsavoury things like prostitution and loan sharking but the real problem is drugs. When he first appeared there was some sort of turf war with the locals but he got the upper hand. Now he's the top of the pile. Taking him down would probably cut the crime rate in the city in half.'

'And you haven't been able to collar him?' I asked.

'He's very canny. Frank Cosgrove has been all over him. Probably thinks that if he can nail him it will restore his reputation. Look Tony, I have to ask how you got these samples because if there is anything to them that could help us catch this guy you need to tell me.'

'John, do you trust me? Because I can honestly say that I acquired these samples because the other chap needed to know about his brother. It had nothing to do with this. He didn't even know about him until recently and I'm damned sure he won't want to after what you've told me. Honestly, there's nothing more to it than that. And I give you my word if I hear anything you need to know I will pass it straight on. Is that alright?'

John nodded reluctantly. 'Ok Tony but please don't ask me to do this again. If Cosgrove found out, I would be out of a job. I hadn't realised how serious this was when you first asked.'

'Nor did I John, I'll disappear now but honestly, if I do discover anything you will be the first to know.'

We parted still friends thank goodness. I hadn't realised what an ant's nest I had kicked over. I made my escape praying I wouldn't bump into Frank again. Luckily, he was nowhere to be seen and I made my way back to the hotel where I had agreed to meet up with Carrie.

When I got to the hotel I was eager to tell her what I had discovered and talk through with her what it would mean to my investigation. The fact that Julian and David did not have the same father seemed terribly significant to me but I still couldn't think the whole thing through. I was sure that talking it over with her would help me clear my mind and maybe she could provide a new perspective.

When I opened the door all thought of murders, angry policemen and parallel worlds fled my mind. Carrie was trying on some of her purchases. One of her many visits had been to a lingerie shop. When she heard me come in she turned and looked at me with a smile on her face.

'So, was it worth me making sure I bought the right stuff?' she asked deadpan.

The underwear she was wearing was definitely the right stuff, what little there was of it. It was red, lacy and hid absolutely nothing yet enhanced her sexiness by an order of magnitude. Carrie was younger than me but still in her thirties. Her figure was that of a teenager. She was one of those girls who seemed to be able to eat like a horse but never put on any weight. I suddenly didn't know what to do or say.

She came up to me and grabbed my shoulders and pushed me onto an armchair. She then straddled my lap and whispered something very imaginative in my ear. What could I do? I was only human. I managed to stand up with her arms around my neck and her legs wrapped around my waist. I just made it to the bed before gravity took over. She fell back with her legs wide open and I, very inelegantly fell on top. We both started giggling but that didn't stop her undoing my trouser belt. I helped by pulling my shirt over my head. Several buttons tore out but I didn't give a toss.

An age later we were lying naked on top of a very rumpled bed. Carrie was nestled under my left arm and I was absently stroking a very pert bum cheek.

'So how was Scotland Yard?' she asked.

'Oh God, you made me completely forget about it you sex mad nympho,' I said. 'Hang on, John gave me a printout. It's in my trousers which I seem to remember you flung over to the other side of the room.'

I reluctantly gave up my bum stroking and went in search of the wayward trousers. I found the folded piece of paper in a pocket and took it over to the bed. I plonked down next to Carrie and she rolled over putting her arm over my chest. 'Come on then what does it say?'

I looked at one side which was covered in writing and numbers, most of which I didn't understand. At the bottom, John had highlighted two sets of digits and underneath had written 'step brothers, same mother different father'.

'There's more though,' I said as I looked at the report. 'One of the samples came up on the Police database as a very active criminal. One who is very much attracting their attention for all the wrong reasons. Apparently, he is into drugs and has a very bad reputation. I can't say I'm surprised.'

'Yes, you told me he was a pretty aggressive sort. I suppose basic character doesn't change in either world.' Carrie said peering at the report over my chest. 'I still don't see how it affects your case though. You said his alibi was watertight.'

'It is dammit,' I said. I turned over the report. John had said the man's photo was on the other side. It was.

It wasn't what I expected at all. 'Oh Fucky McFuck face,' I said. 'Jesus, that really upsets the apple cart.'

'What? Carrie said. 'What's the matter? You look really upset.'

I handed her the paper. 'That's not David, that's Julian Fletcher.'

Chapter 30

Finding out that it was Julian who was the bad guy in my world wasn't the only problem. It also brought another issue to head. One that I had desperately hoped to avoid. As Carrie digested the fact that there were two Julian's or rather there had been, bearing in mind one was dead, it was clear she had started to see the ramifications.

'Hang on a second Tony, when we first talked about this alternative reality you told me that there weren't any duplicate people over there but this person is in both worlds. So there must be others,' she said with a note of suspicion in her voice.

'Actually, I didn't say there weren't any. I only said I hadn't seen any.' I said while I desperately thought of what else I could say. I didn't need this complication at the moment. But as soon as I admitted I had been working with the doppelganger of the policeman I had seen here in London she would know I had been keeping it from her and then would want to know who else was duplicated. How she would take it if she found out she had a double as well was something I didn't want to contemplate, especially when she realised I had been keeping quiet about it. And that was the problem. The more I kept this back, the bigger and worse her reaction was likely to be. I had never felt so strongly about anyone else in my life and the last thing I wanted was to drive her away. Bugger, the only thing to do was come clean.

'And Carrie that was true when I said it. But yes, I have met a couple of people over there who are sort of the same over here. I should have told you at the time. The Chief Inspector who I met at the Yard yesterday and was at least partially responsible for me leaving the police is also the one in Winchester in the other world. Over there he looks the same although he's put on more weight. However, instead of being a mean minded bully, he's quite the opposite. We found that we get on really well and that's why I've been able to work with the police over there so successfully. And there's at least one other person there who you would know about.'

'Oh, who's that?'

'You. There's a Carrie Parks in the other world too.'

There I had said it. I suddenly felt better. I hadn't realised what a burden it had been.

'And are you in love with her too? Carrie asked deadpan.

'What? No. Look Carrie, as I said, people may seem to be the same but they're not. Over here the policeman is a complete idiot but he's a really good man over there. They share the same DNA but are not the same people. That's what seems to be the case with Julian even if it's a bit more extreme. The Carrie over there is a librarian, she likes short hair and you would hate her dress sense. I admit it took me by surprise when we first met but believe me I am not attracted to her one bit. She may look like you but she is definitely not the same person. And it's the person I love and that happens to be you.'

'And she's not attracted to you at all then? You know I've always had a thing for you ever since we were kids.'

Oh well, it was truth or dare time, what the hell.

'I nipped that in the bud. I told her I was gay. And you know what? It immediately changed her attitude towards me. She treats me like a brother now. And look, we've already agreed that once this murder investigation is over, I am not going to spend much time over there. In fact, if you want, I'll never go back at all. It's just not that important enough to me if it would mean losing you.'

Carrie got out of bed and went to look out of the window. I hoped that no one could see in as she was completely naked but we were many floors up. She stood there for several minutes saying nothing then she turned and came back to me. She knelt on the bed and looked me in the eyes. 'Thank you for telling me Tony. I realise you didn't have to and I would never have known. You may find this strange but I don't actually care if there is another version of me somewhere. In fact I quite like the idea, it gives me a sort of immortality. We can never meet. In fact, I wouldn't be that upset if you did have a fling with her, we are the same person after all. How could I be jealous about you and her together when she is also me?'

I had to laugh then. 'Carrie I'm not at all sure I follow your logic but thank you for being so understanding.'

She was still kneeling on the bed in front of me and the view was starting to ruin my concentration so I did the only sensible thing I could and made a grab for her. She didn't resist.

Sometime later we started talking again. 'So these people over there are the same but not the same?' Carrie asked.

'That sums it up quite well,' I said. 'I've been trying to work out why it is and it must be something to do with descendants of people who weren't killed in the wars being in the majority but obviously there will be quite a few who were not involved. Actually, I'm not sure that make sense.'

'It might,' Carrie said. 'I've been looking into their history and there have been several flu pandemics. We had ours at the end of the First World War and they had one at about the same time but they've had two more after that. A lot of people died. So tracing people's genealogy will be a nightmare.'

'Yes, Frank Cosgrove told me he lost his wife to the latest one.'

'Anyway, so someone is born in both timelines and they are effectively the same person. The big difference then will be the environment they grow up in and how they interact. This Inspector and Carrie Two, how much of them is really the same?'

'Very hard to answer that,' I said. 'There is no doubt that they are different people but the basic character is still there.'

'So the same will go for Julian Fletcher? I think you are going to have to dig into his past a great deal more. Maybe he wasn't quite the nice guy you thought he was.'

'I'm beginning to wonder that too,' I said. 'He was very pushy and also seemed to be a bit of a rebel in terms of his social life. I wonder if he upset people of the Venta Society in some way. Which reminds me we must go and look at that building in Aldwych. We can do that tomorrow before we head home.'

I decided we had talked enough about strange alternative realities and dragged Carrie into the shower where amongst other things, we got ourselves clean and then dressed and went out to dinner.

The next morning we got the tube to Aldwych and knocked on the door of the headquarters of the Honourable Guild of Traders. It was exactly what Carrie had discovered. They were very accommodating when we went in and even gave us a pamphlet that outlined a potted history of their organisation. I asked if there was any connection with the city of Winchester but all that got was blank looks. In the end, we left, pretty certain that in this world at least, it was a dead end. So it was a pleasant walk back over Waterloo Bridge to the station to catch the train home. While we were on the bridge I tried to describe to Carrie what the skyline of the other

London looked like. It was quite easy as all you had to do was remove the modern office blocks and double down on the number of older buildings as they hadn't had the bejesus bombed out of them in the last war.

'Take the camera with you next time you come here, over there,' she said and then laughed at what she had said. 'You know what I mean.'

'Yes I do,' I said and for no other reason than that I wanted to, I kissed her.

'What was that for?' she asked when we finally came up for air.

'Oh because the sun is shining, because you are beautiful, and I'm happy,' I said.

'Yes well don't forget you have a funeral to go to tomorrow,' she said.

Suddenly, a cloud covered the sun.

Chapter 31

Julian's funeral was the usual dismal affair. David fletcher did a reasonable job of saying some nice things about his brother. The congregation seemed to be split into two groups. Most of the Venta Society were there in their dark suits and black ties. However, on the other side of the knave were all his friends. It was clear they had decided to honour him in a more modern way and all wore bright happy clothing. They may have got frosty stares from the older generation but I thought it far more appropriate for the man I knew even if I was now having doubts about him.

After it was over we were all invited to his house for a wake and I could indulge in another police technique called 'get the suspect pissed and see what he opens up with'.

Before I could get stuck in, Frank spotted me and came over. 'I've been looking for you Tony. Any news?'

I knew what he meant. 'Yes plenty Frank but now isn't the time or place. What I will tell you is that Julian and David are only half brothers, they only share the same mother.'

'Well that is interesting,' he said. 'But look, I know you are still focused on the brother but as far as we are concerned it's of academic interest. With a watertight alibi, there's no way we can pursue anything further.'

'Understood Frank but there is a lot more to it than that. I can't go into it now how about you come around this evening and we can discuss it in detail?'

He agreed and we both wandered off to mingle. Before I could approach David, Carrie came up and touched me on the arm. 'How was your weekend Tony? I haven't seen you for days.'

'Sorry Carrie, I did say I wouldn't be straight back. It was just business that's all. Did you find out anything else?'

'No, not really. I think the police might be right you know. I can't see how David could be involved. I've not found out any more about the Aldwych house either.'

That's alright, I think a physical visit is required. Fancy a trip to London in a day or two?' I saw her eyes light up at the prospect.

'Yes, that could be fun I don't have to be back at work till Monday maybe we could go at the weekend?'

Oh God, I should have thought that one through before I said it. Two weeks in a row in London with almost the same girl. I wasn't sure whether I was excited or dismayed at the prospect.

Before I could do anything other than nod, David came up to us both. He had very obviously been drinking although he looked fairly steady on his feet.

'David, my commiserations,' I said.

'Yes well, as usual, my dear brother has managed to drop me in it,' he said.

'Oh, what do you mean by that?' Carrie asked.

He turned his attention to Carrie. His expression immediately changed to one of a mixture of longing and annoyance, if that was possible. 'My dear, I know you knew Julian for some time but believe me you didn't really know him. Not many did.'

'What do you mean by that,' I asked intrigued.

'My dear older brother could be a right bastard at times but you would never know that unless you got under his skin.' He stopped and must have realised what he had just said. 'Anyway that's not what I should be saying at his wake I suppose. He's not here anymore.'

'But why has he dropped you in it? Whatever 'it' is,' I asked.

David waved slightly drunkenly around the room. 'I've got all this to worry about now. Then there's the business. I'm sure my father, bless him, would want it to continue but I know bugger all about the stock market. Mind you I'm not that sure Julian did either without your uncle's input. No, I'm going to stick to my aeroplanes. I'll probably just sell the lot, the house the business the whole bloody shebang. What about you Carrie. Got any other men lined up?' He looked back at me as he said that.

'David, you're drunk. I'm not going to answer that,' Carrie said in a very annoyed tone.

'Oops, yes sorry Carrie I didn't mean to be rude. You know I've always liked you. I think I'd better circulate a little more. See you.' At that, he just wandered off.

Elaine, Carrie's flatmate came over. 'Hello you two, pretty dismal way to send off Julian. Some of us are going down to the club this evening to do it properly if you're interested.'

'Sorry Elaine,' I said. 'I have something else I need to do. But tell me, David just mentioned that there was more to Julian than most people knew about. Did either you of Carrie see that?'

'Why are you asking Tony?' Elaine asked. 'This is hardly the place to be having this sort of conversation.'

'Yes I know and I do apologise but if we are ever going to get to the bottom of his murder we need to know as much about him as we can. Frankly, at the moment the police are running out of ideas and so am I.'

The two girls exchanged glances. Carrie nodded to Elaine. 'You knew him better than I did in the early days.'

Elaine turned to me. 'He had a bit of reputation as a bully at school to be honest. He had his own little crowd of friends and they seemed to like picking on other boys and some of the girls on occasions. When he came back when his father was ill he seemed to have changed, to have matured. He did still have a temper though and would sometimes get quite wound up about quite trivial things.'

'He was never violent or aggressive,' Carrie said. 'It was just that he liked to be in control. You probably saw a mild side of that when he organised that party for you.'

'Thanks Ladies,' I said. 'I'm beginning to understand things a little better.' Then a thought struck me, it was one of those things that suddenly flies into your consciousness for no apparent reason. 'Hang on, when David came over a minute ago he said he was going to stick with his aeroplanes. I thought he was in the Marines? Do either of you know what he meant by that?'

Elaine looked oddly at me. 'Yes he's a pilot, surely you knew that?'

'Why would I? The Marines are naval soldiers, not aviators.'

Both girls gave me a very strange look and I realised that , once again, I had said something very wrong but had absolutely no idea what it was. 'Well they are where I was brought up,' I said lamely and then rapidly changed the subject. It was clear that here was yet another very different aspect to life in this world and I needed to find out about it as soon as I could. There was only one person I could ask. It would have to wait until the evening when I could talk to Frank freely. I made my excuses to the girls saying I needed to circulate but promised to ring Carrie later to arrange our trip to London.

That evening Frank came around and we talked about my discovery that in my world Julian was a very different character as well as being only a half brother to David.

'So you're saying he's a gangster over there?' Frank asked. 'Can't say there has been any evidence that he was up to no good here. Of course, that doesn't mean he wasn't. You'd be surprised how many people manage to hide that sort of thing. Actually, maybe you wouldn't seeing as you were a copper as well.'

'But it might mean that he had been up to no good with the Venta Society and they or some of them decided to do something about it.'

'What you mean a professional hit? That makes as much sense as anything else at the moment. We've drawn a complete blank so far, not even found the murder weapon. That would tie in with a contract job. I'll put the word around my contacts and try to see if anyone was asking about a job a few weeks ago. So how about a film seeing as you now seem to be able to charge up that box of yours?'

'In a minute Frank,' I said. 'My ignorance almost got the better of me at the wake today. I was talking to Carrie and her friend Elaine and the subject of the Royal Marines came up. It's clear to me that they do very different things in the two worlds. Both David Fletcher and one of the girls talked about aeroplanes. I thought the Marines were the navy's soldiers.'

'Eh? No, they haven't been for years. They do have an infantry battalion but that is for airfield protection. No, they are primarily the navy's air arm. What are they in your world then?'

'Well, they are the navy's soldiers and nothing else. How on earth did they become the Air Force?'

'What's an Air Force?' Frank asked, which got me totally confused.

'Look, let me tell you what happened in my world,' I said and went on to explain how the two flying services of the Army and Navy were merged after the Great War to become a separate third armed service. 'It wasn't without some serious debate and in fact just before the Second World War the navy got its maritime aircraft back but the Royal Air Force continues to this day.'

Frank snorted in laughter. 'There was some talk about it over here in the thirties but the two services absolutely refused to countenance it. The navy decided that as the Marines acted as an adjunct to the Fleet already then they would focus aviation with them. The army has their own Air Corp.'

'So who flies what?' I asked rather intrigued that this world hadn't seen to invent a dedicated flying service.

'Well, the Army have all the bombers and heavy transport aircraft. The navy have the aircraft that do ocean patrol and a small number of transport aircraft and both services operate their own scouts.'

'What the hell is a scout? I asked.

'Oh, the little aircraft that go around shooting at each other and the bigger machines.'

'Ah, yes we call them fighters. That makes sense, I seem to recall they were called scouts during the Great War.'

'Isn't it staggering the difference just one small change in history can bring about,' Frank said. 'We tend to think of Winchester as a naval town, with the airfields at Southampton, Worthy Down and Flower Down surrounding us but I suppose it's different for you.'

'Yes, my Winchester is or I should say was, an army town. For many years the Greenjackets had their barracks actually in the town. Nowadays the army has all regrouped in the Salisbury area. But what did David mean by sticking to his aeroplanes? Is he a pilot and for that matter was Julian as well?'

'Well I know Julian wasn't,' Frank said. 'He was one of the foot soldiers. He wanted to fly but there was something wrong with his eyesight. I remember him telling me that some while ago. I'm not sure about David. Even if he is a pilot we've looked at travel times from where he was on exercise and there is still no way he could have got here and returned in the timescales we are talking about, even if he flew, aircraft are just not fast enough.'

'That's assuming he was where the marines said he was,' I replied.

'Why would they say otherwise? They were quite clear he was in the north of Scotland. But I'll give them a call tomorrow and see what exactly he was up to. It can't do any harm I suppose. On top of that, I'll start my chaps looking around the Venta people a little more closely. If they did do away with Julian for whatever reason, we may well be able to discover something.'

'Yes and I'm planning to go up to London and look at Aldwych if you don't mind,' I said.

'No, that's fine, you do that and let me know what you find. Now you said you've now got a little gizmo to charge up your computer thingy so what's the film tonight?'

Chapter 32

The next morning I woke up early finding it hard to sleep with all the thoughts crowding my head. I decided to make an early trip to London even though I had said to Carrie we would go at the weekend. For some reason, I had a feeling that things were coming to a head. Also, if Frank was at last going to start digging into the Venta Society I didn't want them to take alarm and shut down whatever operation they had going on in London.

Despite the hour, I rang Carrie but there was no reply. I would just have to apologise to her later. In fact, I was not too upset, my invitation had been a little off the cuff and almost certainly wasn't a good idea.

The train was the usual gliding rocket and I was at Waterloo by half past eight in the morning. If anywhere I had visited over here looked almost the same as in my world it was this station. As I had noticed previously, the same clock hung above the concourse but it was more than that. The shops and cafes could have been in either world. The press of people all purposefully heading somewhere in a wide variety of dress. The only difference was that the arrivals and departure boards were still the old fashioned clicky boards that had been replaced at home with large computer screens. I have to say I preferred the older system. It had a simple charm and still conveyed exactly the same information.

And there standing underneath that famous clock was none other than Mister Alec Jeffries. Why was I not surprised? For a second I was tempted to turn away and disappear in the crush of people. It wouldn't have been difficult but then curiosity got the better of me, not the least to discover how he knew I would be here. I had decided on this trip at the last minute after all.

I walked over and he smiled at me. 'Tony fancy meeting you here.' And he held out his hand.

'Fancy indeed. I suppose I should ask how the fuck you knew I was here?' I saw him wince at my language. Good, I wanted to get under his skin.

'Come and have a cup of tea with me Tony, we need to talk,' he said deadpan.

I followed him over to a café that had seats on the concourse itself. In my world it would have been a Costa or Starbucks. Here is seemed to be a franchise of the Lyons Corner House that used to be near Trafalgar square in my world. All the waitresses were dressed in black dresses with white aprons and white lace caps.

'Tea?' Alec asked.

'Coffee please.' I replied. I knew that asking for a latte or cappuccino would be a waste of time. I had already discovered they didn't do fancy stuff like that over here.

While the waitress went off to fetch our order I looked at Alec carefully. He didn't look quite the urbane gentleman I had met last time. In fact, he looked as though he had dressed in a bit of a rush.

'To answer your rather crudely put question,' he said. 'I was informed that you were taking the train to London this morning so I decided to hop on myself. You were in First Class at the rear so I went into Second at the front to make sure I was waiting for you when you got off the platform.'

Just then the waitress arrived and put our orders down. I sipped the brown sludge they called coffee and realised I could probably make a fortune opening up some decent coffee shops. The only problem would be weaning everyone here off their addiction to tea.

'So you've been having me followed?' I asked. 'That's a bloody cheek. Unless you've got something to hide that is?'

'Yes I do have something to hide but now I want to show it to you. I'm hoping that once you see it you will be less judgemental.'

'Does it have anything to do with the murder of Julian fletcher?' I asked. 'Because if it has I will be very judgemental indeed.'

'What? No nothing. Well, nothing that I know of. You mentioned the Aldwych property when we last spoke and I admitted that not all the members of my society knew about it. I want you to understand why I was worried and what it means to me.'

'Fair enough but as you're here, I have a couple of questions about Julian.'

'Go ahead, I have nothing to hide.'

'Firstly, how well did you and the rest of the society get on with him? Was he hard to deal with? Was he ambitious, maybe angling for more power within the group?'

'That's a very perceptive question if I may say so,' Alec said with a look of surprise on his face. 'How did you even come up with that suspicion? Because you're right he was very much into taking control when he could. He was quite different in that respect to his father. His big problem was that the Society is full of men who could also play that game. I believe he was quite frustrated. In some ways, we were glad when you turned up because it diverted his not inconsiderable energies elsewhere.'

'So there weren't any thoughts of removing him in a more permanent way?'

Alec barked with laughter. 'Oh come on, who do you think we are? We're businessmen not some East End gang of thugs. The worst sanction we would ever come up with would be to throw him out of the Society, we have byelaws for that. But arrange his murder, please Tony that is just madness.'

I've listened to some very consummate liars in my time but Alec Jeffries did not seem to be in that league. I couldn't tell you exactly why but I believed him about that at least. Of course, that's not to say that other members of his Society hadn't thought differently.

'And if you lost him then your access to me would be greatly diminished.' I said deadpan.

'The truth be known, you're right Tony. Julian wasn't really that good a stockbroker. It was purely his relationship with your uncle and hopefully with you that gave him any leverage in the group. And as a group, we didn't just rely on him for investment management anyway. Plenty of the Society have their own arrangements, me included.'

'Good, I'm glad to hear that because I'm not sure I am going to be able to continue in the same vein as Uncle Peter. I'm like Julian in that respect, I'm no expert on stock markets like he was.'

If Alec was worried about that he kept a straight face. I suspect he would be leaning on me in the future but for now, he seemed far more preoccupied with whatever it was he was going to show me.

We'd finished our drinks and he stood. 'Come on let's go for a short walk. I know that you know the way.'

As we walked over Waterloo Bridge I suddenly remembered something I had seen written on Julian's notes and a thrill of concern shot through me. 'Alec, this doesn't have anything to do with a company called Digitalus does it?'

Alec turned to me. 'How on earth did you know that?'

'It was written on one of the papers that Julian left on his desk when he was murdered along with a name. Bill gates.'

He laughed. 'Well you'll meet Bill in a minute, your uncle recruited him for me. Not far to go now.'

Jesus, what exactly had my uncle been up to? Up until now I had thought that he had been very careful with his investment strategies and had understood the risks even better than I did. Yet here I was about to meet someone who could possibly be the analogue to one of the richest men on my planet. One of the men who had been responsible for the digital revolution.

With a thousand questions churning through my mind, we went in the crescent of Aldwych. To the house I had seen Mister Brown Suit disappear into all those weeks ago and which I had visited only last weekend on another world.

The front doors were not modern glass, instead they were made of wood ornately carved with some sort of flower design. Alec went up and knocked. The door opened and a middle aged man stood there. I recognised him immediately. It was Mister Brown Suit.

Alec turned to me. 'Tony, let me introduce you to Mister William Gates. You almost met a while ago.'

With a rueful smile William held out his hand. 'Sorry about that,' he said in a broad Scottish accent. 'I don't think I'm cut out to be a spy. But welcome to Digitalus. I'm sure your uncle would be very pleased that you are here at last.'

Chapter 33

'I am totally confused William,' I confessed as I shook his hand. 'What the hell is Digitalus and what is going on here?'

'Please call me Bill, everyone else does,' he said and then turned to Alec. 'What have you told him Alec?'

'Very little,' Alec said. 'I thought it would come better from you. It's your project after all.'

Bill turned back to me. 'Well, the name is easy. Did you notice the flowers carved on the door? When this place was built for some reason, someone in the original guild liked flowers, Foxgloves to be precise. The Latin name for a Foxglove is Digitalus. And the building has been called Digitalus House ever since.'

I was starting to wonder whether my misgivings were all wrong. This chap didn't look or talk anything like the Bill Gates I was familiar with and far from being something to do with digitisation it appeared that flowers were the other link. I thought it a little odd that I hadn't picked up on the Digitalus name from the building in my world but there again it hadn't been a question I had thought to ask.

'Look, come on and have a cup of tea and I'll explain it all,' Bill said and led me through a large oak panelled lobby into what was clearly an office. There was a desk and a couple of chairs and kettle on a shelf at the back. It was clear I wasn't going to get coffee so I settled for a large mug of tea instead.

We all sat down. 'What you need to understand first Tony is that a lot of this was your uncle's idea.' Bill said. 'I took the proposal and turned it into a practicality with the support of Alec. You see this place had been empty for some time. The Venta Society own it and one of the problems was that they couldn't come up with a consensus about what to do about it when it became vacant. Some wanted to sell, others to lease it and while all the wrangling was going on nothing was being done. I knew your uncle from some of the charity work he did in Winchester and here in London as well and we came up with the idea.'

I hadn't known that Uncle Peter was into charity work but let that slide. 'Alright but what is it? What are you doing here?' I asked in increasing frustration.

'It will be easier to just show you. Come and have a look.' Bill said.

We put down out mugs and he led me back out into the lobby and then through two swinging doors at the rear.

The room we entered was long and thin. By my reckoning it covered the full length of the building and at half its width. It looked like a hospital ward and I said so.

'Because that is exactly what it is,' Bill said.

As I looked, I could see that some of the beds were screened but at least half of those I could see were occupied. Several women in blue dresses, who I assumed were nurses, were tending the patients.

'What? But why?' I asked in confusion. 'What's wrong with regular hospitals? Why on earth do you need this?'

'Because many in society cannot afford them,' Alec said. 'There's more to this as well come on.'

A door in the middle of the ward led to more rooms. 'We've got consulting rooms, a radiology suite and a simple operating theatre down there.' Bill said. 'In reality for anything serious, we would have to go to a regular hospital. Let me show you upstairs,'

We walked down the ward and I was led out of the rear to a staircase. I could see it went up at least two floors. However, we stopped at the first one. The corridor here was narrow with a regular row of doors on both sides. It looked like a simple hotel corridor. Bill opened one door and showed us in. Inside was a simple bed, washing facilities and a wardrobe. It all looked brand new. The smell of paint was everywhere. Someone had spent a great deal of money converting this building and quite recently.

'General accommodation.' Bill said. 'We got the hospital running first and then went on to convert the upstairs. Not the best way of doing things but financially it made sense as the hospital pays for itself very quickly.'

'Hang on, I thought you said people downstairs couldn't afford normal hospitals?' I asked.

'No they can't but the government has had a guilty conscience about this for many years and at last are starting to do something about it. Your uncle talked regularly that there ought to be some sort of universal medical provision for everyone. We agreed to set this up with a large grant from central government, some of his own money and some charitable donations. Then, because we had the space, we were able to do these upstairs conversion. The rooms are partly for people convalescing but we also hope to offer some hostel accommodation. The homelessness problem in London had been another scandal for years. This will help greatly.' Bill explained.

'And I take that some of the Venta Society wouldn't like this idea?' I asked turning to Alec.

'Exactly but now it's almost finished it's a done deal. The place will be financially self sufficient and a tremendous advertisement for your uncle's dream. Now, do you see why I was so keen to keep it a secret?' Alec said.

'Well yes but it can't be a secret much longer surely?'

'No, we have a grand opening in two week's time. We've taken in a few patients quite quietly to make sure that everything is in order. We are even trying to convince the King to come down and make a formal ceremony of it. It's looking likely that he will agree and I can't see any of the Society complaining after that can you?'

'Which is why you wanted to show it to me,' I said. 'You didn't want me nosing around and upsetting the apple cart.'

'Something like that,' Alec said with a smile.

A thought occurred to me. 'Did Julian Fletcher know about this? I don't think this is the sort of thing that would have impressed him.'

'No, he was one of the people we wanted to be kept in the dark.'

'Yet, as I told you, I found something about this written on my uncle's notes, he must have seen them. They were pretty cryptic but could they have got him investigating? How many others in the Society actually know about this?'

'Only five of us out of the whole membership,' Alec said.

Shit, another five suspects at this stage of the investigation but they all would have had a motive. Frank was going to be delighted.

'Alec, I am going to need those names.' I said firmly. 'Surely you can see if any of them thought Julian was going to scupper this plan then they might try and to stop him.'

'I suppose you now include me on that list?' he asked. 'Look this is a charity. It's to make people's lives better. And as I said I was not aware that Julian even knew about it, But alright, I'll write you a list when we go back to the office.'

I realised that now was not the time to push further. 'Alec thank you and please don't let them know until I or the police have spoken to them. However, you are probably right and this is a fantastic thing you've done here. I assume you hope it will become a model for more these?'

'Absolutely, we even have a property in Winchester in mind but please keep that to yourself. Once this become public we are hoping for a large and positive response.'

We went back downstairs to the front office and Alec gave me the names. I also made a solemn promise not to tell anyone apart from the police about the hospital and keep the whole thing under wraps until the formal opening.

Alec and I shared a compartment on the train back to Winchester. We spoke amicably but I also reflected on my uncle's motivations and his dark sense of humour. I hadn't realised there wasn't a National Health Service in this world but once again it was one of things that was born out of the Second World War. Although I didn't know, I guessed that Uncle Peter was trying to put something back as a recompense for all that he gained from here. Good for him. Unfortunately, it opened up a whole new world of possibilities for discovering Julian's murderer. Alec may have been sanguine about his colleague's innocence. I wasn't.

It was late morning when I got home. Before I contacted Frank I decided to call Carrie and ask her to see what she could find out about the names I now had.

Elaine answered the phone. She sounded frantic. 'Tony, thank God you called. Do you know where Carrie is? Is she with you?'

'No, I've been up to London I tried ringing before I left but got no reply. Why are you so worried?'

'We were meant to meet up for coffee this morning, when she didn't turn up I went back to our flat. She wasn't there. Her bed hadn't been slept in. I know that because she was dreadful at making it in the morning, she never did.'

'When did you last see her?' I asked as I started to get concerned as well.

'Yesterday after the funeral was over. I went off with my friends to the club as I said we would. Carrie said she wasn't feeling up to it. I got home late and just assumed she had gone to bed.'

Suddenly all thoughts of investigating middle aged businessmen fled my mind. 'Ring the police and then stay there Elaine, I'll be right over.'

Chapter 34

I arrived at the house where the girls had their flat within minutes. It was at the city end of Christchurch Road, a long and rather up market road that led from St Cross into town. The house was the standard brick and flint design that had obviously been some wealthy man's family home in the past but had now been converted into three flats. Elaine and Carrie had the whole top floor.

Elaine let me in as soon as I pressed the buzzer and I went straight up the stairs where she greeted me.

'This is just not like her,' she said, clearly very upset as she ushered me into what was obviously the shared living room. 'Have a look at the bedroom.'

I did as I was bid and indeed the room was unused. The bed was made and everything seemed neat and tidy.

'Are there any clothes or bags missing?' I asked.

'You think she might have just run off? Elaine asked. 'That just doesn't make sense.'

'I know but we have to check.' I said. 'Do you share a bathroom? Maybe you could see if any of her toiletries have gone.' I knew my Carrie would never leave home without at least one bag full of various potions, lotions and God knows what else.

Elaine had a look. 'No, everything's there. She can't have come home last night and I can't think of where she might have gone.'

'Elaine, I don't want to be indelicate but could she have gone to someone else's place for the night. She had been drinking yesterday afternoon.'

'She wasn't like that. Anyway, she had just gone to her boyfriend's funeral, surely you can't think that of her?' Elaine sounded really annoyed at the suggestion.

'No I don't but we have to consider all the possibilities,' I said firmly. 'Even the unpalatable ones.'

Just then we heard a car crunching up the gravel of the drive. I looked out of a front window and saw Frank getting out of a car. 'Look, the police are here they will ask the same questions.'

The door buzzer went off and Elaine went over and pressed the door release. Within a short time, a slightly puffing Frank Cosgrove arrived. Clearly, a couple of flights of stairs was a bit of a challenge but for some reason I didn't think it was the time to mention fitness to him. Instead, I filled him in on all I had found out. He had another look around and then asked the same questions that I had.

When Elaine had run out of answers, he turned to us both. 'Look, under normal circumstances I would not consider looking any further into this until at least twenty four hours had passed. However, because of the on-going murder enquiry, I am going to take this more seriously. Miss Smith I would like you to come down to the station and give a statement if you have the time and Tony I need to talk to you as well. Do you mind coming with me as well?'

'Actually, Frank I've got some news for you too. I'll follow you down in my car.'

Half an hour later, Elaine had given her statement and a car was running her home. She wasn't too happy but there again nor was I. However, there was nothing to be done in the short term and I knew Frank's people would be doing their best.

We regrouped in his actual office for a change. 'What do you think?' he asked me.

'If you mean about Carrie going missing, it worries the hell out of me,' I said. 'There's no reason for her to wander off. She wasn't suicidal, just very upset as you would expect.'

'I've already asked some of my team to start interviewing everyone who was at the wake but that's going to take time. I take it you didn't see anything?'

'Nope, although David Fletcher did come over at one point and was quite obnoxious. Mind you he had been drinking and it was his brother's funeral. I assume he will be heading off to Scotland again soon.'

'Probably, although I did discover something yesterday. He was on exercise in Scotland but is actually based at the test flight school at the Naval Air Station at Worthy Down, just up the road. It still doesn't help your theory though because he was definitely over five hundred miles away at the critical time. Now tell me what you've discovered.'

I told Frank all about my visit to London and the surprise I got when Alec Jeffries showed me what they had been doing. I also said that I thought it possible that Julian had cottoned on to what was going on which could have given someone a motive.

Frank didn't look too impressed. 'I can hardly see why exposing such a charitable enterprise would be a motive for cold blooded murder. There again I've got bugger all else to go on at the moment. Do you have the names of these five potential assassins?'

I handed him my list which he studied for a few seconds before snorting in derision. 'We have here, the Chairman of the Bench of Magistrates, a solicitor, two prominent and very successful businessmen and the Headmaster of Winchester College. Do you really think any of them are capable of this?'

'Not really but don't forget Jeffries as well, he can be pretty hard nosed. But yes I have to agree. And sa you say, what else is there to go on?'

Just then the phone rang. Frank picked up the receiver and listened for several minutes. 'You're sure?' He said briefly. 'Can we come over and talk about it? 'We could be there in half an hour.'

After a few more seconds he put the phone down. 'We need to get to Worthy Down as fast as we can. I'll brief you on the way there.'

On the way out of the town I wasn't sure whether Frank was trying to kill me or the rest of the car driving public of Winchester. He turned on the blue lights on the roof and put his foot down. The police car was remarkably rapid compared to its contemporaries but seemed to handle like a cart and horses. I spent the whole trip clutching onto the seat for dear life while trying to listen to why we were on the suicidal mission.

'David Fletcher's gone AWOL.' Frank said cheerily as he overtook another car on a blind bend on the way towards the village of Kings Worthy. 'He was due back at the air station this morning. Also, they've just discovered some discrepancies in the flight log of the aircraft he was flying during the exercise when his brother was killed. There's a Lieutenant Commander Evans wants to show us. He's David's boss apparently.'

Luckily at that point we had cleared Kings Worthy and were on a decent straight road that didn't exist in my world but obviously led directly to the air station which I could see in the distance.

We pulled up in a screeching halt at the main gate and a sailor came over and asked who we were. Frank showed his warrant card and told him where we wanted to go. After giving us directions, the sailor lifted the large red pole barrier to let us through.

Within a minute we pulled up in front of a long low building that was built onto the side of a massive hangar. I breathed a sigh of relief. I was going to have to talk to Frank about his driving style sometime. Maybe after my pulse had reduced from over two hundred.

'Well that was fun,' Frank said grinning like a Cheshire cat. 'I rarely get the chance these days.'

Before I could query Frank's use of the word 'fun', an officer in uniform came out of the main door of the building. He must have been waiting for us to arrive. I tried to work out what uniform he was wearing. He had a dark blue reefer jacket with gold rings and buttons around the sleeves but his hat was unusual with a very small peak. Strangely, his shirt had a wing collar. It all looked like an old black and white photo from a hundred years ago.

He came straight up to us. 'Inspector Cosgrove I presume,' he said in a very cut glass accent and held out his hand. 'Glad you could come so quickly. And who is this?' He asked turning to me.

'My name is Tony Peterson, I'm working with the police on this case.' I said. 'And sorry but you are?'

'Oh yes, please forgive my lack of manners. Lieutenant Commander Daniel Evans but please call me Dan, everyone does. I am David Fletcher's Commanding Officer and something very odd has happened which is why I rang the police. Please, why don't we go into my office and I can explain.'

We followed him into the building. There was a long corridor that ran the length of the whole place. The walls were covered in posters most of which seemed to be focused on flying safely or technical drawings of aircraft none of which looked familiar.

Dan's office was at the far end and had large windows which looked out over a sweeping area of concrete. As we walked in, I could see the massive doors of the hangar off to one side. They were open and a small aircraft was being towed out by a tractor. It almost looked familiar, it had the lines of one of the early jets from my world, rather like a Hawker Hunter but with straight wings.

Dan saw me staring with interest. 'Beauty isn't she. Our latest and finest Turbine Scout, the Sopwith Petrel. She's far ahead of anything else in the world. Our job here is to evaluate new aircraft in an operational sense before they enter service. To see what they can do and how many of the manufacturer's claims stand up to real service.'

I had to do a quick mental translation. For 'Turbine Scout' read 'Jet Fighter' but it was very clear what she was just by looking at her sleek lines.

'Was this the machine that Fletcher was flying?' Frank asked getting straight down to business.

'Yes, he was the project officer for her. For the last few weeks, he and a maintenance team have been based up in Stornoway, in the Hebrides, north Scotland. The Army and a Marine battalion were on exercise on the mainland and the aircraft was being used in the ground attack role. By having it operate from an offshore island we were simulating it flying off one of our new aircraft carriers.'

'So that's where he was when his brother was killed?' I asked.

'Good question,' said Dan. 'One of the things we were assessing was getting the machine flying out of a forward base on the mainland with very limited facilities. There is a small strip close to the exercise area with a refuelling capability. The idea was that he would fly there, fuel up and be on call for the pongos when they wanted him. Apart from anything else, it was very much a test of the reliability of the machine. The day his brother was killed he was meant to be ashore. However, when the army called on him to fly a support mission they got no reply on the radio. It wasn't unusual apparently, with all the high ground around, they just assumed he hadn't received the call. Later that night, Fletcher flew back to Stornoway. He claims it was only then that he heard about the missed call.'

'I'm sorry,' Frank said. 'But what's odd about that?'

'We have an automatic recorder on the aircraft. It's something that's always fitted to preproduction machines. It logs information for the boffins to look at later. In this case it recorded almost three hours of flight time that can't be accounted for.'

'How long would it take for that machine to fly the five hundred odd miles back to here?' I asked as the penny started to drop.

Dan just looked at me. 'It cruises at four hundred and seventy five and has fuel for just over three hours if it had external tanks fitted, which it did.'

172

'So it flew somewhere that evening and returned later having used most of its fuel.' I asked. 'But could it have actually come here? Presumably, someone would have noticed the latest and shiniest machine coming in to land.'

'Correct, it didn't come here but it could have gone to Chilbolton.'

I looked blankly at Dan.

'It's our satellite airfield.' He said. 'It has runways and a control tower but that shuts at four. He could have landed there and parked up quite securely. A main road runs past some of it and there's a garage with a phone box nearby.'

'Look, I'm sure all this military technical stuff you two are talking about makes sense,' Frank said. 'But let me summarise. You're saying that David Fletcher flew somewhere the evening of his brother's murder and it could have been here. His machine was fast enough and had enough fuel to do that. He would then have had to get into the city and if he did I suspect he used the telephone in that garage and called a cab. So I can do some very simple and old fashioned police work and find that out very quickly. Dan, can I use your phone please?'

Dan just handed him the receiver. Frank dialled and immediately started issuing instructions, it didn't take long.

When he finished he put the receiver down. 'It should only take a little while to get to the bottom of this. But this is not just why you called me is it?'

To my surprise, Dan looked embarrassed. He reached over and pressed a button on a box on his desk. 'Brian you can come in now.'

A few seconds later the door opened. A young man dressed in what looked like a flight suit came in. He had tousled blonde hair and was quite tall. However, what caught my attention was the magnificent black eye he was sporting.

'Gentlemen this is Lieutenant Brian Janes. He had an encounter with David Fletcher early this morning. Brian, these gentlemen are from the police. Please tell them exactly what happened.'

The Lieutenant looked at us both and then started to talk. 'It was early this morning. I was in because I have the first slot of the day and I like to get ready in good time.' He must have noticed our slightly confused expressions. 'I was due to fly the Petrel on a test flight. Anyway, I was in the crew changing room when David

Fletcher came in. He didn't notice me at first just went over to his locker and started pulling things out. He seemed in quite a state. When I called over to him he looked startled. I don't think he realised that I was there. When I asked him what he was doing he got really agitated and told me to mind my own business. I've known David for several years and if I hadn't known better I would have said he was either drunk or high.'

'You knew about his brother? The funeral was only yesterday,' I asked.

'Oh yes, which is another reason I was surprised he was in so early. I knew he wasn't programmed to fly so it all seemed rather odd. Then I noticed he had taken out a pistol from his locker. We all have them but they are meant to be kept in the armoury when we are not on operations so I asked him what the hell he thought he was doing. He just came over to me and punched me. I was so surprised I fell back and hit my head on a locker. I was a little dazed then but I watched him take a bag and stuff some clothes, flying boots and the pistol into it and he left.'

'Did he say anything to you as he went out?' Frank asked.

'Funny you ask that, yes he did. He said he was sorry and we wouldn't meet again. I managed to get to my feet and follow him out. He had a car parked out front and jumped in and drove off. I'm pretty sure there was someone in there with him. It looked like a girl to me but I couldn't be sure.'

Chapter 35

The phone rang and when Dan answered it he just passed it to Frank. Frank listened for a minute and then hung up. He turned to us. 'The garage confirm that a man in some sort of military clothing used their phone the evening of Julian's murder. They also recognised the taxi firm that sent a cab. The taxi company confirm a man was taken to Winchester although there is no record of it being used to take him back. We've got our man. Sorry Tony, you were right all along I should have paid more attention.'

'I guess we'd better get back into town,' I said. 'Won't the military police want to get involved Dan?'

'For being absent yes but his assault on Brian is a civil matter. I had to consult with the legal people and they say you have precedent which is why I didn't contact you straight away so I'll leave you chaps to get on with it. But look, up until this incident David Fletcher has been a fine officer and a damned good pilot. Something must have sent him over the edge. Please give him a chance to explain himself.'

'Of course,' Frank said. 'Just as soon as we have him in custody. I don't suppose you would have any idea where he might go?'

'No sorry old chap,' Dan said. 'Brian any ideas? You knew him better than me.'

'Well I know there was a girl in Winchester he was keen on. His problem was that he was rarely ever here. He only joined this unit a few months ago before that he had been working in Plymouth. I remember him complaining once that the navy had never given him time to settle anywhere. Sorry, can't be of more help than that.'

We thanked the two officers, went outside and climbed back in the car. After a brief debate, we agreed that we didn't need the blue lights this time, mainly because I told Frank I would be walking back if he repeated the outbound journey.

As we travelled a great deal more sedately back into the city I tried to arrange my thoughts.

'Frank you're not going to like this but something about this whole scenario doesn't add up.'

'Please don't tell me you don't think he did it now. You're the one who's been doing all the digging.'

'Yes but why? I don't get why he suddenly felt the need to break all the rules to come down here and murder his brother. Something must have happened. I can't see that it would have been pre-planned so what suddenly made him do it? We know he had motive in that he would inherit but would hardly have generated such an urgent reaction.'

'Maybe Julian rang him and told him something that sparked it off. Something that he felt he needed to react to immediately.'

'I guess it had to be something like that or that someone else contacted him with the same result. What's more urgent now is that we find out where the hell he has gone with Carrie. I'm assuming that was who was with him in the car.'

'Agreed, I'll get my team together as soon as we get back.'

I continued to gnaw at the problem as we drove through the city. It was clear to me that David had some sort of crush on Carrie and probably had had it for some time. His sister's reaction to his name had been quite illuminating so there was some bad blood in the family. There again if there were any comparisons to be made it was Julian who was more likely to be the rotten apple. Why was none of this making sense?

As soon as we got back to the police station Frank called all his team together. We listened to their reports but in reality there was little more to go on. Frank put out an all persons call to look out for David and Carrie. We also knew that the car they were in was almost certainly Julian's and so made everyone aware of its licence plates.

'Can we check with the telephone company here or in Scotland and see if there is any record of a call to David on the day he flew down here?' I asked.

All my question got was blank looks. Someone said, 'I suppose we could ask the local exchange operators if they remember anything but it was ages ago now.'

I realised that they must still use manual exchanges. I needed to be careful not to let my ignorance show.

Thankfully Frank stepped in to cover my gaff. 'Who was it who checked with the taxi firm?

A hand went up near the back of the room.

'You didn't say where the person was dropped off. I assume it was in Edgar Road where the victim had his house?'

There was a second's silence as the man checked his notes. 'No Inspector, it was half way down Chilbolton Avenue.'

Frank and I looked at each other as the penny dropped. 'Oh bugger,' Frank said. 'Right, let's go.'

'Oh bugger,' I said to myself. He was going to turn on the blue lights again. He did. As we headed up the Stockbridge Road I suggested we turn them off as a covert approach might be more sensible. Frank agreed and as we turned into the avenue I knew I was going to live to tell the tale.

We parked clear of the gates. 'What do we do?' I asked. 'How do you want to play this? When I was here last he had a butler and a bruiser of some sort. He almost kidnapped me.'

'They won't be here today,' Frank said with confidence. 'The butler is only for show when the Society meet and the other chap you are talking about actually works in one of his warehouses in town.'

'You're very well informed,' I said. 'Are you a member as well?'

'Hah, the day I join any secret society will be my last,' Frank said with a snort of derision. 'But I do like to know what's going on in my patch. The butler works for the catering company that does the food when they all meet up and the heavy is well known to us for other reasons.'

'So, it should just be Alec there?'

'Guess so, unless he has any domestic staff. He was married, she left him some years ago for a much younger man and they had two kids but they are both out of the country. Bloody big house for a man on his own but I guess he keeps it on for the Society meetings. So we keep it simple, we ask him why David came here that night and see what he says. If he clams up we might have to intimate we know more than we actually do. Are you alright with that?'

I nodded.

'Then depending on what we establish, we might just invite him down to the station for a cosy chat.'

With that agreed, we climbed out of the car and approached the gates which were well over head height and firmly shut. I tried the latch and to my surprise the gate opened easily on well oiled hinges.

The large drive inside was empty although I did notice a big double garage off to one side of the house that was shut. The whole place was quiet and possibly even deserted. I just hoped the Alec was in because finding him would not necessarily be easy especially if he did have something nasty to hide.

Frank strode up and knocked firmly at the door. I went up and pressed the doorbell off to one side. 'One of these methods should work,' I said.

Frank gave me a sour look just as we heard footsteps approaching. There was the sound of the door being unlocked and Alec Jeffries looked out at us.

Before he could say anything Frank pushed past. 'Good afternoon Alec,' he said. 'My colleague and I would like to have a little chat. If that's alright with you of course.'

To my surprise, Alec didn't object. Either to the way Frank had barged in or the way he had been spoken to.

'Come with me,' was all he said and he turned and led us through a door on the right of the entrance hall. The room we entered was obviously a dining room with a large highly polished dark wood table surrounded by ornate wooden chairs.

Alec pointed to the chairs. 'Please take a seat, sorry we can't use my living room my cleaner is there at the moment. Now, what is it you wish to discuss?'

Frank got straight to the point. 'We have strong evidence that David Fletcher flew to an airfield near Worthy Down and took a taxi into Winchester at just about the exact time his brother was murdered. The strange thing Alec is that the taxi didn't drop him at his brother's house. It came here. Care to explain?'

If Alec's reaction to Frank's claim was going to be of any help we were quickly disappointed.

'Sorry Frank, I've absolutely no idea what you're talking about. Fletcher may well have been dropped off in this road but he never came here. I suggest you ask him what he was up to.'

'We will,' Frank said. 'Just as soon as we find him. He appears to have done a runner. Not only that but he seems to have taken a young lady with him under some form of duress.'

'That's all well and good Frank,' Alec said. 'But what evidence do you have that he came here apart from some taxi driver's story that this was where he was dropped off? I'm sorry but that's hardly going to stand up in court is it?'

'Alec, what are you hiding?' I asked, as I looked hard at him. It was quite clear to me that he was under some sort of duress himself. There were drops of sweat on his top lip and his finger was tapping nervously at the table top. He looked back at me and then down at his tapping finger.

'Who said anything about going to court Alec,' Frank said. 'It seems to me you are being defensive over nothing. If he came here then you could be of great help in solving the murder. Unless of course you were involved in the first place?'

'Look, I wasn't involved in anything.' Alec protested. 'Maybe David wanted to walk the last part of his journey so that no one would spot the taxi dropping him off. Maybe he has other friends down this road. It could have been anything.'

'Oh, so you admit you were friends then?' Frank said with a note of triumph.

'I've known both the Fletcher boys since they were children,' Alec said in exasperation. 'They went to the same school as my sons, they used to come and play here when they were young.'

I suddenly realised I could see through a very small gap in the door behind Alec. I wouldn't have noticed except a small movement caught my eye. Before either man could speak again I broke in. 'I think that's all we can get out of this meeting.' As Frank was about to object, I managed to kick him sharply on the shin. He turned and gave me a startled look. I looked hard back at him and mouthed the words 'trust me' at him.

'I think you need to think this over Alec.' I said. 'We'll leave you now but this isn't over. It seems to me that you have a great deal more to tell us. We'll be in touch.' I said the last words firmly. I then grabbed Frank by the arm. 'Don't worry we'll let ourselves out.'

I almost had to drag Frank the first few yards but when we were in the hall I whispered in his ear. 'Out, now.'

We went back outside. 'There had better be a good reason for that Tony,' Frank said. 'I wasn't even warmed up.'

'There is,' I replied. 'Hold on a second.' I quickly ran a couple of paces to the garage and looked through a side window then doubled back.

'There was someone in the room behind Alec. Remember he said that he had his cleaner in which was why we didn't use the living room.'

'So?'

'Did you see any sign of him or her for that matter? Surely they would have had a vehicle of some sort.'

'So what are you saying?'

'He wanted us in that room for a reason and the only one I can think of was that was where we could be overheard. There was an adjoining door which I would bet went into the kitchen it was slightly open. I caught a flash of something yellow moving. Just for a second. Carrie was wearing a yellow dress at the wake. And what sort of car was David driving?'

'Eh? A Lanchester I think, one of the sporty ones.'

'There's one of those parked in the garage.'

Chapter 36

'Oh shit,' Frank said. As soon as we were back outside the gates, he grabbed the radio and made a call that he wanted as many of his team up here as soon as possible. They were to come armed and ready for a hostage situation. We backed off down to the end of the road and waited. It didn't take long for four police cars to arrive each with four policemen inside. They were all in uniform which was a shame but this world seemed to have the vast majority of the force dressed formally. However, they all carried pistols and several had mean looking sniper rifles.

One of them came up to Frank and handed him a pistol. Frank said something and he went to the back of a car and gave me one as well.'

'I take it you know how to handle one of those?' Frank asked.

I looked it over. It was vaguely like a standard issue military Browning nine millimetre. The safety catch was obvious and the rest was simple. 'No problem Frank but I hate using these things. In my opinion, they cause more problems than they solve.'

'I tend to agree,' he replied. 'But would you want to go back in knowing who is in there, without one?'

'Is that what we are going to do?'

'Got a better idea?'

'Well, I assume that David's not a welcome guest and it's hardly a place he can stay in indefinitely. We could just wait until he makes a break for it.'

'You may well be right there but whatever happens we need to get the place secure first.' Frank said.

He called to three of his men and instructed one to go to the Golf Course which was at the rear of the house and tell them to close it immediately and get players away from the area of the house. The other two were to go to the neighbouring houses and explain what was going on and get them evacuated. The rest of the men were to surround the place and make sure all the exits were covered. 'And no one is to do anything without my clear instruction. Is that clear?'

The men nodded and ran off to their positions. All we could do was wait.

'The bigger question is what the hell does he think he's going to achieve?' Frank said in a worried tone. 'All I can think of is that he's going to try and leave the country. He must realise we now have a pretty good idea of what happened after being discovered at the air station and then us visiting Alec. I bet he wasn't expecting that.'

'Good point, so how the hell did he know it was us at the door?' I mused.

'Maybe he didn't. He could have been waiting for someone else. Or he saw us through one of the windows as we came in through the gates.'

Just then a police van rolled up and a sergeant got out. 'Got the full kit here now Sir, anything you need straight away?'

'Yes, let me have the directional microphone. I think we'll try to have a little listen in to what's going on.' Frank said.

Intrigued, I watched the Sergeant go to the back of the van and pull out a large box. Inside was a large parabolic shaped aerial and a box which was attached to it with a wire. The aerial had a pistol grip and there was a set of old fashioned looking headphones connected to it.

'I expect you use something more sophisticated where you come from,' Frank said quietly. 'But this is pretty sensitive and if we can get a line of sight on a window of a room where people are talking we should be able to hear them from one of the adjoining houses. At least we know where they were so we might just get lucky.

Just then Frank's radio came to life and reported that the building was covered from all angles. We walked up to the neighbouring house on the right hand side. The owners, a middle aged couple were talking to one of Frank's men. We asked if they minded if went in to their house to oversee what was going on. They seemed keen to help. Let's face it, this was probably the most excitement this City had seen for years and they would be able to dine out on the story ever after.

There was a tall wooden fence separating the two gardens so Frank led the way upstairs. We found what was obviously a spare room, with windows that allowed us to look down on the side of the house where we had been talking to Alec. Behind the dining room window was a larger one that looked like our target. Unfortunately, there appeared to be a blind covering the window so we couldn't see in.

Frank opened our window and was able to point the dish with a good line of sight. He put on the headphones and started to twiddle the knobs on the control box. When satisfied, he took off the headphones and gave me one earpiece to listen through while he used the other. At first, all I could hear was hissing and what I assumed was distant traffic. However, I soon realised I could hear distant voices as well. Initially, I couldn't make out what they were saying but by putting my finger in my other ear and concentrating hard I was able to start making some sense out of the conversation.

'South... ton and we can ...... ship to South Ameri... Leave as soon as possible.'

The voice was clearly David's and he didn't sound particularly rational. There was someone else talking back to him but I couldn't make out what he was saying. Both voices were male.

I turned to Frank. 'Looks like he's going to make a run for it to Southampton. But what about Carrie Parks? We don't even know if she's in there.'

As soon as I said that, I heard her voice. 'Never, why the hell do you think I would come with you?'

A wave of relief washed over me. Her voice sounded much clearer, so I surmised she must be closer to the window and she was still alright. Any reply was impossible to hear but it was clear that a vigorous and acrimonious debate was taking place.

I turned to Frank. 'Let them go or contain them?'

'Once they leave we have lost a large degree of control, it's too risky.'

'Totally agree,' I said.

'I think I need to go and have a chat before they get too prepared to leave. There was a phone downstairs.'

We went down and found the phone in the hall. However, Frank went outside and spoke to the house's owners. When he came back, he got on the radio and warned his men he was about to make contact and they were to stay vigilant but on no occasion were they to use their weapons without prior approval.

He then picked up the receiver and started to dial. 'Had to ask for Alec's number,' he said. Once again I realised how different these two worlds were. I would simply have used my mobile and gone on line to get it.

I could hear the phone ringing faintly through the earpiece as Frank listened. Eventually, it was answered. It sounded like Alec.

'Mister Jeffries, this is Inspector Cosgrove. We are now aware of what is going on in your house. We have also surrounded the place so there is nowhere for anyone to go to. Please inform Mister Fletcher and ask him to come out. All my officers are armed. Do you understand?'

I didn't hear the reply but Frank stood there with the phone to his ear for some time. Then a new voice came over the line. Frank listened and then replied. 'Not going to happen David. Now don't be silly, you're just making it worse for yourself.' There was a long muffled reply and the phone went dead.

'Bugger,' Frank said. 'He said he has Carrie Parks as his hostage and he wants a police car and escort to Southampton. He wants us to take him to a Chilean ship that's there. They don't have an extradition arrangement with Great Britain. He says there is one docked and due to leave on tonight's tide at midnight. He's given us half an hour. Not going to happen.'

'Why the hell does he think a Chilean ship will even take him?' I asked.

'Because we don't have good relations with them and he has plenty of military secrets they would want to hear about. Once he's on board he's on Chilean territory and we can't touch him. We're going to have to get the War Office in on this as soon as we can. We're going to have to stall him somehow. What's the time now?'

I looked at my watch. 'Just past six, we've got until half past to come up with some sort of delaying tactic.'

Suddenly it all became irrelevant. The radio bust into life. 'Shot fired,' someone said but we had heard it clearly ourselves anyway.

A few seconds later the telephone rang. Frank answered. 'Shit, alright get some pressure on the wound we'll be over straight away. Where is he now?'

I barely waited for him to put the phone down as I sprinted out of the house and along to the gates of Alec's place. She may not have been my Carrie but somehow that made it even worse. If that sod David had hurt her he would have me to deal with. Frank was well behind me by now and yelling to me to stop. I ignored him. The front door was open and the scene that greeted me caught me by surprise. I almost felt guilty when I realised that Carrie was alright, as it was Alec sitting slumped against the wall. Carrie was kneeling by him. There was a lot of blood and she was holding something against his arm, presumably where he had been shot. There was no sign of David. I realised that I had the pistol in my hand as I scanned the hallway.

'Where did he go?' I asked just as Frank and two constables came in behind me.

She pointed to the large door that I knew opened into the Venta Society's meeting room. The two policemen ran towards it so I put the gun down and knelt by Carrie and Alec.

'It's alright,' Carrie said. 'I'm first aid trained and I've stopped the blood for the moment.'

Frank had grabbed the phone and was calling for an ambulance.

'What the hell happened Carrie?' I asked.

'David is what bloody happened. I'll tell you the full story later but this was my fault. He was pointing the gun at Alec and getting more and more angry. He said the police would have no choice but to let them go. Alec was trying to pacify him but it wasn't working. David was so focused on Alec that when he pulled his gun up and pointed it, he didn't see me grab a walking stick from by the door. I hit him on his gun arm but it wasn't hard enough to make him drop it. It went off and hit Alec in the arm. He must have realised that the shot would be heard and that the police would probably have no choice but to come in. He tried to grab me but I just kept backing away from him. He pleaded for me to go with him. When I said exactly what I thought of him, he seemed to make a decision and made a run for it through the doors over there. I went to help Alec and then you got here.'

I sat down and put my arms around her. Despite her efforts to help Alec, I could see she was shaking and close to breaking down completely. I gently took her hand off the pad of cloth she had been holding on the wound and put the pressure on myself.

'It's alright now,' I said. 'He's gone and the police will find him very soon.'

Just then, two men dressed like paramedics from my world ran in. I explained what had happened and they took over in a very professional manner.

I lifted Carrie up and we went over to a small chair, I seated her in it and knelt down beside her. 'It's all over Carrie. He won't get far.'

Just then one of the policemen who had gone after David came back. He saw Frank and came over. 'No sign of him Sir. We've no idea how he did it but he's got away.'

Chapter 37

'How the hell did he manage that?' Frank said in an accusing tone to the policeman. 'The whole bloody place was surrounded. Didn't anyone see him at all?'

'Sorry Sir, he's just vanished.'

A weak voice came from one side of the hall. It was Alec. 'He probably used the old tunnel. It goes from below the rear veranda which used to be the kitchen area of the old house here and across to the other side of the golf course. David and my sons discovered it years ago and used to play down there until I stopped them because it was too dangerous. We always thought it was something to do with hiding priests in Tudor times, it was certainly that old.'

'Shit,' Frank said. 'Where does it come out?'

'There's a copse of trees the other side of the fairway behind the house. There used to be an old building there possibly a chapel.'

Frank turned to the constable. 'You still here? Get over there now.'

The man didn't waste any time and disappeared back through the double doors.

'He'll be long gone,' I said.

'Yes but he's on foot and we know where he's trying to get to.' Frank said.

The two paramedics now had Alec in a stretcher and were taking him out.

'I'll get a constable to go with him and get a statement as soon as he can,' Frank said. He then used his radio and instructed that an all persons call be put out to apprehend David Fletcher. He also told the radio operator to contact Southampton police and warn them that Fletcher might well be heading their way.

He then turned to Carrie. 'Are you able to tell us what happened Miss Parks? It could be of great help.'

I could see that Carrie was trying to pull herself together and finding it hard. She was clearly in shock. 'Just give us the bare bones Carrie,' I said. 'The detail can wait.'

'Here, have a pull on this,' Frank said and handed her an open hip flask.

She looked at it dubiously but put it to her lips and took a swig. Once the coughing stopped, she actually had some colour in her cheeks. She handed the flask back.

'It started at the wake at David's house. Tony, you saw how drunk he was. Well, he got worse. I'm afraid I also got a little tipsy and when I realised it was time to leave I was just about the last person there. That was when David started pestering me again. I agreed to have a final drink with him just to get him to stop and I don't remember anything after that until the middle of the night. I woke up in a bed and someone was trying to take my clothes off. It was David, I don't think he expected me to wake up. When I started to fight him off, he became all apologetic saying I had passed out and he was just getting some of my clothes loosened to let me sleep it off. I didn't believe a word of it and we ended up having a screaming match. Then he suddenly burst into tears. I got the whole story then. How he hated his brother who had bullied him terribly as a kid and how he had always loved me. He said Julian had even turned him against his sister. He joined the marines to prove he was a better man than Julian but then Julian had left and started making money like his father. He really had a chip on his shoulder. By then it was starting to get light and I told him I had to get home. He offered to drive me. When we got in the car he said he needed to go out to the air station first as there was something he needed to collect urgently. I suppose I should have just got out and walked but I had a serious headache by then so just agreed. Anything to keep him calm really. However, when we drove back into Winchester he came here instead of my place. He seemed to know the house quite well and knew there was a key to the kitchen door at the back under a plant pot. I started to argue with him but he pulled out this gun and forced me inside and locked me in the pantry next to the kitchen. There were no windows and no way of getting out. I just had to wait. Then, sometime later the door opened and Alec was pushed inside.'

'Any idea what he was doing while you were locked up?' I asked.'

'No, we couldn't hear or see anything. I asked Alec why he had come here and all he would say was that David knew him from years back and presumably needed somewhere to hide. We tried to work out what the hell was going on. All we could think of was that it was something to do with Julian's murder. To be honest, I was pretty sure there was more to it than that but I wasn't really in a position to insist. At least we had some water and food in the pantry. I've no idea how long we were in there. Then he let us out but before we could start talking he must have seen something because he told Alec to go and let whoever it was at the door come in and talk to them in the dining room so that he could hear what was being said. He threatened to shoot me if Alec didn't comply.'

'Yes we worked most of that out,' I said. 'Go on.'

'I realised who it was as soon as I heard your voices but there was nothing I could do. Then you left. After that things got really desperate. Alec was trying to convince him to give himself up but he wasn't listening. He said he had arranged to go to South America and he even thought he could convince me to go with him.'

'Then we called on the phone,' Frank said.

'Yes and you know the rest. I tried, I'm so sorry I couldn't stop him.'

'Hey, you did alright Carrie. It was very brave of you to try and disarm him.' I said and gave her a hug.

'What are you going to do now?' she asked.

'The first thing is to get you home,' Frank said. 'I'll get a car to take you there.'

'Will your friend Elaine be there?' I asked.

'Yes, she should be,'

'Good, then get home and I suggest you get some sleep,' I said. 'I'm sure any need to give statements can be left until tomorrow.'

'Absolutely, young lady,' Frank said. He picked up his radio and ordered one of his cars to come over.

A shaken looking Carrie was escorted out. I gave her a smile as she left and she gave me a tentative half smile back.

'So what the hell do we do now?' I asked Frank.

'Get the docks at Southampton sealed up,' he said. 'But he's no fool, he'll know that we now know that was his plan so maybe he'll do something else. But whatever he does he's going to need transport and I've got an idea about that.'

'Oh, is this some coppers hunch?' I asked.

'Maybe,' Frank said. 'Let's get things underway and then we need to have a talk.'

We went back to the police station where Frank started issuing more orders and then spent some time on the telephone to the Southampton police.

'He'll know that we know he's expected there to get on this ship.' I said when he put the phone down.

'Yes but he's a pretty resourceful chap. The docks are a massive place.'

'But they don't need to cover the whole dock area, they know which ship he is trying to board. They just need to put a cordon around that.'

'Yes and that's what they say they are going to do. But if he's got any sense that's the last thing he'll attempt. If it was me, I'd try and get hold of a boat of some sort and board her while she is going up Southampton water or in the Solent. Don't forget we are pretty sure the Chileans want to get hold of him. They will do everything they can to get him on board.'

'So the obvious thing to do is to stop him getting away. What was this idea you were working on?'

Frank smiled. 'He's going to need transport to get to the port. We've already got his car. He could try and thumb a lift but that would be very risky. I've got all the train stations covered where he could get to on foot and he doesn't have time to walk all the way to Southampton, it's just too far.'

'So you think he will risk trying to steal a car?' I asked. In my world that was a difficult proposition these days but from what I had seen over here the cars were pretty basic. 'He'll be on foot, have you got a helicopter you can use to track him down?'

'Oh, you mean one of those things I saw in that film the other night? We call them ornithopters and they are only just being used by the military.'

'Shame, all our police forces have them and they have cameras that can pick up a person's body heat. He wouldn't get far in our world. Mind you, I might just be able to help if we can nip over to my house. So where do you think he will head for? What was this hunch of yours?'

'Yes I've a pretty solid idea where he will go,' Frank said with a feral grin. 'The Chalk Pit.'

Chapter 38

His look of disappointment when I didn't react was priceless. 'Please tell me you have the same over there?' He asked.

'Sorry Frank, haven't a clue what you are talking about.'

'Farley Mount, the Chalk Pit something must be there surely?'

The penny dropped. 'Yes it's a country park just to the west, there's some sort of monument to a horse there if I remember. I used to go for walks there as a kid.'

'That's all? No country club, no golf course, no history of excess? No stories of wild parties and debauchery?'

'Sorry old chap nothing like that.'

'Well, we need to get there and quickly.' Frank said as he stood up. 'I'll tell you more in the car.'

'And we need to go via my place,' I said. 'I've got something there that might just help. It's not far out of the way.'

'Alright but be quick, it will be getting dark soon and if I'm right that's when he will be making his move.'

Once again, I had to suffer the excitement of Frank's driving but luckily the traffic was quite light. We pulled up outside my house and I jumped out. 'Just give me a few minutes,' I said as I left him in the car. I ran up to the study and jumped through the mirror. To my surprise, Carrie was sitting behind my desk reading something. I don't know who was more startled.

'Tony what are you doing?' she asked.

'No time to explain in any detail,' I said as I gave her a quick peck on the cheek. 'But with any luck, this investigation will soon be over and then you and I are going on a long and very expensive holiday.' As I said it, I was rummaging through the pile of electronics that we had acquired from London. The box I wanted was easily found.

I turned back to Carrie 'Should be back in a day or two,' I said and went back into my other study and ran downstairs to the waiting car.

'What the hell is that?' Frank asked as I opened the box and started to put things together. Luckily I had made sure the batteries were all fully charged.

'I'll show you once it's assembled. 'Now tell me more about the place we're going to.'

'Very well. It goes back to the mid seventeen hundreds. Some chap called Paulet St John an Earl by all accounts was riding his horse and chasing foxes when they fell into a twenty five foot deep chalk pit. Amazingly, they both survived and the next year he raced the horse in a local race at Worthy Down and won. He renamed the horse 'Beware Chalk Pit' for the race. He must have had a great sense of humour and when he died he put up the monument. It all changed in the early Thirties when the whole area was bought by the Riley family. They built a private club there and called it the Chalk Pit. It became quite notorious for many years. The family were Irish and from Liverpool and were into all sorts of barely legal activities. In the end, it was closed but not before it had gained its famous reputation for lewd behaviour and outrageous parties.'

'You mean it became Winchester's knocking shop? I can just imagine how well that went down with the City fathers.'

'Something like that but it was way outside the city boundaries so there was little anyone could do. You'd probably have found most of the city fathers there on a Saturday night anyway. The family also built a racecourse which is now part of the golf course. It was derelict for some years after the Rileys left but then it was bought by a hotel chain and refurbished. It's incredibly popular now as a country club. There's a spa and an excellent five star restaurant. They've been really clever with the marketing and managed to retain the atmosphere of the original place, at least in the décor. Hopefully, not in the behaviour. And luckily for us, it has a really large car park and it's the only one around for miles. To get there from Alec's house is only about three miles and that was the direction David was heading.'

'Damn it sounds like there are aspects to this world that are far more fun than mine,' I said only half-jokingly. 'But what happened to the memorial? That's all there is in my world.'

'It was incorporated into the building and it's now the centre piece of the bar. I'm not sure what the original owner would have thought about that but bearing in mind his sense of humour, I suspect he would actually have been delighted. Now what the hell is that thing you've got there?' Frank asked.

'You remember I asked if you had a police helicopter? Well, this is the next best thing,' I said. 'It's called a drone and it flies under remote control and this one has a special camera.'

'What sort of camera?'

'Infra red, it can see variations in temperature and that includes the body heat of a person.'

'Yes we've got that sort of camera too but they are ten times the size of that little contraption. So how do you think we should use it?'

'Before I answer that will there be many of your men there as well?'

'No, it's just you and me. This is still a long shot in some ways and most of my spare men are working with the Southampton lot or out on patrol.'

'So what are we trying to do? Arrest him? He's armed don't forget.'

'Not necessarily. If we can identify him and see what he does, we can follow and get my men in position to make an arrest. That cuts down the risk for everyone.'

That sounded fine to me. Confronting someone like David when he was armed was a very bad idea. Especially as I had been asked to return my pistol and I knew that Frank had as well.

The road that led up to Farley mount was wider than my version but was still not the sort of road to drive fast along as there were plenty of blind bends. Mind you, Frank didn't seem to worry about them overmuch. Thankfully, it didn't take long to get there. We pulled into the large car park and I could see the country club building and the restaurant over to one side. It looked very impressive. The car park was packed, there must have been over fifty cars as well as a couple of coaches. You would need half a dozen people patrolling to catch a thief and anyway we didn't want to discourage him. We wanted him to make his escape and see where he was heading and then stop him safely away from any other people and any chance of collateral damage.

Frank parked as close to the entrance as he could and we both got out. 'How long can that gizmo fly for?' He asked.

'On one battery about forty five minutes,' I replied. 'But I've got three more in the box.'

'So where's a good place to operate it from?'

I looked around. The main buildings were to the north of us and most of the approaches were open country. However, to the west, back towards Winchester it was quite heavily wooded. If I was waiting to make a covert approach that is where I would be hiding.

There was a low earth bank surrounding much of the car park. 'Let's just go the other side of the bank,' I said. 'No one will be able to see us there and we are close to the car if we need to give chase.'

We clambered over the bank and sat down the other side. We were well out of sight. I put the drone down clear of us and got the controller ready.

'Sit next to me Frank,' I said. 'And watch this screen.' I then moved the controller levers and the drone started its deep buzzing and leapt into the air. It was clear that Frank didn't know whether to watch the drone or the screen.

'That is just amazing,' he said.

'I took the little machine quite high so it would be hard to hear. Not that anyone here would have a clue what it was and moved it slowly towards the wood. It was the sort of drone I could fly by looking at the controller screen which was lucky because it was soon out of sight. With no GPS or mobile phone signal it was not as easy as it could have been but once over the woods I was able to use the hover function and using its gyroscopes it was able to hold position reasonably accurately. The picture on the screen was black and white but there was enough temperature difference in the trees to create a picture.

We waited. I flew the drone very slowly along the edge of the wood but nothing showed up. After half an hour I brought the machine back and changed batteries. It could have lasted longer but I didn't want to risk it. As soon as it was back in position there was something that hadn't been there only minutes before.

'Bingo,' I said and pointed to the screen. The edge of the treeline was quite clear and there at the edge was a large white shape. 'Someone is hiding just inside the woods,' I said to Frank. 'What you're seeing is the fact that he is a lot warmer than the surroundings. Looks like you were right.'

'Fair enough but it could be anyone, let's not assume anything at this moment. Mind you I'm not sure who else would be hiding there at this time of evening. Can we get closer do you think?'

'That's going to be hard because he's right over the other side of the car park,' I said. 'You could take a radio and investigate but remember if it is David, he's armed.'

'Good point we'll wait here and see what he does.'

It was starting to get quite dark by now although there was a good moon rising behind me. However, our target didn't seem inclined to move. I wondered if he had fallen asleep. I have to say I was starting to find it hard to keep my eyes open and concentrate. It had been a long day. Suddenly, the white blob started to move. As soon as it was clear of the undergrowth we could clearly see it was a man but there was no way we could identify who it was.

'What the hell is he doing?' Frank asked.

Instead of creeping around checking car doors as we expected, the person was walking boldly up to the front of the main building. Within a short time, he had disappeared inside.

I recalled the drone. It was of no use now. 'What the hell do we do?'

'We wait. There is still only one way out. We don't go in knowing that he's armed. Let's go back to the car.'

As we got in the car the radio came to life. Frank immediately answered it. 'Boss this is Sergeant Jones. We've just had a message from the hospital. Alec Jeffries discharged himself half an hour ago in spite of the doctors advising against it. We've been up to his house and his car is missing. The neighbours say it left only a few minutes ago.'

Chapter 39

'This is not going to plan,' I said.

'It never bloody well does,' Frank said bitterly. 'Where the hell does Alec think he's going?'

'Here maybe?' I said. 'Look we know that David had a different father to Julian. Could it have been Alec?' It would explain a lot.'

'Then why did David shoot him? That's hardly the actions of a loving son.'

I suddenly reflected back to what Uncle Peter had told me about his relationship with my mother. The circumstances were different but maybe the result was the same. 'Maybe he didn't mean to. Carrie said it was because she hit his arm with the walking stick. Suppose they were just acting for her benefit. Don't forget Alec and David were in the house together before Alec was locked in the pantry. They could have been planning it.'

'But why? What's the logic behind all this?'

'What do we actually know about Alec's past? Maybe he's not what we think.' An idea was starting to form in my mind and it was logical in a rather chilling sort of way. 'Look we haven't got time to speculate at the moment. We need to arrest David and probably Alec by the sound of it. Despite what you said just now, we really need to get inside the building and see what the hell David is up to.'

'Agreed,' Frank said and we left the car and walked towards the main building where David had entered.

The entrance lobby was simply awesome. I had to stop and stare to take it all in. A large square room with a balcony on three sides. Dark red curtains with massive gold tassels hid most of the downstairs walls. In between the drapes were oil paintings of a definitely indelicate nature. The staircase that led up to the balcony was simply magnificent with ornate gold bannisters. Dotted all around were velvet armchairs and settees. To say it looked like the archetypal brothel from every male fantasy was doing it a serious injustice. Luckily, it wasn't that busy, I suppose most people were in the bar or restaurant.

Frank turned to look at me. 'Told you they wanted to keep the original theme going. You should see some of the bedrooms.'

'Bloody hell Frank. What was it like when it really was a knocking shop?'

'By all accounts, it was pretty damned good. But come on we need to track David down.'

Off to one side of the stairs was a rather incongruous reception desk. I don't know whether I was relieved or disappointed to see that the rather pretty receptionist was dressed in modern clothes rather than in keeping with the décor.

We went up to her and Frank showed her his warrant card. 'Inspector Cosgrove, Winchester Police,' he said. 'We are looking for this man and believe he may have come in a few minutes ago.' He showed the girl a photograph he had been carrying in his jacket pocket.

'Oh yes Sir,' she said. 'He asked for the toilets and said he wanted to use a telephone. I directed him to the phone booths. They're in the corridor behind me as well as the toilets.' She pointed to a door that obviously led further into the building. 'Is there something wrong?'

'No, not really. I just need to have a talk with him,' Frank said. 'Thank you for your help.'

He led me off to one side where we could sit unobserved but still see the door the receptionist had indicated.

Frank got out his portable radio and talked quietly into it. 'Yes, I want backup here now. And once they are on their way I want someone to look into the background of Alec Jeffries, right back to when he was in his bloody crib.'

I was just about to say something when the door opened and David came out. There seemed to be a look of relief on his face. He looked at his watch and clearly came to a decision because he started walking purposely towards the door to one side that must lead to the bar. The clue being the word BAR in large, ornate, gold letters over the top.

'If Alec turns up, do we try to apprehend them?' I asked.

'Not unless backup has arrived,' Frank replied. 'Let's get out of here and watch from outside. We can cover the exit to the car park.'

We both got up and were only a few feet from the front door when it opened in our faces and Alec Jeffries came in. I don't know who was more surprised. We all froze for what seemed like an eternity and then Alec turned around and ran. Frank started after him. Even with Frank's bulk, Alec wasn't going to get far. His arm was in a sling and even from the glimpse I got, he was clearly in pain. However, what stopped me from charging on was the feeling of something hard poking into my back and words whispered in my ear.

'Don't even think about going after them,'

Oh shit, David must have seen us confronting Alec.

'Now let's go out to the car park please Mister Peterson. I'm sure your colleague won't have gone far chasing a wounded man.'

I was pushed forward. There was nothing I could do and sure enough only half way down the line of parked cars Frank had his hands on Alec. I gave him an apologetic look as we walked up.

'You can let Alec go now Inspector,' David said. 'Your colleague here will testify to my resolve.'

Frank did as he was told and turned to face us. 'Give it up David. I've got back up on the way and anyway, where the hell do you think you can go where you will be safe? We know all about you wanting to get to Southampton. It's sewn up tighter than a duck's arse. There's nowhere you can go.'

David didn't answer directly instead he turned to Alec. 'Are you alright?' he asked with concern in his voice.

'Yes, I'll be fine,' he replied although he looked quite the opposite. 'Trust me.'

'Plan B then?' David said.

Alec just nodded.

'Where's the car? David asked.

'Follow me,' Alec said and David gave me a shove in the back as we all walked down the line of parked cars until we reached the end. I was desperately looking to see if there was anyone else in the vicinity. Any distraction might be enough for me to turn the tables. But the place was eerily quiet. Everyone who was coming must have already arrived and no one was in the process of leaving just yet.

Alec's car was nearest the entrance.

'I think the good Inspector will make the best insurance policy,' David said and before I could react, he had shoved me forward and was pointing the gun at Frank. 'In the car please Inspector. I think one hostage is enough. Mister Peterson would be too much of a handful. Are you sure you're alright to drive Alec?'

'Yes, the car has an automatic gearbox. And I don't think I would be much use holding a gun.'

'Do you always do as your son tells you?' I asked Alec. 'Are you sure you want to do this?'

A strange look crossed Alec's face. For a second I felt I was looking at a complete stranger.

'Not even a good try,' David said before anyone else could speak. 'Don't worry he's just trying to get us off balance. Now into the back please Inspector. Goodbye Mister Peterson.'

I tried one last throw of the dice. 'Give the Ambassador my regards.'

All that achieved was another dirty look and then the doors slammed and the car's rear wheels spun as it drove clear.

I only had seconds to react. Luckily, I wasn't far from Frank's car which was mercifully unlocked. I wrenched open a back door and grabbed the drone and controller. Alec's car wasn't exactly hard to see. It lit up the screen like a flare. As I suspected, they weren't heading back towards Winchester but had turned the other way. That was a quicker route to the main road to London where I was pretty sure they were now going but not if I could help it. I accelerated the drone to get ahead of them. This wasn't going to be easy and I only had one shot at it. Once the drone was further down the road, I turned it around and took it as low as I dared. I was counting on surprise and the driver not having a clue what was happening. The glare of the heat from the car was starting to fill the controller's screen when it suddenly went dead. I ran into the road as the sound of crumpling metal could be heard.

It was several hundred yards and I was panting hard when I got there. The car had swerved into a ditch and was on its side. As I arrived the rear door opened and a rather battered looking Frank clambered out.

'You alright?' I asked as I went to help him climb clear.

'No thanks to you,' he said. 'What on earth did you do?'

'Crashed the drone into the windscreen. Bet it gave Alec a fright. We'd better go and see how they are.'

As I finished speaking blue lights appeared behind us. 'Or maybe we could just let the cavalry do that,' I said.

Chapter 40

It was going to be a long night. A soon as the back up squad arrived I sneaked away to look for the remains of the drone. Luckily, it hadn't gone far but was quite smashed up. Just in case, I made doubly sure by stamping on it and removing the battery and all the printed circuit boards. The rest was just a heap of mangled plastic and I was sure there was nothing to start a technological revolution if someone found it.

Alec was pulled out unconscious. I idly wondered if I could start up a business making air bags. None of the cars here had them. The only concession to safety were seat belts and most people didn't seem to bother with them anyway. David put up more of a fight as soon as he was hauled out but four burly constables were quite capable of restraining him while Frank read him his rights. Then it was back to the police station, all except Alec who was taken back to the hospital by ambulance. He wouldn't be checking himself out this time as a constable went with him.

As we drove back into the city, Frank and I talked.

'What did you arrest him for?' I asked.

'Two counts of kidnap, wounding with intent although that might not stick and assaulting a police officer. I also warned him the military would be looking to charge him with being absent without leave. I think that should do for the moment.'

'But not the murder of his brother?'

'Can't at the moment but let's just let him stew for a while and then see what we can get out of him.'

'You might want to consider treason as well,' I said.

'Yes that was in the back of my mind too but what proof is there? It will be very hard to come up with any evidence.'

'If I'm right we will find out back at the station.' I replied. 'We did get all the luggage out of the car?'

'Yes of course.'

'Then we need to search it very thoroughly but I suspect what we need will be on his person.'

'You are being very mysterious Tony.' Frank said.

'Just let me run with this,' I said. 'I could be wrong but if I'm not then we should be able to wrap this all up quite quickly.'

'Alright, I'll let you have your way for the moment. I can't ask you to physically attend any interviews but I do have one interview room with a one way mirror and you're welcome to observe. Then if your idea comes to fruition you can let me know.'

By then we had arrived and we made our way back into the station. David had already been brought in and was waiting in the interview room. I went up to the desk sergeant. 'Have the suspect's clothes been searched?' I asked.

'Only for weapons or other dangerous objects,' he replied. 'But we've put him in a boiler suit now that we've processed him. It's for his and our safety so you can have the lot.'

I turned to Frank. 'Could I have those clothes so I can look at them? Honestly, this could be very important.'

Frank nodded to the sergeant. 'Please do as Mister Peterson asks,' he said. 'Take him down to the evidence room. Meanwhile, I intend to have a long talk with our new guest.' He then turned to me. 'If you find what you are looking for come to the observation room and let me know.'

I nodded to him and the Sergeant got a young constable to escort me. We waited in the small room for several minutes before another policeman came in with a bundle of clothes.

'Here you are Sir,' he said and he dumped them all on the table and left.

I turned to my escort. 'What's your name constable?' I asked.

'Jameson Sir but everyone calls me Jamie.'

'Right Jamie, we're looking for something very important but I'm not sure exactly what form it will take. So we are going to have to look at everything here, in extreme detail. It could be stitched into a seam or hidden in plain view but it's very important that we find it.'

He didn't look convinced. 'Sounds a bit vague Sir.'

I knew that but couldn't tell him that I wasn't familiar enough with the technology of this world to know what format it would take. 'Just look at everything. We'll do it together. Two pairs of eyes are better than one.'

We made a start with the trousers and then moved on to the jacket and found absolutely nothing. In desperation we tried the socks and shirt but still nothing. Time was passing and I was getting more and more frustrated. I was sure I was right and it would be here rather than in the luggage. David would definitely not want to risk it away from his person.

'Funny label on the shirt Sir,' Jamie said.

'Eh, what's wrong with it?' I asked as a glimmer of hope passed through my mind.

'Well it feels stiff, that's not right.'

I felt it and saw immediately what he meant.

'We need a razor blade or sharp knife,' I said.

'Here you are Sir,' Jamie said passing me a pocket knife with a very sharp blade.

I sliced very carefully around the label and cut it free. It comprised two sheets of cloth with what I took to be washing instructions on it but there was definitely something inside it. I carefully cut one end and teased it out.

'Is your Oracle system working this time of night?' I asked.

'No Sir but I'm trained. I can operate it,' he said as he saw what I was holding.

'Let's go.'

Twenty minutes later, Jamie escorted me up to the observation room and then interrupted Frank in his interview.

'How's it going?' I asked him when he came in.

'Nowhere, he's in there with his counsel and saying no comment to everything I ask. But I'll wear him down don't you worry. Some testimony from Alec would help but apparently, he's still out like a light.'

'I think I just might be able to help you out then and I held up the data sheet. 'This was sewn into the label of his shirt and we've just been down to the Oracle to see what was on it.'

'And?'

'He wasn't just trying to escape the country with his life. He was trying to steal some of your best secrets. His first plan was to sneak away quietly by sea and get to a country with sympathies with your enemies. He even thought he could convince Carrie to go with him. But when Alec arrived and you told him that the port was sealed, he talked about plan B remember?'

'Which was?'

'Go to London and get diplomatic protection in the German or Russian Embassies. With what he had they would welcome him with open arms. And anyway his father was almost certainly one of them and has been for years.'

'Bloody hell Tony where are you getting this all from?'

'I'll lay a bet now that when you look at Alec's past he hasn't got one. You might have to go a long way back but I reckon that at some point he came here, probably as a young man to be a deep cover agent. I'm guessing now but I would lay odds on that he had an affair with Julian's mother. We know David was only a half brother. Then something happened recently to change things. Quite possibly Alec's masters found out about the work David was doing and decided to activate him. Alec convinced David to fly down urgently. He used Julian's investigations into the hospital charity or possibly Carrie's engagement to get him to confront Julian. It's quite clear he has been besotted with Carrie for years. There was no love lost between the brothers. Something happened and Julian was killed by David and now Alec had the perfect lever to get David to do what he wanted.

'That's all pretty thin Tony,' Frank said. 'And there' absolutely nothing to prove any of it.'

'No but confront David with this evidence and there will be nowhere for him to go. Treason is presumably a capital crime here?'

'You bet your life it is,' Frank said. 'Sorry about the bad pun. Now, what the hell is on that data sheet.

'The full specifications of the Sopwith Petrel, its engine and its weapons.'

Chapter 41

Are you sure you don't want a job in my Force Tony? We pay very well, the hours are good and there's plenty of time off.' Frank said with a smile.

'Not a fat chance in hell Frank,' I said. 'You know why but I appreciate the offer.'

We were sitting back in the pub the next day. Frank had been up nearly all night but once again he somehow looked fresh and ready for anything. Maybe it was the adrenalin high of cracking the case. Even worse, I had given in and was sipping at a pint even though it was lunchtime. After I had done my bit the previous evening I had left to get some sleep. I was sure I had provided Frank with all the ammunition he needed.

'In fact, you should know that I'm going to be away for some time. As you well know there are a few things I have on my agenda that are literally not of this world.' I didn't tell him that I may not even be coming back at all.

'I had to ask,' he said. 'But please give your Carrie my best wishes.'

'Thanks. Now was I right? As you said at the time, much of what I suggested had happened was pure guesswork. I did have some things to work on though, like David being left handed and the way he behaved when he first came down after the murder. It was almost as if he was playing a part rather than being genuinely involved. Then there was Alec's attitude. He virtually had me kidnapped to come and meet the Venta Society. I never liked him he was just too regimented, too dare I say it, Germanic.'

'Actually, he was Russian so you weren't quite right there,' Frank said. 'And there is no real evidence that he was an agent. He did come over forty years ago but so did many Russians and Germans for that matter. There was quite a diaspora in the middle of the century. Our intelligence people are talking to him now so I don't expect we'll ever get the full story. As for David, well there you were pretty much right. Once I had confronted him with the evidence of his treachery he completely folded and told me everything. I think the totality of what he had done suddenly hit him. Maybe he had been in denial up until then. Anyway, he confessed the whole story. Alec had rung him to tell him about Julian and the hospital and that Julian and Carrie had got engaged. The engagement was what really got to him and made him take the risks he did. I actually think that Alec only wanted David to stop his brother spilling the beans about the hospital. However, when he got there it seems that he just lost it. Julian taunted him about Carrie. David seems to have had a long history of being bullied by his brother and this was the final straw.'

'Yes, I got that impression from the way he acted at Julian's wake,' I said. 'And knowing what we do about his brother's counterpart in my world I can't say I'm surprised. So was I right about the knife?'

'Yes, Julian kept his old Commando knife on his desk as a letter opener. Apparently, Julian was quite dismissive of everything David said. He said he was going to tell the rest of the Society about the hospital, he was just waiting for the right time so that he could do maximum damage to Alec's reputation. When David asked about Carrie, Julian just laughed and said he'd only become engaged because he knew David had a thing for her. At that point, David cracked. He picked up the knife and used it just as you described. He struck from behind with his left hand.'

'Did he tell you what he had done with the knife?'

'Yes, he took it back with him and it was with his personal effects at the base. A good place to stash it as wouldn't arouse any suspicion. They are all issued with them when they join up and many keep them with them.'

'So what was the whole espionage thing about?' I asked

'Well, once David came back after the murder, Alec finally told him that he was actually his father. Don't forget the Fletcher kids spent a lot of time at Alec's house. I can understand why now. Anyway, they both agreed at that point that there was a high risk of David being identified as the murderer and Alec as an accomplice so David suggested that they defect with the aircraft plans. They would be well rewarded. The Germanic Empire has nothing like either the jet engine or the aircraft for that matter. It would have been a hell of a coup for them. It seems that David was getting thoroughly fed up with the military anyway. Personally, I think he had had some sort of breakdown. As I said earlier, whether Alec was an agent and being far cleverer than we give him credit for is now neither here nor there. You were right about the shooting as well. It was purely accidental when Carrie intervened and thank God she did. It could all have ended differently if Alec hadn't been shot. So, I've done my job thanks to you. In fact, I would go as far as to say that I couldn't have done it without you. Another pint?'

'What the hell, why not.'

It was past four when I managed to extricate myself from the pub. It hadn't helped that all of Frank's team arrived and it turned into quite a celebration party. I was asked quite a lot of pointed questions about my role in the whole thing but Frank and I simply kept to the line that I was a retired cop who just got caught up in the whole thing. When I finally got outside I was able to hail a cab. There was no way I was fit to drive. I would ask Michael to collect the car tomorrow because I wouldn't be there. I was going home.

Nothing is ever simple and when the taxi dropped me off there was someone waiting for me at the house.

'Hello Carrie,' I said as I saw her when I came in the hallway.

She gave me a funny look. 'I didn't know whether you were coming to see me or not,' she said. 'So I decided to make the decision for you.'

Oops. In all the excitement of the last day, I had simply not made the effort to call her this morning. I suddenly felt guilty. 'Come and grab a seat. I'm so sorry but yesterday was so hectic and then I really needed some sleep.'

She only looked partly mollified but followed me into the drawing room.

'At least the police have been in contact,' she said. 'They told me what happened when you went to the Chalk Pit and afterwards. It seems you had a big hand in it all.'

'So did you. That was a very brave thing you did with that walking stick. If Alec hadn't been injured when he drove off, who knows what would have happened.'

I went on to tell her everything, including how Julian had behaved towards his brother, she needed to know.

'And this hospital they were setting up in London was that all a fake?' she asked.

'That's' a very good question Carrie,' I said. 'And no it can't be a fake. I've been there and seen what's been done.'

'So what happens now?' she asked in a small voice. 'Is that it? Does life just go back to normal?'

'No of course not. How could it?' I said with sympathy. 'But we all have to make adjustments.'

'And what are you going to do?' She asked.

'I'm going away,' I said. 'But before that, there's something I have to do.' Then a thought struck me. 'And I would be really honoured if you were my guest.'

Chapter 42

A week later and things were very different. The sun was shining, and the whole of the street had been cordoned off. Flags were flying everywhere and crowds of people were waiting expectantly behind barriers. This was going to be a good day for many people. I was standing with Carrie next to me. On my other side, Bill Gates was standing looking proud and a lot smarter than when he was in his old brown suit. Behind us and to one side were all of the members of the Venta Society, bar one of course. They were all formally dressed and looking very solemn.

The day after the arrests and after I had said goodbye to Carrie, I had gone home. I hadn't been away for long but after the chaos of the last few days, it seemed like it had been forever. I needed a dose of sanity after the madness I had just been through. I called my Carrie and she came straight over. She quickly spotted that I was slightly the worse for wear but I sat her down and told her the story from when I had attended the funeral, to the events of the night up at Farley Mount. We also cracked a bottle of red which kept me going. Until I fell asleep that is.

The next morning, after we had become properly reacquainted, we went over the whole story again but in all its minute and gory detail. She was particularly taken with the idea of the Chalk Pit and I was given strict instructions to take some photos of it if I ever went there again. I also explained that I would need to go back one last time. At least in the near future. Once that discussion was over, we both went on to plan our future lives together.

So here I was today, standing on the steps of the Digitalus building, dressed in my finery. When I had told Michael and Mavis what it was all about they went into a frenzy of organisation. An urgent visit to a tailor was first on the list. I had absolutely no idea what would be needed for such an occasion but the tailor did. Which is why I ended up in something resembling a morning suit with a mauve cravat and starched white shirt with wing collar. I also had to wear odd shiny shoes with absolutely horrible white spats. Apparently, I also had to wear a hat. The damned thing looked like a cross between a top hat and bowler. To say I felt like a stuffed penguin was no exaggeration.

If the Thompsons were in a tizz, it was nothing like the panic that Carrie had got into. I told her it was my treat for her to buy whatever finery she needed. She insisted I go with her. They may have been the same girl brought up in totally different environments but my God did this young lady and my Carrie know how to 'shop'. We must have walked the whole length of Winchester High Street at least three times. I drew the line at special trip to London and as I was paying, I got my way but only just. And yes, in the end, the dress and all the other stuff Carrie bought was from one of the first shops we went in to. Mind you, I hadn't seen her so happy for a long time and I think the whole experience was just what she needed to put the past behind her.

We went up to London the night before and stayed in the same hotel that my Carrie and I had stayed only a week or so ago. That was weird. It was the same in some ways and very different in others. I actually thought that the understated elegance of this version was far better. I know that my girl said she wouldn't be jealous if I misbehaved but that is not how I looked at it. There was no way I was going to be unfaithful even if it was with the same girl, if that makes sense. Don't think I wasn't tempted though. This young lady scrubbed up just as well as my version. The temptation to come clean and tell her that my stories about being gay were just that, stories, was enormous. However, the next morning when I woke up on my own, albeit with the usual thick head, I felt a great wave of relief. Not just for being faithful but because I didn't want this girl to get her hopes up over me. I really felt that I was going to have to be very frugal coming here in the future and therefore there was no hope for us even if I had succumbed to temptation. We all had to be in place by ten thirty although things weren't due to kick off until eleven. It gave me some time to talk to the Venta people. Not one of them seemed upset with the change of use of their London property. Not only that but they all seemed inordinately embarrassed that the head of their organisation was now languishing at His Majesty's pleasure. So much so that most of them wouldn't even talk about him. I was a little naughty bringing up the subject with some of them but it was a guilty pleasure seeing them squirm with embarrassment.

But now the time was approaching eleven. The media, who had their own little enclosure, started to stir themselves. From where they were sitting they could see down the road better than us because we were standing right next to the building.

Suddenly, the crowd started clapping and cheering. Hundreds of little Union Flags were being waved and three large black cars came into view. The middle one had a flag on the bonnet and it drew up opposite the red carpet that had been laid down on the building's steps to the curb. I turned to look at Carrie, she seemed almost mesmerised.

'He's only an old bloke. At times like this I always try to think about what they look like with no clothes on. It sort of takes the drama away.'

'Shut Up Tony,' she whispered.

'Look, he's getting out.'

A flunky had come around to the rear door of the limo and opened it. Out got the stately figure of His Majesty King Edward the Ninth, eighty year old son of Edward the Eighth. In this world there had never been a vivacious American divorcee to turn his father's head and he had retained his crown and bred a son and a daughter. The son was walking slowly up to us now as clapping and cheering continued even louder than before. I idly wondered if there was a branch of the family somewhere with a couple of daughters. I suppose there must have been. I made a mental promise to myself to see what had become of Elizabeth during another visit.

Then the great man arrived. I did as all the other men did and bowed and Carrie curtsied just as she had been practicing all week. I took a sneak look as I bowed. He was a tall man who had the carriage of someone much younger. Piercing blue eyes seemed to take in everything that was going on. He even sported the famous Windsor beard that so many of his forerunners had worn although now it was a snowy white. His immaculate grey suit was unadorned with any regalia except for a star of some sort on his right breast.

Bill Gates then stepped forward. 'Your Majesty, we are honoured that you could attend and officially open the first free public hospital in the country. If you would be so kind.' And he indicated the rope with the gold tassel attached to a purple cloth covering the plaque on the wall next to the main doors.

The King had not been programmed to give a speech. The plan had been for him to say a few quick words, pull the string and then accompany us lucky few inside where he would be given a short tour and then a buffet lunch and drinks.

He did nothing of the sort. He turned to the crowd. 'People of London, this hospital was the brainchild of several people one of whom is no longer with us.'

'*Oh God,*' I thought. '*He's going to mention Alec.*'

'I am speaking of a great philanthropist.'

Not Alec then.

'I'm speaking of someone I knew quite well. Mister Peter Peterson who unfortunately left us some short time ago and without whom I'm pretty sure this wonderful facility would never have been built. I am very glad to see that his son is here to represent him.' He turned to look at me.

'*Good God,*' I thought. '*How many sides to Uncle Peter were there? Friends with the King for goodness sake, he never mentioned that. And for that matter how on earth did he recognise me?*'

I wasn't given any time to think further. The King gestured to me to come to his side. 'I think we should pull this rope together,' he said. 'And later on, you can tell me how my cousin is getting on ruling in your world.'

Epilogue

'He said what?' Carrie asked in amazement. We were lying on a beach in Antigua. I had deliberately not told her about what the King had said on that amazing day until now. I wanted to surprise her. It looked like I had been successful.

We were on honeymoon and we were both very happy about that. I had managed to get her to give in her notice at the school. Neither of us needed to work any more although we both tacitly agreed that we would find some way of doing some good with all our spare cash. But that was a debate to be had some time in the future. The wedding had been spectacular. Neither of us wanted a religious service but we did want a formal event. In the end, we did the deed in the grounds of our house. Many of my friends from the Met came. I even invited Inspector Frank Cosgrove, although for some reason he didn't attend. Carrie's family came in droves. There was even her sister, my old girlfriend Hannah, with her husband and three kids. She seemed very happy for us.

Of course, my parents were long gone but I did manage to rustle up a few distant relatives if for no other reason than to balance out the numbers. It didn't really matter. Carrie and I were more than happy. And I know it had been a great day because of how I felt the next morning. My only one sadness was not being able to invite some of my new friends from a certain other place. That Fank Cosgrove would have attended and been the life and soul of the party.

So here we were lying on a beach in the sunshine and it was time to come clean. 'Yup, he asked me how his cousin was getting on over here.'

'So he knows about all this. About the mirror and everything. How on earth did that happen?'

'Uncle Peter told him of course. I didn't manage to find out exactly how the two of them got together and exactly how much he knows because there were just too many people vying for his attention. He knew that I would not always be around but he did invite me to Windsor when I was next back for what he called a proper chinwag.'

Just for once, Carrie was speechless. She lay back on her sun lounger and took a big swig of her rum and coke.

'Well the future is going to continue to be interesting,' she said. 'There's no doubt about that.'

Author's Notes

I grew up in Winchester and many of the elements of this book (and those to come) arise from my youthful experience of this beautiful city.

For some reason, my childhood bedroom had a full length mirror on one wall. As a kid, I would often dream about whether I was seeing a reflection or an actual alternative world just out of reach on the other side of the glass.

My previous novels tend to be based on real events which I weave into the plot. It was a refreshing change to do something different this time. That said. I have woven parts of the city into the narrative quite deliberately. In fact, in this book, I had to force myself to be sparing as there are many more stories to come and I want to base them around different aspects of the city.

I've always loved books about alternative histories. Take one little event, change it and then, as Einstein would say, conduct a thought experiment about it. So here we have a bad driver running over one of the most notorious assassins in history and everything is changed.

Being able to mix and match the resulting technology was fun but don't think that it will all be one way. The world through the mirror has much to teach us – their trains do 400 for a start!

I hope you enjoyed it. Please look on Amazon at my other titles. Most of my books are self published although I do have some non-fiction work published through a main stream publishing house. As an 'Indie' author, reviews are the lifeblood of our success so if you feel strongly enough I would love to read your comments in the review section on the book's Amazon page.

Larry Jeram-Croft

Printed in Great Britain
by Amazon

79551712R00130